THE BITTERROOTS

C.J. BOX

HEAD
of ZEUS

First published in the UK by Head of Zeus in 2019
This paperback edition published by Head of Zeus in 2020

Published by arrangement with Minotaur Books,
an imprint of St. Martin's Publishing Group

9 7 5 3 1 2 4 6 8

A catalogue record for this book is available from
the British Library.

ISBN (PB): 9781786693402
ISBN (E): 9781786693372

Cover design: Ghost design
Photographs: Shutterstock.com
Typeset by Adrian McLaughlin

Printed and bound in the UK by
CPI Group (UK) Ltd, Croydon CRO 4YY

Head of Zeus Ltd
First Floor East
5–8 Hardwick Street
London ECIR 4RG

WWW.HEADOFZEUS.COM

For Laurie, always

THE BITTERROOTS

PART I

The root of the kingdom is in the state. The root of the state is in the family. The root of the family is in the person of its head.

—MENCIUS (MENG-TZU), *Works*

Going home must be like going to render an account.

—JOSEPH CONRAD, *Lord Jim*

ONE

THE CRAZY MOUNTAINS were on fire and Cassie Dewell sat alone in her car at night on McLeod Street across from the Grand Hotel in Big Timber, Montana, looking for a twenty-four-year-old reprobate known as Antlerhead.

That's when the call she'd been dreading came on her cell phone.

It was from Rachel Mitchell, the primary defense attorney in the firm of Mitchell-Estrella in Bozeman. It was from Rachel's personal cell phone rather than from her office, which was unusual in itself. The attorney was working late and it meant a chit had come due.

The call created a stab of cold dread in Cassie's gut. She didn't need the distraction of a call from Rachel Mitchell at that moment. A call from her meant Cassie's life could be altered one way or another. She declined to answer and let it go to voice mail so she could return it later.

*

SHE BRUSHED CRUMBS from a half-dozen chocolate-covered mini-donuts from her lap and lifted her gaze from the empty sidewalk that led to the front door of the hotel to the fire on the distant mountain. It was mesmerizing and officially out of control.

The long fire line extended across the entire southern face of the range like an orange zipper. It dipped into canyons and emerged on the other side. It raced down over meadows and plateaus in spots but never broke contact with the extended fire line itself.

Because it was dark, there was no delineation between the fresh fuel in front of the blaze and the smoking cinders behind it. The fire seemed like a living thing, a snake, a nocturnal beast more alive at night than during the day. It burned bright enough that it stained the bellies of low-hanging clouds with pink hues. When Cassie closed her eyes, the fire lingered as if imprinted inside her eyelids.

She could imagine the line of fire eating its way down through the timber and eventually consuming the grassland of the prairie all the way to I-90 and Big Timber itself unless the wind turned it west or south.

Like most of the summer, the September air was thick with smoke. It haloed the few downtown streetlights and she could smell it on her clothing. She had a sore throat from breathing it in all day. On some mornings, she brushed a thin film of white ash from the hood and windshield of her Jeep Cherokee as if it were snow in the winter.

It had been the Summer of Fire in Montana, and it wasn't over yet.

She thought about how many fires there were—seventeen at last count throughout the state—and how they'd likely keep burning until the snow finally put them out. They could be seen from space. Both the state and federal budget for fighting them had run out of funds in mid-August.

Hundreds of thousands of acres of timber had burned. So much that the numbers no longer had meaning. Several hundred mountain cabins and homes were destroyed and dozens of towns had been evacuated more than once.

Against the backdrop of the Summer of Fire the case for finding Antlerhead seemed very small in the grand scheme of things. She felt small as well.

The phone in her lap chimed and lit up again and Cassie was afraid it was Rachel again. Instead, it was a text message from her fourteen-year-old son Ben, who was home in Bozeman, sixty-one miles to the west.

When R U home?

She replied that it would be a few hours, that he needed to do his homework and go to bed and to not wait up for her.

She's feeding me brown rice again.

She meaning Cassie's mother, Isabel, a free spirit and self-proclaimed progressive who had recently returned from North Dakota where she'd been participating in protests against an oil pipeline opposed by indigenous people. Since getting back she'd refused to cook or serve anything white.

Cassie pondered her response. At least Ben was getting dinner when his own mother wasn't home to prepare a meal. There was that.

5

Before she could tap something out Ben asked,

Can I ride my bike to McD's?

It was warm enough outside and Bozeman was safe enough to say yes. McDonald's was three blocks away. But giving Ben permission to skip Isabel's meal would undermine her mother's authority. It would fan the flames on the tension between them that was already smoldering like one of the fires in the mountains.

Cassie texted:

We'll go there tomorrow.

Ben replied with:

Like U'll be home for once.

It was followed by an angry face emoji.

Good night. I love you.

The words "I love you too, Mom, and I realize you have to work late so we have a nice home to live in and food on the table" didn't appear on her phone.

In fact, Ben didn't text back at all and Cassie sighed and swallowed a lump in her throat. She could stare at the screen and wish for those words to appear but this was Ben's way when he was angry with her. He knew that the meanest thing he could do to her was to withhold his affection. That it would hurt her more than anything he said.

When she looked up, she saw a rail-thin form emerge from the alley behind the Grand and dart back into the shadows to avoid being seen by a passing car.

Antlerhead.

She'd guessed right.

ANTLERHEAD'S GIVEN NAME was Jerry Allen. He'd received his nickname several years before while on work release from the Montana State Prison in Deer Lodge after his conviction for a series of house and cabin burglaries. Allen was assigned part-time at a wild game processing facility outside of Anaconda during hunting season. That's where he hefted the newly delivered severed head and the set of six-by-six antlers onto his shoulders and said to his co-workers and fellow inmates, "Look at me—I'm an *elk*!" seconds before he slipped on a smear of blood and his strength and balance gave out. A hundred and twenty pounds of antlers crashed down on top of him and laid him out on the loading dock. One of the sharp tines entered his skull just above his right eyebrow and another halved his clavicle and punctured a lung.

His next job, once he was released from the hospital after a two-month stay and ten months of physical rehab courtesy of Montana taxpayers, was in the prison laundry.

Antlerhead later went on to become one of the most inept heroin dealers in Gallatin County. He'd been arrested along with two others for selling heroin laced with fentanyl to three male Montana State University students in Bozeman. All three Bobcats were rushed to the emergency room at Bozeman Health Deaconess. While two recovered, the third went into a coma and lingered for months before regaining consciousness.

That the third student survived meant Allen avoided additional homicide charges to those already levied against him: felony charges of criminal possession of dangerous drugs, criminal manufacture of dangerous drugs, criminal possession with intent to distribute dangerous drugs, and conspiracy.

The recent arrest photos of him showed a rail-thin, gaunt-faced man with a mop of brown hair, a long crooked nose, and dull feral eyes. Above his right eyebrow was a sunken red dent of a scar that was no doubt the spot where the antler tine had penetrated his skull that resulted in his nickname.

Cassie was reminded that in just about every instance losers *looked* like losers. Allen was a poster child for losers.

Antlerhead Allen was going to go back to prison in Deer Lodge for a very long time, which was fine with Cassie. That's where he belonged.

Except that following his arraignment hearing two days before, after his parents scraped together the $150,000 bond that allowed him to walk out of the county jail until his criminal trial, Antlerhead had vanished.

And his parents were on the hook for the money.

CASSIE SHIFTED her weight on the seat and winced. She'd been sitting in her car so long that her right butt cheek had gone numb. Her stomach rumbled from her dinner that consisted of a box of Hostess chocolate-covered donuts and an energy drink from a convenience store. She'd vowed to stop eating like that until she dropped twenty pounds. Unlike Ben, who wore slim-fit jeans and didn't have an ounce of fat on him, Cassie *should* be eating Isabel's brown rice.

Like always when she was on the job, she wore her unofficial Montana PI uniform: jeans with enough play in them that she wasn't uncomfortable sitting in a car for long hours, a roomy blouse, and a tunic or jacket. She always wore her tooled cowboy boots for a couple of reasons. One was a nod to her state and her upbringing. The other was that she could tuck a backup weapon into the shaft of her right boot. Plus, she *never* stood out in Montana because of her clothing.

She'd kept a close eye on the alley behind the Grand Hotel for another glimpse of Antlerhead. She didn't want to try and go after him if he was there in the dark. Instead, she wanted him to appear on the illuminated sidewalk and his identification could be confirmed before she took any kind of action.

Several people had left the Grand, climbed into their vehicles, and driven away. There were now five autos parked diagonally at the front of the hotel—a sedan, a crossover, and three pickups. All had Montana plates. She knew from walking around the block before dark that employee parking was next to the building on a gravel lot. There were four cars in the lot. From where Cassie had strategically parked her Jeep, she could see the front and side doors of the hotel as well as the employee lot.

If Antlerhead was lurking in the alley as Cassie suspected he was, he would be blocked from viewing any activity from the front and side doors. But he'd have a clear angle on the employee parking from the back corner of the building.

Which, if her working theory was correct, would be what Antlerhead cared about most.

Nayna Byers. The waitress Cassie had met who worked at the Grand.

TO FIND ANTLERHEAD, Cassie had placed a call to the administration office of the Montana State Prison and asked for Johnny Ortiz. She'd worked with him when they were both deputies at the Lewis and Clark County Sheriff's Office in Helena. Since then, she'd moved to North Dakota and Ortiz had taken a job with the Department of Corrections.

Ortiz had provided background and unofficial intel to her before, and in turn Cassie always left a dozen cinnamon rolls from Wheat Montana at the front desk for him every time she passed through Deer Lodge.

After small talk about the fires, Ortiz tapped on his keyboard and told Cassie that during Antlerhead's incarceration he had only four names on his approved visitor list: his parents Buford and Nadine Allen, his defense attorney, and Nayna Byers of Big Timber.

Cassie wrote down the name and thanked Johnny for his help. She could tell from his hearty, "You bet, Cassie," that he was grateful she hadn't asked him for anything dubious or untoward. Visitor lists for prisoners were public records.

It took less than two minutes on the internet to find her.

APPREHENDING ANTLERHEAD and delivering him back to his parents' house could get tricky. Cassie couldn't legally arrest him or detain him without cause and Antlerhead hadn't actually broken any laws that she was aware of.

She'd notified the Big Timber PD via email from her phone of her presence there earlier in the afternoon but she hadn't said what she was doing other than "investigating a case."

She'd done it as a courtesy. There was no requirement to alert the locals but it was good policy if things went haywire or if she was questioned by the police as to why she was in their town with an array of equipment and weapons.

She didn't want to call them now. A police car might spook Antlerhead and she might lose him. Or the cops might provoke him into doing something stupid like resisting arrest that would result in another charge and another bail for his parents.

HER STRATEGY was simple: confront him and firmly persuade him to go back to his home with her. She would tell him about the financial consequences his parents faced if he refused to come with her and she hoped he'd feel some guilt about that. Additionally, she'd let him know that she was duty-bound to inform the court that he'd disregarded the judge's instructions to stay home. Which meant he'd go back to lockup.

She knew Antlerhead was not a smart person. She could only hope he was smart enough to realize that the best thing he could do for himself was to let her take him back.

Nevertheless, Cassie patted herself down to check her gear and weapons. Her .40 Glock 27 was on her hip and her five-shot .38 snub-nosed Smith & Wesson was in an ankle holster. There was a Taser in her large handbag on the passenger seat as well a canister of pepper spray, a Vipertek mini stun gun, and several pairs of zip ties.

Since she'd opened her agency she'd never once been in a situation where it was necessary to draw any of her lethal or nonlethal weapons. She hoped the streak would continue.

The most important tool she had on her person was the most innocuous—her cell phone. She'd activate the recording app before leaving her Jeep and keep it running during her confrontation and conversation with Allen. Digital audio records had come in handy dozens of times in her career when it came to proving what had actually transpired. If nothing else, she could play it back for the Allens to prove that she'd earned her fee if Antlerhead didn't bite.

CASSIE CAUGHT a glimpse of yellow light from the shadowed side of the Grand as a side door opened and someone exited. It wasn't one of the public doors and Cassie assumed it accessed the kitchen. When it closed she couldn't see the figure well.

Cassie had a night vision scope in the back of the Jeep but she didn't want to call attention to herself by climbing out to get it. So she waited, narrowing her eyes and hoping they'd adjust to the dark or that the person would move into the light.

It wasn't necessary, though, because Nayna Beyers thumbed a lighter and raised it to the tip of a cigarette in her mouth. Cassie could identify her clearly.

The flame went out and was replaced by the lone red cherry of Nayna's smoke.

The cherry on the end of Nayna's cigarette was suddenly bobbing up and down and advancing down the sidewalk. Then Nayna appeared in a pool of yellow from the streetlight near the front of the Grand. She was walking quickly and looking over her shoulder toward the back.

Antlerhead was right behind her, loping from the alley.

Apparently, he'd seen her come out for her smoke break as well and when he caught up with her, he grabbed her by her arms and spun her around to face him. Her cigarette dropped into the gutter with a display of sparks.

Cassie cursed herself for not seeing it coming and she opened the door of the Jeep and pushed herself out. The call from Rachel had thrown off her concentration. She fumbled for the recording app on her phone as she walked quickly across the street toward Nayna and Antlerhead. Nayna struggled to break his grip.

Cassie took a deep breath to calm herself. She hadn't expected Antlerhead to escalate the situation so quickly.

"I just want to talk to you," Antlerhead said.

"Let me go, you asshole."

"Nayna, please. I just want to talk."

"There's nothing to say. Let me go or I'll call the cops. I'll start *screaming*."

He prevented that by wheeling her around again so he could clamp her in a headlock with his left arm across her throat.

Cassie heard a muffled yell, and Antlerhead said, "Stop it, Nayna, goddamn you. I don't want to hurt you. *I fucking love you.*"

Nayna's eyes were wide open and panicked but they locked on Cassie's approach. Antlerhead hadn't seen her yet because he was so focused on getting Nayna to stop struggling.

Cassie gave up on turning on the recording app—too many wasted seconds, too many stupid swipes of the screen—and she thumbed the icon for her camera. A red dot appeared and she punched it. She was now recording video and she raised her phone to chest level and aimed it at Antlerhead and Nayna with her left hand while reaching back for the grip of her Glock with her right.

"Jerry, let her go."

Antlerhead's head bobbled at the sound of his name and he glared at Cassie. He kept Nayna in the chokehold. Cassie hoped the waitress could get enough air to stay conscious.

"Who in the hell are you? This is a private conversation." He even sounded dumb.

"It's not a conversation, it's an assault," Cassie said. "Let her go right now or I'll blow your stupid head off."

She drew her gun as she said it and leveled it at Antlerhead. The front sight was aimed squarely at the dent above his eyebrow.

"Shit, man," he said. He sounded offended. "Put that down and turn that camera off."

Cassie steadied the weapon and hoped her hand wouldn't tremble.

Then he relaxed his grip on Nayna and she twisted away. As soon as she got her balance she coughed, then turned on her heel and kicked Antlerhead so hard between his legs it lifted him off the ground. He wheezed—it was a pathetic sound—and he dropped to his knees.

Nayna cocked her leg back for another kick and Cassie said, "Back off, Nayna. It's over."

"It ain't over," Nayna said as she kicked him in his sternum. "He was choking me."

Antlerhead moaned and fell over in slow motion.

"I'm not kidding," Cassie said to her. "That's *enough* or I'll call the cops on both of you."

"He's supposed to be in jail anyway," Nayna said. "He won't leave me alone."

"I get that."

"Who are you anyway?" Nayna asked. Then: "Oh, I remember you from earlier. Are you some kind of cop?"

"I'm a licensed private investigator. My name is Cassie Dewell. I'm here to take our friend back to his parents' house."

"He ain't my friend."

"He used to be."

"Well, he ain't no more. He's an asshole."

"I'll give you that."

Cassie neared Antlerhead and holstered her weapon. He writhed on the asphalt with both of his hands clamped between his thighs. His clothing was white from the film of ash on the ground.

"Did you hear that, Jerry? It's time to go home. We can do this without getting the police involved. How does that sound?"

"Just get him out of here," Nayna said. "I don't ever want to see his stupid fucking face again for the rest of my life."

From Antlerhead, a childlike sob. His body shook as he cried.

"Come on, Jerry," Cassie said. "Let's go over to that Jeep across the street."

"Nayna," he cried. "*Nayna.*"

Cassie could see that Nayna was positioning herself for another kick so she stepped between them. The waitress backed away.

"Please get back to work," Cassie told her.

ARM IN ARM, they staggered across the street toward her Jeep. Antlerhead was unsteady on his feet and he hadn't stopped sobbing.

Cassie saw the Big Timber PD unit turn the corner and drive slowly down McLeod Street toward them.

"Straighten up," Cassie said sharply. "Act like a man."

She guided him into the passenger seat and closed the door. Antlerhead slumped forward and put his head in his hands. Cassie would have preferred to cuff him and stow him in the back for the drive to Laurel but she didn't want to draw attention from the local cop who passed by.

"That was close," she said as she climbed in and turned the key to the ignition.

"*Nayna.*"

"Oh, please," Cassie said as she drove cautiously out of town toward I-90. "You're not the victim here."

"The hell I ain't," he said. "She told me she loved me once and now she *kicks me* in the *nuts.*"

That struck Cassie as funny and she looked away so he couldn't see the expression on her face. The release of tension from the situation and Antlerhead's perceived victimhood made her want to laugh out loud.

After a few minutes, she said, "Let me know when you stop crying and can hold it together long enough for me to return a phone call."

TWO

THE LAW OFFICES of Mitchell-Estrella were on the second floor of a newish office building on Main Street on the western flank of downtown Bozeman. It was a cool sunny morning tainted by the brackish odor of smoke from the forest fires in the mountains. Not until the temperature climbed to forty-five degrees would the inversion layer open up and allow the smoke to disperse into the atmosphere.

Cassie parked in the first visitor space in the lot and fished a notebook out of her handbag. She left the tools and weapons and stuffed the bag under the passenger seat so it couldn't be seen from the outside.

Before getting out, she paused and sighed heavily. She was tired and it wasn't even nine in the morning. She'd not arrived home until one thirty after delivering Antlerhead to Buford and Nadine Allen, and she'd been up at six forty-five to make breakfast for Ben and spend some time with him before he went to school and Isabel got up.

Of course, her son had barely spoken, and when she asked him about school, wrestling practice, and his friends he'd said all were "fine."

"Just fine?"

He rolled his eyes, exasperated with her. "What do you want me to say, Mom?"

Fourteen-year-old boys were a challenge.

And so was making the effort to see Rachel Mitchell, even though Cassie had known this day would come.

Climbing the stairs to Rachel's office, she fought the feeling that she was crossing a line that she didn't want to cross.

EVERYTHING that happened in western Montana happened in one of the valleys between mountain ranges. The towns, the roads, the rivers, and the railroads were all funneled into the valleys between the Absaroka and Beartooth Range to the southeast, the Gallatins and Crazies to the southwest, the Bridger, Big Belt, and Elkhorn ranges to the north, and the Bitterroots to the northwest.

Cassie worked those valleys on a daily basis, and it wasn't unusual for her to drive three hundred miles in a day as a private investigator working several different cases at once. She was the owner and principal of Dewell Investigations, LLC. She was a fully licensed private investigator and her services included skip tracing, asset searches, background checks, fraud, criminal defense investigations, domestic cases, and surveillance. Her Montana PI license number was number 7775.

After years of existing in the backstabbing bureaucracy

of local law enforcement, she'd decided to strike out on her own. She thought it would be a good move for her and a good thing for Ben. Cassie liked the ideas of setting her own hours, choosing her own cases, and being her own boss.

Her career in law enforcement had been intense and tumultuous. She'd pursued and taken down Ronald Pergram, the infamous Lizard King, who was a serial rapist and murderer who operated as a long-haul trucker. He'd also become her obsession.

She'd also shot and killed Montana state trooper Rick Legerski who was a coconspirator of Pergram's and the murderer of Cassie's mentor, Cody Hoyt.

Her work as chief investigator in North Dakota both saved the life of a then fourteen-year-old boy with fetal alcohol syndrome and dismantled a violent MS-13-financed drug ring.

But instead of kudos and promotions, Cassie had been made the scapegoat by a politically ambitious county attorney for a sting operation that went horribly wrong and resulted in the deaths of several fellow deputies including her fiancé at the time. She'd eventually been cleared and offered her job back, but she couldn't make herself put on a badge again.

Although her sense of justice and respect for the law remained intact, her enthusiasm to "ride for the brand" had been crushed. There had been too many self-aggrandizing officials, too much misanthropy among the good old boys in the system, and too much politicization instead of investigation. She still wanted to put bad guys away and protect innocent people, but she could no longer fight the bureaucracy in order to do that.

It had all worked, sort of. Her idea of setting her own hours and not being beholden to a departmental superior had resulted in longer days, fewer vacations, and serving the toughest boss of all—herself.

Setting up shop had been more difficult than she thought it would be. She hadn't given enough thought about how tough it was to deal with landlords or the city administration when it came to leasing space and setting up shop. There were so many taxes and fees it was as if the system was set up to make her fail.

The hardest part, though, was overcoming her aversion to private investigators due to her years in local law enforcement in Montana and most recently North Dakota. Jon Kirkbride, the sheriff of Bakken County and her boss in NoDak, once told her, "TSA agents are folks who were too dumb to pass the test for a job at the post office, and private investigators are folks too dumb to qualify for the TSA."

Nevertheless, she met the minimum license requirements in Montana and passed a background investigation and finger-print check, she had the requisite experience in spades, and she could afford the two-hundred-fifty-dollar application fee and the premiums for a half-million-dollar commercial liability policy. Her references included cops she'd worked with in her native Montana as well as Kirkbride, who wished her well. She'd passed the examination for private investigators with the highest score ever recorded, according to the clerk who'd administered it. And for another fifty-dollar fee, she'd automatically received a firearms endorsement because of her previous qualification certificates on the range in both states.

She was a neophyte when it came to hiring competent clerical and administrative help. In the two years since she'd launched Dewell Investigations, she'd been through five administrative assistants. Two had left on their own and three had been fired for incompetence.

If it wasn't for Isabel filling in—her mother justified the hours as "assisting the downtrodden of society"—Cassie might have given up or gone to work for someone else. Or even put aside her revulsion and applied with the local sheriff's department or police department.

Income hadn't been an issue after the first four months of her new enterprise. Word got around that she was professional, efficient, and honest. She had more work than she could handle and she had the luxury of not taking unsavory cases—usually.

She'd been told more times than she cared to be told that she "didn't look like a private investigator" and she was never sure how to take the comment. Cassie was in her mid-thirties, five foot four, ten to fifteen pounds overweight, and her hair was thick and unruly. She didn't have the commanding presence that would instantly bring a room to order, and she was more of a listener than a talker. Since she no longer wore a uniform, she was rarely taken for a cop.

The only person in her life who thought otherwise was Ben, who said she had "cop eyes." Whatever that meant.

Cassie had quickly become the PI of choice for several bail bondsmen, a half-dozen insurance companies, two car dealerships, the county realtors' group, and one criminal defense firm: Mitchell-Estrella.

MITCHELL-ESTRELLA was gaining both prominence and notoriety in Montana legal circles. Although partners Rachel Mitchell and Jessica Estrella were Cassie's age and the firm was less than ten years old and the majority of their clients were still lowlifes looking for plea deals, Mitchell-Estrella had recently won acquittals in several high-profile criminal trials. The most lurid case involved Monte Schreiner, the ex-governor of the state who'd been accused of hiring a transient to murder his mistress near his vacation cabin by hitting her over the head with an oar, loading her unconscious body in a drift boat, and pushing it out onto Flathead Lake where she was later found dead of exposure. Cassie had carefully followed the trial in the *Bozeman Daily Chronicle*.

The blustery Schreiner, who was known for his frequent appearances on cable television news shows wearing a bolo tie and who brought his dog along to every event, came across in news reports as likely guilty to most Montanans, Cassie included. In a state where nearly everyone had met the governor and seen him in action on a personal basis, it just seemed like the kind of thing he would do. Cassie had once seen the governor work a room and put his hands on every person in it, lingering just a little too long with the younger and attractive women whether they were married or not.

The transient, who admitted to the crime and agreed to turn state's witness against Governor Schreiner, was shredded on the stand and caught in a half-dozen lies by attorney Rachel Mitchell. Mrs. Schreiner, who eagerly wanted to see her husband sent to prison and had agreed to testify against him, was forced to admit under Rachel's cross-examination that she had conducted multiple affairs in the past and that she'd exchanged text messages with a fly-fishing guide promising to be with him if "she could just get rid of Monte."

Monte Schreiner was found not guilty and Mrs. Schreiner had moved to Seattle.

After the verdict, Rachel gave a press conference on the courthouse steps declaring that justice had been done.

Cassie saw the clip on the news and thought that a guilty man with a sharp and aggressive lawyer had beaten the system. Although the prosecution's case had some holes in it—didn't they all?—this was the kind of thing that had soured her about the criminal justice system in the first place. She'd vowed not to ever be a part of it.

BUT CASSIE and Rachel Mitchell had history. Rachel's father, Bull, had been a cantankerous outfitter who had guided both Cassie and her mentor Cody Hoyt into the Yellowstone wilderness. Cody had been in pursuit of a client on a multi-day horse pack trip who was also a multiple murderer. Cassie had later hired Bull to go after the Lizard King.

Rachel had been in the middle of both situations, both trying to look out for her father's welfare and providing local legal counsel.

Against her better judgment as well as Rachel's admonitions, Cassie had persuaded Bull to come out of retirement one more time and even though he was excited to go and at the time was rejuvenated by the adventure, his physical and mental health deteriorated rapidly upon his return. Although still in Rachel's home in his own special wing, Bull rarely ventured out of his recliner and frequently forgot the names of his daughter, son-in-law, and grandchildren. He only came to life during prime time on Fox News, when he awoke to rail and shake his fist at liberals.

Although Rachel didn't blame Cassie outright for Bull's rapid decline, Cassie felt tremendous guilt for her direct role in it and she knew her requests of him had accelerated his physical and mental decline.

She felt she owed Bull and Rachel, but she'd also made it clear to Rachel that she didn't like the idea of helping to exonerate Rachel's criminal clients no matter who they were. Rachel had assured Cassie that she'd never ask her to do work that would "offend her sensibilities." She'd said it in a wry and irritating way, Cassie thought.

Shortly after that conversation, the firm of Mitchell-Estrella sent the first monthly retainer check to Dewell Investigations. Cassie weighed the decision but cashed it. She needed the money to get started. By doing so she acknowledged her obligation.

Which was why the phone call the night before had thrown Cassie off her game. She knew at the time that Rachel was calling to collect.

RACHEL MITCHELL stood up from behind her desk as Cassie entered her office. Rachel was slim, stylish, and graceful—everything Cassie was not. The attorney had auburn hair, a sly smile, and green eyes. The credenza behind her desk was filled with framed photos of her teenage boys white-water rafting, fishing, and skiing at the local mountain called Bridger Bowl. There was a large shot of Rachel and her handsome husband waving from the basket of a hot air balloon taken somewhere tropical. A black-and-white still showed a much-younger Bull Mitchell astride a horse guiding a long string of pack horses into the Yellowstone Park wilderness.

"Cassie, you look tired," Rachel said after grasping both of Cassie's hands in hers in a firm greeting. Right to the point.

"You don't," Cassie replied. She knew Rachel either ran or swam every morning before coming to work to stay healthy and fit.

"I was up late on a case," Cassie said as she sat down in one of two leather-bound chairs across from Rachel's desk. She dropped her handbag on the surface of the other.

"Anything I should know about?"

"I don't think so. A skip trace in Big Timber. He's back home with his family for the moment awaiting trial."

"Sounds like one of our clients," Rachel said with a smile.

"I can't say." Cassie knew that Antlerhead's attorney had been assigned through the public defender's office for his new trial and that Rachel took fewer and fewer of those kind of charity cases. Either way, it was unprofessional for Cassie to discuss her clients.

"Well, I'm glad you're in one piece," Rachel said. "It can't be fun going after desperate people."

"It isn't. But it's part of the job."

"You're doing well for yourself," Rachel said as she glided into her chair. "I'm very pleased to see how well you've done here."

"Thank you."

"I think it's important that we stick together as much as we can, you know?"

Cassie nodded her agreement. They'd had this conversation before. Like her own small private investigations firm, Mitchell-Estrella was owned solely by women. Rachel seemed to be more concerned about the fact than Cassie ever was, but it was certainly a bond between them and something Rachel often brought up. This was Montana, after all—the land of big skies, Gary Cooper, ranches the size of small countries, and barely a million people. Cassie had grown up there and was pleased to be back. But there was no doubt that prejudice and misogyny lingered in backwards pockets.

A criminal defense firm run by women was a rarity. Rachel had once told Cassie that when she got together with Jessica Estrella to form their partnership, they were both known by their middle name of Angela. Angela Estrella and Angela Mitchell. They'd agreed to change their professional names to avoid being marginalized and lumped together in the legal community and law enforcement as "the Angelas."

"And how is Ben?"

"He seems to be doing all right," Cassie said. "It's hard for a teenager to fit into a new place and a new school but he seems to be doing fine."

Rachel nodded her approval. She'd remembered Ben's name and Cassie couldn't recall any of the names of Rachel's boys. She felt her neck flush red. Rachel had a way—whether intentional or not—of making Cassie feel inadequate. Cassie thought it might be one of Rachel's techniques for getting what she wanted out of people, and it likely served her well with witnesses in the courtroom.

"Jake, Van, and Andrew are doing well," Rachel said breezily as if to bail her out. "They grow up so quickly, but I'd be lying if I said I wanted all my little boys back. Jake and Van have discovered girls and I'm lucky to see them at all. Andrew, though, is like a young Bull. All he wants to do is go up into the mountains to fish and kill animals. He's been hardwired like that since he was a baby."

"Ben's a wrestler," Cassie said. "He's not very good but he's trying."

In fact, he'd lost every match thus far in the season. She

hoped he'd stick with it. Isabel disliked sports and encouraged Ben to "find his passion," whatever that was. It was one of several items of contention between Cassie and her mother in regard to raising Ben.

Cassie contemplated trying to get Ben together with Andrew Mitchell because Ben complained about never having the opportunity to go fishing. Cassie felt guilty about that but she didn't know how to teach him and at the moment there wasn't a man around who could. She wondered if Andrew would take Ben under his wing or if that was a disaster of an idea cooked up by a sometimes desperate single mother.

There was a pause and Rachel said, "We've got a new client and I'd like you to investigate the circumstances of his arrest."

There it was.

Cassie raised her eyebrows. "The circumstances of his arrest?"

"Everything about it. From the charge to the investigation to the arrest. I'm very interested to hear what an experienced investigator like yourself thinks of everything that has happened to date."

"Who are we talking about?"

"Our client is Blake Kleinsasser."

Cassie jumped in her chair as if poked from behind. "*No way.*"

"Hear me out," Rachel said without a smile.

CASSIE HAD READ about the case and heard officers gossip about it. Blake Kleinsasser was the oldest son of a very prominent ranch family that owned a huge cattle and hay operation in the shadows of the Bitterroot Range up north in

27

Lochsa County. Kleinsasser had been away for years under a black cloud but had recently returned under mysterious circumstances. He'd been accused of molesting and sexually assaulting the fifteen-year-old daughter of his younger sister—his own niece—at a distant outbuilding on the ranch and leaving her there when he was through. The victim had come forward and named her uncle as her assailant. His arrest had created a great deal of attention because of the Kleinsasser name and their influence in the area.

Fifteen years old, Cassie thought. Just a year older than Ben.

"No way," Cassie repeated as she shook her head back and forth. "I won't help you defend a child rapist. I put bad guys like him away, Rachel. I don't get them off. We talked about this. You agreed."

"We talked about finding justice," Rachel said evenly. "Everyone deserves that."

Then she asked, "Why are you so sure I'm asking you to help a guilty man go free? Are you saying the cops and over-zealous prosecutors don't make mistakes?"

Cassie paused. "What mistakes?"

"I don't know and neither do you," Rachel said. "This arrest took place up in Lochsa County, and I wasn't there to see it go down. Until I talked to him and reviewed the charges and the evidence—or lack of it—I knew as much about this case as you do right now and it all comes from newspapers and gossip.

"Up until a week ago he wasn't on my radar at all and I probably had the same view of him as you do," she said. "This was all a Lochsa County crime and I don't know my way around up there. Blake Kleinsasser hired a local attorney named Andrew Johnson for the arraignment and preliminary hearing and he wasn't my client. We didn't get involved until a week ago when the trial was moved here and Blake's counsel removed himself from the case for health reasons."

Cassie smirked. In her experience the only time defense attorneys resigned or stepped aside was because their client was either supremely difficult to work with or so obviously guilty that they didn't want to be associated with the accused. It happened more often in rural communities than urban environments, Cassie knew. Small-town attorneys had to live there after the trial.

"Why was the trial moved?" she asked.

"There are some highly unusual circumstances in this case but they're not all bad. My client was arraigned up there and entered a not guilty plea and bail was denied because Kleinsasser is considered a flight risk. During the pretrial hearing, the judge did a loop-de-loop and agreed with the defense that it was unlikely my client would get a fair hearing in Lochsa because the Kleinsasser family is an institution of some kind up there. I agree with that decision.

"Then after the case was assigned to here, my client's lawyer withdrew from the case for health reasons."

"What health reasons? That sounds hinky."

"I agree but I can only guess because my client won't share much with me," Rachel said. "But after looking at the charging documents and the evidence I think the attorney made the right decision for whatever reason. Let's just say that in my opinion there were a lot of things his previous counsel *didn't* do, and a lot of evidence he didn't challenge for some reason. Maybe he was just out of his depth with these kinds of serious criminal felony charges. I'll leave it at that because I'm hesitant to disparage another defense attorney."

"You people do stick together," Cassie observed.

"It's a small community. Too small to burn bridges, Cassie. Blake Kleinsasser's ex-lawyer may turn out to be the judge I'm trying a case for one of these days. You never know.

"Have you been to Lochsa County before?" Rachel asked.

"A million years ago. Not since our girls' basketball team played there in high school."

What Cassie could remember was murky. She recalled a bus ride on narrow country two-lane roads through miles of dark timber, the emergence of the snow-capped Bitterroots through the windshield as they neared the rural high school, and a foreboding sense of claustrophobia within the town of Lochsa Springs itself. It had been so unlike the rest of the state with its open vistas and wide skies that it stuck in her memory.

The game itself had also left a bad taste in her mouth. It was played in a tiny and ancient gymnasium and the stands were packed with local fans who booed the interlopers from Helena with a vehemence that rattled all the players. The Lochsa Springs girls were rough and nasty, and Cassie's team got killed.

"Lochsa County is an odd place," Rachel said as if reading Cassie's thoughts. "Some people might say it's about as backwards and inbred as you can find in this state. It's like the twenty-first century passed it by. Maybe even the twentieth."

She continued, "We can be grateful that the judge up there agreed to change the venue of the trial and we don't have to go up there for it. Did you know that there has never been a murder conviction in Lochsa County if the accused is from there? I've heard from prosecutors that if you're a local and you shoot someone in that county it's probably because they deserved it. Seriously. But if an out-of-stater is on trial for doing something to a local you can be pretty much assured that they're going to end up in Deer Lodge. So, we dodged a bullet there."

Cassie squirmed in her chair. "So, you think he's innocent?"

"I didn't say that. But I think he's entitled to a fair trial. Don't you agree?"

"A fifteen-year-old girl said he did it," Cassie said. "I don't want to be in the position of impeaching the testimony of a scared fifteen-year-old girl."

"It may not come to that."

Cassie sat back in her chair and grimaced. She wanted no part of this.

"WE'RE WAITING for all the prosecution discovery evidence to arrive," Rachel said. "In my opinion they're slow-walking everything, which unfortunately isn't that unusual. We're also waiting for the files from my client's ex-attorney that he prepared for the case before he withdrew. But I *can* tell you what the prosecution's case consists of because we have the transcripts from the preliminary hearing."

Cassie nodded for her to go on. Although Cassie knew it was lawyer-speak, she found Rachel's constant use of the term "my client" interesting. Cassie guessed that if she used "Kleinsasser" it would be confusing because the case was filled with Kleinsassers. If she said "Blake Kleinsasser" each time it would sound stiff. And simply "Blake" would convey familiarity that could come across as unprofessional.

Rachel consulted no notes and she met Cassie's defiant glare with a no-nonsense look of her own.

"According to the prosecution, my client arrived back in

Lochsa County three months ago—in June. For years he's been on the East Coast working in the financial industry. I don't know the details of what he did except I take it he made a small fortune for himself and apparently didn't keep in contact with his immediate family. It's well known up there that he's the black sheep of the Kleinsasser clan and apparently no one was very happy to see him come back."

"Why?"

"My client's problems with his parents and siblings go way back," Rachel said. "I don't have many details but I think it boils down to the fact that he's seen as a turncoat—a climber—who abandoned his multigenerational family legacy as well as the area. He's the oldest and firstborn son. You know how that goes."

Cassie was well aware of the phenomenon known throughout the Mountain West as "the curse of the third generation," wherein the founders of the ranch passed it on to their children, who later passed it on to *their* children. But it was that third generation where the situation sometimes went nuclear: family members who either did or didn't want to carry on the tradition, members who wanted to sell the whole place to get out and avoid taxes, members who went to war with brothers and sisters for what they saw as their rightful inheritance.

Lawyers and accountants had made their careers representing different factions of the third generation because the legal battles often went on for decades. It was the nastiest kind of war: brother versus brother, brother versus sister, sister versus sister.

"So, your client came back to reclaim his inheritance?" Cassie asked. "Sort of a backwards prodigal son thing?"

"Unclear, but that's the assumption. Look, I'll cut to the chase," Rachel said. "The prosecution alleges that on the night in question, July second, Blake got in a big fight with his younger brothers and ended up drunk at a local bar. From there, he left in his rental car and picked up the fifteen-year-old victim—his niece—after a church event and drove her to a remote outbuilding on the property where he assaulted and raped her and left her to fend for herself. Her name is Franny Porché."

"That's exotic," Cassie said. "Not Kleinsasser?"

"She's from my client's sister's third marriage. The sister, named Cheyenne, is divorced from what I understand."

"Okay," Cassie said. She already knew that if she went forward one of her first tasks would be to sketch a family tree. Not that she intended to go forward though.

Rachel said, "The other side claims they have a mountain of evidence and the Lochsa County prosecutor agreed with them. So did the judge, obviously. They say they can place Blake in the bar that night and later at the church. They say they have witnesses who will testify they saw the niece get into his rental car and drive away. They say the niece gave a statement that led to his arrest at a motel in Horston the next day.

"Of course," Rachel said, "They're throwing the book at my client and overcharging him as usual. We're talking felony sexual assault, kidnapping, criminal endangerment—the gamut."

Before Cassie could ask about the credibility of Franny, Rachel held up her hand palm-out to quash the question.

"The charges go well beyond he said, she said if that's what you were wondering."

"I was."

"According to the charging documents, the Lochsa County sheriff's department have four pieces of physical evidence to bolster their case. One is a whiskey glass found in the cabin where the girl was raped that's covered with my client's fingerprints. Two, they've got tire tracks from his rental car on the dirt road from the highway to the cabin. Three, they say they have semen residue and DNA on her underwear that matches up with my client. And four, they say they processed a conclusive rape kit with hair, fiber, and DNA evidence pointing to my client."

Cassie snorted and said, "Is that all?"

"I don't appreciate the sarcasm," Rachel said quickly.

"He's guilty," Cassie said. "Every box has been ticked. There's motive: a dispute with his family. There's opportunity: he was there. And there's both direct *and* circumstantial evidence that he did it."

"He says he doesn't think he did it," Rachel said. But her tone was tentative, not strident.

"You mean he says he doesn't know?" Cassie asked.

"He says he remembers getting in the argument with his brothers and later getting hammered at the Hayloft Saloon in Lolo. I've been there—it's a classic dive.

"My client recalls drinking shot after shot and then apparently blacking out. He didn't come to until the Lochsa County deputies were banging on his motel room door the next morning."

Cassie whistled. Open and shut.

Rachel sighed. "He insists on pleading not guilty, despite my advice."

"Of course he does. Ninety-five percent of criminals think of themselves as victims, not perpetrators. He's no different."

Rachel leaned forward and steepled her fingers. She said, "I know how it sounds. It sounds that way to me, too. But you yourself just said there's a five percent chance."

"I was pulling that number out of my butt," Cassie said. "I've spent my life around these scumbags. They blame everyone but themselves for the things they do. Of course he's not going to admit it."

Rachel lowered her hands to the desktop as if showing a hand of cards. "I'm not asking you to compromise yourself. I don't want that. I don't want you to set out to free a child rapist."

"Then what do you want from me?"

"I want you to step back a couple of years in time. You're once again the chief investigator for Bakkan County and this horrific crime is presented to you. I want you to do the same things you'd do if you wanted to put this guy away for the rest of his life, which you probably do. Interview the witnesses," Rachel said, tapping the tip of one manicured finger with her other hand to indicate *one-two-three*. "Examine the evidence. Go through the arrest warrants and the police reports. Look twice at everything you find to see if there are inconsistencies or holes. Do it not from the standpoint that you're trying to help a defense attorney blow holes in the prosecution case against her client. Do it as if you want to assure the prosecutor that every step you've taken as lead investigator is by the book and one hundred percent legit."

Cassie blinked.

"When you're through I want you to brief me on what you've found," Rachel said. "I want it straight, warts and all. If I learn from you that the prosecution's case is as bomb-proof as it sounds, well, I'll try a different tactic like a plea deal if I can convince my client that's the only way he can go. I need an airtight argument to convince him.

"But if mistakes were made—I need to know that, too. And if you discover new evidence or inconsistencies, well, I need you to share them with me as well."

Cassie thought about it. Rachel seemed sincere. It was almost as if she didn't know what she was asking.

"Based on what you've told me I think he's guilty as charged and he needs to go down for it," Cassie said. "I can't imagine a scenario where I'd change my mind."

"There might not be one," Rachel said with a sigh. "But I need to know that before the trial starts and we have to give our plea. That way I'll know how best to proceed."

Cassie hesitated. She weighed the likelihood of confirming the prosecutor's case and sending a scumbag to prison against the very dubious possibility of discovering gaping holes in the case.

"He's going to spend the rest of his life in Deer Lodge," Cassie said.

"Probably."

"That's where he belongs."

"Probably."

"This will all be an expensive waste of my time and your client's money."

"So it's a yes. Good."

Cassie nodded.

"How does your schedule look for the next couple of weeks?" Rachel asked.

Cassie didn't need to consult the appointment app on her phone. "I've got several jobs in the works right now— two insurance fraud investigations and a whole stack of background checks. Most of that work can be done from my computer in the office, although I do need to do a little surveillance of an insurance claimant up in Missoula."

"Is anything urgent?"

"Not really. Of course, I can't anticipate when someone will walk through the door like my skip trace job last night."

"You might have to turn them away."

Cassie squinted, trying to discern the reason for the rush.

Rachel said, "Please clear your calendar starting today. We came late to this case and we're behind the eight ball. I need the intel you can get as soon as I can get it."

Then it came to her. Cassie said, "If I find something to derail the prosecution's case you want to be able to use that information at pretrial motions. Before jury selection."

Rachel sat back. "When did you get your law degree?"

"I didn't. But I've been fighting people like you—over-aggressive defense attorneys—for a long time. I know some of your tricks."

"I'd call it a legitimate legal procedure. Not a trick."

"Whatever."

Rachel stood up and handed an inch-thick file to Cassie. The meeting was apparently over.

"If I do this, we're square," Cassie said, accepting the file. "No more obligation to you and your dad."

Rachel hesitated a moment and then nodded in agreement. "You might want to get reading," she said. "We're scheduled to meet with my client at ten in county lockup."

Cassie looked at her watch. She had forty-five minutes.

THREE

BLAKE KLEINSASSER was led into the interview room adjacent to A Pod of the Gallatin County Detention Center by a uniformed county correctional officer with a buzz cut and a wad of chewing tobacco in his lower lip. Kleinsasser had to shuffle from the door to the chair across from Cassie and Rachel because of the shackles and chains on his ankles. He held his hands out in front of him as if he were making an offering—but that was due to the handcuffs.

As he approached, Cassie had a severe hot flash that made her gasp for breath. Kleinsasser's entrance had immediately taken her back to a similar room in a similar jail in Wilson, North Carolina, when the Lizard King was in custody and she was sent there to identify and interrogate him. The man responsible for perhaps hundreds of rapes, murders, and mutilations of truck stop prostitutes and other innocent victims had loomed over her as he approached and had assessed her with dead shark eyes. He was operating under a new name and he'd added glasses and a beard to change his features, but there was no doubt it was him.

A few minutes later, after Cassie baited him, the Lizard King tried to crush her windpipe.

The scene in that room came back to her. She took a breath and felt her eyes flutter. She could feel the prick of perspiration under the collar of her blouse and she hoped her face hadn't flushed red.

Even though she knew the Lizard King was dead on this earth, he was still very much alive in her everyday thoughts and nightmares. He might always be. He was partially to blame for the fact that she could never go back to North Dakota, why she didn't want to be rehired by a law enforcement agency, and why she shuddered every time an eighteen-wheeler roared by her on the highway.

CASSIE TRIED to shake it off and observe Kleinsasser carefully. He was fairly tall and slim, six foot even, with longish sandy hair and hooded blue eyes. He had wide shoulders and he looked at them both with a kind of self-aware, self-satisfied smirk. His orange jumpsuit was several sizes too large so that the short sleeves of his top extended past his elbows and the fabric bunched around his jail-issued slip-on boat shoes. The effect made him look younger than his forty-three years, Cassie thought. He looked like an adolescent forced to wear adult clothing.

Jailers liked to humiliate prisoners in subtle ways, she knew. Especially high-profile inmates who arrived with attitude. They were issued clothing that was laughably too small for them or, in this case, much too large.

"Will you please unlock him for our meeting?" Rachel asked the CO.

"I can unlock his wrists but not his ankles."

"Then please unlock his wrists."

Kleinsasser nodded his appreciation as he sat down. The CO leaned over his shoulder with the cuff key and Kleinsasser held up his hands but didn't look over at the officer. Cassie noted the arrogance of the gesture, like holding up an empty glass at a passing waitress but not making eye contact.

When his wrists were unshackled, he rubbed them with his opposite hands before dropping his arms to his sides.

"I'll be right outside the door," the CO said to Rachel.

"I know you will. Please respect our privacy."

"Sure, ma'am," the CO said with a roll of his eyes.

Rachel waited for the *clunk* of the door lock before speaking. She turned in her chair and addressed the closed-circuit camera that was mounted in the top west corner of the room behind them.

"If this camera is live and somebody is watching this feed, now is the time to shut down your system. Observing an interview between the accused and his counsel is illegal and provides a basis to vacate the charges. Not only that, but I'll go after anyone snooping with everything I've got in a court of law."

Cassie couldn't swear to it, but she thought she heard a barely audible *click* from the direction of the camera.

Rachel turned to face Kleinsasser, who seemed amused by what was taking place.

"This is Cassie Dewell of Dewell Investigations," she said. "She's my investigator on this case."

Kleinsasser nodded his head slightly to Cassie, but didn't give her the focus she was giving him at the same time.

He didn't *look* like a rapist, Cassie thought. But that meant nothing. Some criminals, like Antlerhead, looked the part. Others simply didn't. The Lizard King looked like an overweight mid-western blue-collar worker, but he'd exuded menace despite his outward appearance. Kleinsasser gave off an air of bemused resignation.

After reading the file on the case, Cassie had Googled his name and looked for images. The disparity between what she found was striking. The most recent shots of him were of a gaunt and disheveled man being led across a motel parking lot to a sheriff's cruiser the morning he was arrested. In those photos, he looked confused and lost. His hair was pasted to the side of his head and he had a three- or four-day growth of silver-flecked whiskers. His eyes were dull.

Prior to that string of images, though, were many from what appeared to be New York City. In those, he wore stylish suits and ties and his hair was groomed. He was pictured with other hedge fund executives and bankers at social events, IPO launches, and financial instrument rollouts. He looked brash and above-it-all, a man almost too comfortable in his own skin. He looked smug and confident—a man used to winning, a fast-talker. There wasn't even a hint of Montana in his bearing.

He looked smug and confident, kind of like he looked today.

Before he opened his mouth and judging solely on his presence, she put herself into the role of a jurist in his upcoming trial and asked herself, *Is this man before me capable of raping his fifteen-year-old niece?*

As if reading her mind, his eyes darted toward her and then back to his lawyer in a dismissive way that set her on edge.

And she thought, *Yes. He's capable of that.*

"I'M FUCKED, aren't I?" he said and almost smiled.

"Let me answer your question this way," Rachel said as she dug into her briefcase for the file Cassie had read and a fresh legal pad to take notes, "you're charged with a half dozen Class A felonies. If you're convicted of even a couple of them, say kidnapping and forcible rape—you could be sentenced to two hundred years. But the bright side is you're going to get the best defense possible."

"Anywhere?" he asked with a sarcastic grin. "The best defense anywhere? Or the best defense in Podunk, Montana?"

Rachel froze for a moment and then her eyes narrowed into slits. Cassie felt the tension and fought the urge to slide her chair away from Rachel.

Rachel said, "Podunk, Montana, is where you've been arrested and charged for kidnapping, conspiracy, and the assault of your own niece. If you want to reach out to one of your high-priced New York criminal law firms and pay for them to fly out here and save your ass, I'll gladly step aside like your last lawyer and leave this hot steaming piece of shit case to them."

She set her jaw and said, "If you think a Montana jury would be impressed with the thousand-dollar-an-hour fast-talking New York lawyers, you're sadly mistaken."

Kleinsasser didn't flinch, as Cassie had. It said something about him, she thought. He was used to that kind of hyperbole. She wasn't.

"Color me impressed with that little speech," he said to Rachel. "People talk around here. I heard you were a bulldog."

He had a flat and fast New York accent that he must have picked up in the years since he left the ranch.

Rachel opened the file. "To answer your question: yes, based only on the prosecution's evidence and the charging documents, I think we're fucked. But that's why we're here today. So, try to keep your attitude in check long enough that maybe I can figure out a way to mitigate your situation."

Kleinsasser cocked an eyebrow.

"As usual, the prosecution has overcharged in this case," Rachel said. "As I think you know, you're looking at conspiracy, kidnapping, sexual assault, and rape. In Montana, section 45-5-503 of the criminal code for rape allows the judge to put you away for a hundred years if the victim is less than sixteen years old."

Kleinsasser snorted. "That ought to do it. Why all the other charges?"

"They always do that because it makes better headlines and they hope that if the judge or jury doesn't buy some of the charges, they'll find guilt with at least one major crime.

"I'll be blunt," Rachel told him. "It doesn't look good. There's nothing I've seen or nothing you've told me that even gives a whiff of hope for an acquittal. So, what we need to establish is whether or not we can base our defense not on your innocence, but somehow mitigating the worst of the charges so it'll result in fewer years in prison."

Kleinsasser tapped his fingertips on the tabletop. "You mean so I'll only go away for ninety years instead of a hundred."

"Ninety would be generous, Mr. Kleinsasser."

"Like I said, I'm fucked."

"Have you given any thought to changing your plea?"

Kleinsasser sat back and blinked. "Changing my plea?"

"That's what I asked."

"Why would I do that?"

"To avoid a trial. The county attorney *might* be willing to drop a couple of the charges and you *might* face less time in prison if they'll offer a plea bargain."

Kleinsasser glared at her. "No thanks to that."

"I had to ask," Rachel said, breaking their stare down. "If at any point you change your mind please ask the administration here to get in contact with me."

"Yeah, I'll sure do that if I change my mind." He rolled his eyes as he said it. "Don't ask me that again, Counselor."

Rachel took a deep breath, obviously trying to stanch her annoyance with him. "Look, Cassie here has reviewed your case and she has some questions for you. Please take your time and answer them in full. That way, when she goes up to Lochsa County she'll be better informed."

For the first time, Kleinsasser turned his full attention on Cassie. His eyes did a full assessment of her and Cassie could tell he found her less than impressive.

"You're going up to the ranch?"

"Probably."

He slowly shook his head. The grin that formed on his mouth was terrifying.

"Do you believe in God?"

"Yes, I do."

"Then may God have mercy on your soul. You have no idea what kind of fucking snake pit you're going to fall into."

SHAKING OFF the implications of the statement as best she could, Cassie reviewed her notes. It was a way to avoid Kleinsasser's withering instant negative impression of her appearance and abilities. "Let's get some background to start. Why did you come home, Mr. Kleinsasser?"

He narrowed his eyes and shook his head. "I didn't come *home*. I came *back*. There's a big fucking difference."

Cassie said, "Look, we don't have to make this difficult. I can do without the sarcasm, attitude, and profanity. Just answer the questions so I have some kind of basis on which to operate."

Kleinsasser briefly closed his eyes as if trying not to snap. Then he opened them and spoke in a lower, more modulated voice.

"I guess I forgot you're on my side," he said.

"I'm not on your side. I'm doing investigative work for your attorney. There's a big fucking difference."

"Gotcha," he said with an approving nod. "Using my own words against me."

"Get used to it," she said. "It's likely to happen in a court-room, too."

Rachel nodded her agreement.

"So again, why did you come back?"

"My parents are old. They're on their last legs and even though they're truly awful people all hell will break out when they're gone. As you probably know, I have experience in finance and I thought maybe I could broker a deal among everyone because whatever they think of me, I'm still the oldest son. I guess I foolishly thought I could help out with transition within the family. Obviously, I've been away too many years and I wasn't thinking clearly. If I had it all to do over again, I would have stayed in New York."

Cassie shook her head. "Broker what?"

"The inheritance. I thought I might be able to figure out a way to divide up the assets of the ranch and all of their enterprises in a way that would make everybody happy. I guess I figured I was the only one who could pull it off since it was obvious I had no interest in getting anything myself."

"Why is it obvious?"

He started to roll his eyes again but caught himself. "It's obvious because I left as soon as I could get out of that place. That isn't done in the Kleinsasser family. No one ever leaves. It doesn't matter if you make your own way in the world and don't ask them for anything. The problem is you left in the first place. That's considered the ultimate act of disloyalty. With them, if you leave or strike out on your own it means you look down on them and they resent you for it. Like I said, it's a snake pit."

Cassie glanced down at her notes. "I assume you're referring to your sister Cheyenne and your brothers John Wayne and Rand."

Cheyenne was the next oldest in the Kleinsasser family at thirty-nine. John Wayne was thirty-five and the youngest brother, Rand, was thirty-two. All still lived in Lochsa County.

"That would be them," Kleinsasser said through gritted teeth. "They all want the ranch for their own twisted reasons. They're so wrapped up in the legacy of the place that they think it's worth something—which it's not. I tried to tell them that."

"But how can that be?" Cassie interrupted. "The Klein-sasser Ranch is nearly eighty thousand acres."

"Over half of that is mountains," Kleinsasser said. "No good for anything besides scenery. Cows can't eat scenery, and the area is too remote to develop. There's no oil or gas on the property and not even enough wind for a damned wind farm. If you split that place up everybody would go broke separately.

"I tried to reason with them that it made the most sense to prepare to put the whole place on the market and we could split up the proceedings. Sell it to some billionaire land collector and forget about trying to make it work as a cattle ranch. I told them I didn't want any part of the payout but my share, that I'd sign any document they wanted attesting to the fact that I didn't want more.

"That just made them even more suspicious of me," he said. "My brothers, especially. They knew that because I was the oldest, I was entitled to the lion's share and they couldn't believe that I was willing to lower my inheritance to twenty-five percent. They figured I must be involved in some kind of big scheme to screw them or freeze them out. They figured I must know something they didn't—that it was a money grab by me because I don't love the place the way they do, which I don't.

"That's what you need to know about my family," Klein-sasser said. "It's all about two things: legacy and resentment. If you know that going in everything will be clear to you. It'll start to make some kind of sense."

"Since you claim to be wealthy, why do you even want twenty-five percent?" Cassie asked. "Why not just stay away and let them fight it out?"

"If only it was that easy," he said. "I wish it could work that way. But as I said—I'm the oldest son. They'd suck me in so they could pick the meat off my bones. I could see being involved in litigation for the rest of my life with people I never want to see again. I wanted to head off the coming war.

"Besides," he said, "Twenty-five percent isn't as much as you might think it might be once you go through all of the legal crap, all of the taxes, paying all the creditors—everybody with their hands out. In the end I figured I'd get a couple of hundred grand. That's chump change in my world, and it sure as hell doesn't compensate me for the years I spent growing up around those people."

Cassie tapped the tip of her pen on her notes. "Okay, there are a lot of family issues. I'm not sure us knowing them helps your case."

"It explains everything," he said defensively. "I haven't even told you about the Kleinsasser Family Trust."

Cassie cocked her head and Rachel leaned forward.

"The Kleinsasser Family Trust?" Rachel asked.

"It was established by my grandfather, Horst Kleinsasser. He was the so-called leader of a breakaway Hutterite cult who established the ranch in 1916 after being shunned by the rest of his colony. He was a strange and twisted dude, which maybe accounts for why my family is the way it is. But yes, he wrote a long document and deed establishing how the ranch would be passed down through the generations. My dad has it memorized and so do my idiot brothers."

Cassie wrote down the words *Kleinsasser Family Trust* for later research.

"Going by the Kleinsasser Family Trust, I should get everything," he said. "I'm the oldest son. It's all mine if I want it.

It's up to my discretion whether my siblings get a piece of it or not. But there's a catch. The only way the heir can be expelled from the trust is by denouncing the family name or committing 'moral turpitude.'"

Rachel sat back. "Like rape."

"That's correct. Like rape."

Cassie was intrigued but suspicious. "Are you saying they conspired against you in some way to establish moral turpitude?"

"I guess that's up to you to prove," he said. "But they already tried to get me kicked off the trust. They said that by leaving the ranch I'd denounced the family name. They hired attorneys and everything, but the judge concluded that going to work some place other than Lochsa County, Montana, isn't the same as formally denouncing the family, even though to my fucked-up family it was. So this is the next best thing."

"Again," Cassie said forcefully, "you're trying to convince us that they hate you so much that they *forced you to assault your underage niece*?"

With that, she dropped her pen on her notes and sat back with her arms crossed across her breasts. She wasn't buying it.

"I'm telling you what I know and what I suspect," Kleinsasser said. For the first time, there was a hint of desperation in his tone.

"Did you pick up Franny Porché from church that night?"

He nodded. "I did. I thought she was innocent. I thought she might be redeemable because she's of the fourth generation and that the magical hold the ranch has on the rest of them might not be as strong with her. I guess I thought that she might be able to talk some sense into J. W. and Rand."

Cassie switched her glare from Kleinsasser to Rachel. Rachel responded by looking away.

"You took a fifteen-year-old girl to an old outbuilding on the ranch because you wanted to talk with her?" Cassie asked. She couldn't keep the incredulity out of her voice.

"I know how it looks," he said, "but that cabin is where I spent the only good years of my life growing up on that place. I guess I wanted to show her that I did have a connection to the family after all these years despite what her mom and her uncles told her."

"You guess?"

"I'd been drinking for three days," he said looking down at his hands. "I can only remember bits and pieces of those seventy-two hours. I remember picking her up and I remember waking up when the deputies pulled me out of my bed at the motel."

Cassie shook her head. She disliked Blake Kleinsasser and she thought he was pathetic.

"How do you explain the whiskey glass they found at the cabin with your fingerprints on it?"

He shrugged.

"How do you explain your semen found on her underwear?"

To his small credit, he cringed. But he shrugged again.

"You're not going to claim that the sexual intercourse was consensual, are you?" Cassie challenged. Because if he did, she thought, she'd walk out of the room.

"There was no sexual intercourse," Kleinsasser said. "It didn't happen. Believe me, if it happened, I'd remember it. That's something even a drunk remembers."

There was no reason to ask him about the tire tracks from

his rental car. He'd already admitted picking Franny up and taking her out there.

"Have you been accused of assaulting underage victims before this incident?"

"God, no."

"So, when we dig into your past there won't be similar incidents? I ask because for sure the prosecution is looking."

"I'm not a monster," he said. "I'm just a stupid drunk uncle who thought he was doing the right thing."

Cassie bit her tongue. The sudden shift to victimhood in his tone rankled her. Like Antlerhead, like most criminals, nothing was ever their fault.

"Why did your lawyer quit?" Cassie asked. Out of the corner of her eye she could see Rachel tense up at the question. It was likely out-of-bounds. Cassie didn't care.

"You'll have to ask him," Kleinsasser said. "But as you'll find out, everybody in Lochsa County is connected to my family in some way. Maybe he figured that if he wanted to continue his practice into the future he needed to step aside."

"Cassie," Rachel cautioned, "do you have any more questions about the facts of this case?"

Cassie slumped in her chair. Her disgust with Kleinsasser and her role in his defense made the bile rise in her throat.

She asked him, "Can you give me the names of people who might have witnessed you during the time you started drinking to when you were rousted out of your bed at the hotel?"

He squinted as if trying to remember. "There's a man I met at the Corvallis Tavern."

"What is his name?"

"I think it's Frank."

"Anyone else?"

"I met a woman there. Lindy. Blond, late twenties, nice... figure. We spent a lot of time together before I blacked out."

"Last name for Lindy?"

"You think I got her last name?"

Cassie sighed. "Anyone else?"

This time, he closed his eyes while apparently trying to recall more details.

"There was a goofy old cowboy—a ranch hand. He was the foreman back when I was a kid but apparently he got let go. Named Hawk. He was nice to me. I remember sitting next to him at the Corvallis Tavern. He seemed to know me from my youth but I couldn't remember him as well as he remembered me. One of those old-timers, you know? He had a hard-on for my dad and my brothers. We talked about what assholes they are."

"Was this the first night of your bender?"

"No, the second, I think. But don't hold me to that."

"Did you spend time with Lindy that night?"

"Yeah."

"Anyone else?"

"Probably, but I can't think of anyone right now. It's all kind of a blur, like I said."

In her notes, Cassie wrote down: *Hayloft Saloon / Lolo / Lindy. Corvallis Tavern / Hamilton / Hawk.*

"You're less than helpful," Cassie said. "Can you help me with a time line from the hour you entered the Hayloft Saloon to when you were arrested?"

"Not anything other than what I told you. I was blotto."

Cassie sat back. "How often does this happen—these blackout periods when you're drinking?"

He shrugged. "Back when I was a young big swinging dick on Wall Street it was every couple of years, but it hasn't happened in a long time. This place isn't good for me, I guess.

"I don't know what it is about coming back to Montana," Kleinsasser mused. "But whatever it is—the big sky or the bad memories—it makes me want to find a bar stool as fast as I can."

Cassie looked over at Rachel again. The attorney looked as exasperated with Kleinsasser as Cassie felt.

He said, "They used to tell me when I went on a bender that the people I talked to didn't even know I was drunk," he said. "They described me as 'lucid.' But afterwards, I couldn't remember a damned thing."

"Let's say there was a scheme against you," Cassie said to him. "Who would likely be the prime mover in it?"

"J. W.," Kleinsasser said quickly. "Absolutely John Wayne. He thinks of himself as the keeper of the family name. Rand is unstable and he worships J. W., so I wouldn't be surprised if he were in on it."

"What about your sister?"

He shook his head. "Cheyenne and I have the same problem. We tend to go on benders where we can't remember what we did. Except when Cheyenne goes on one she comes back pregnant."

"Your parents?"

"I wouldn't put anything past them."

"And why would Franny lie?"

"I wish I could tell you. I *liked* her. She's a little off in the head but anyone would be growing up in that family."

"So, in conclusion," Cassie said, "everyone in your family is poison, twisted, and paranoid except for you. Your role is to show up and try and help everyone out of the goodness of your heart after twenty-five years of being away. Did I get that right?"

Kleinsasser started to talk but caught himself. Then he turned to Rachel. "I don't have to listen to this bullshit."

Rachel said, "This is nothing compared to what you'll hear in the courtroom."

"I'm not copping a plea," he said. "There's no way I did this."

"I thought you said you couldn't remember what happened," Cassie said.

CASSIE WAITED on a worn bench in the jailhouse hallway for Rachel to finish her meeting with Blake Kleinsasser. She couldn't spend another minute with him.

When Rachel came out she flashed her palms up. "Don't say it, Cassie. I know."

Cassie nodded.

"If you go up there and come back with corroboration maybe, just maybe, I'll be able to convince him to change his plea and we can move past this."

"How do you do it?" Cassie asked. "How do you look at yourself in the mirror?"

"I don't."

"We're on the wrong side here," Cassie said.

Rachel didn't disagree. She looked out the smudged jailhouse window and said, "The fires are bad this morning. My throat feels like I smoked a pack of cigarettes."

"I'll go tomorrow," Cassie said as she stood up.

They walked down the hallway together but didn't say

another word until they parted for their separate cars in the parking lot.

"Sometimes, they're not guilty," Rachel said over her shoulder.

But most of the time they are, Cassie thought to herself. Like Blake Kleinsasser.

FOUR

THE DINING ROOM still smelled of soy and MSG as Cassie gathered the dishes after dinner that night with Isabel and Ben. She'd stopped at Chinatown Restaurant on West Main on her way home and picked up cartons of sweet and sour pork, cashew chicken, fried rice, and hot and sour soup. Chinese was a compromise of sorts: Ben liked it because it was still exotic to him after living in North Dakota, and Isabel tolerated it because in her mind it was the product of struggling indigenous immigrants in a Caucasian world even though Chinese had built the railroads and had been established in Montana for generations.

Dinner had been quiet: Cassie with her thoughts, Ben with his, and Isabel scrolling through her iPad. But they'd all eaten together and not argued about anything, so it was a win. Often, lack of tension was all she could ask for.

While she scraped off the dishes and placed the half-full containers in the refrigerator for future meals, she tried to fend off feeling dirty for what she'd taken on. It had hung with her throughout the afternoon after meeting with Blake Kleinsasser. She hadn't mentioned a word of it to either her son or her mother because she wasn't sure she could defend herself against their questions.

CASSIE, BEN, and Isabel lived in a three-bedroom ranch-style home on West Kagy Avenue in Bozeman that was south of Montana State University and within sight of the Museum of the Rockies. The neighborhood was old and established, and the homes in it ranged from well-appointed to worn-out. Cassie's thirty-year-old house was closer to the latter. She knew she needed to get it painted and reshingled, replace the carpets and drapes, and update the kitchen.

Someday.

It wasn't her dream home by any means but it was good enough to be a placeholder until she could afford a rural property with some space around it. Maybe even a horse or two. The idea of grooming a horse seemed restful. Riding one at dusk and letting the tension of the day melt away...

AFTER DINNER, Ben had gone straight to his room without a word and Isabel had moved into the family room and turned on the television. The only three channels she watched were CNN, PBS, and MSNBC.

Her mother stood near the bookcase shaking her head at whatever the president had said or tweeted that day. As usual, Isabel wore a flowing full-length dress and her long white-gray hair was bound in a ponytail. The bare nubs of her toes stuck out from the sandals she wore most of the year. For as long as Cassie could remember, she'd never seen her mother wear makeup.

Isabel, who refused to answer to "Mom," or "Grandma" in Ben's case, was a stubborn caricature of what a sixties radical should look like two decades into the twenty-first century and she knew it and it didn't bother her. Once, after several glasses of wine, she'd mused about "changing her look" but she never had. Cassie was so used to it she was only reminded when strangers gaped at her mother when they saw her for the first time. It must be, Cassie thought, like suddenly meeting an actual cartoon character in the flesh.

"Don't let yourself get worked up," Cassie said as she entered the room drying her hands on a hand towel.

"It's impossible not to," Isabel said. "Just look at that orange clown. Just *look* at him. What is wrong with you people?"

It was a mantra. The current president had won Montana by nearly twenty percent. It was a source of apoplexy for Isabel and her small circle of like-minded friends.

"Has your life changed in any way?" Cassie asked, despite herself. "Mine hasn't. Is there something in your life that has gotten worse since he got elected?"

Isabel didn't look away from the screen. "I'm waiting for the internment camps. I'm waiting for the armies of intolerance to take over the streets and round up the gays and brown-skinned immigrants."

She was only partially kidding.

"In Bozeman?"

Cassie regretted even bringing up politics. She knew better. Plus, she had a favor to ask.

"Isabel, I might need to be away for a few days. Are you able to look after Ben?"

That got her attention. "How many days?"

"I'm not sure. It's for work. I may have to be gone a week at most."

"A *week?*"

"It may not be that long."

"Where are you going?"

"North," Cassie said. "I've got to do an investigation in Lochsa County."

Isabel's eyes left the television and narrowed on Cassie. "Have you ever been there?"

"In high school but I'm sure you don't remember."

Isabel didn't. She'd never paid any attention to high school sports or attended any of Cassie's games. That wasn't Isabel.

Cassie added, "Since then I've only driven through."

"Let me tell you about that place. I went there once with your father and it was horrible."

Cassie's dad had been a long-haul truck driver who was away weeks at a time, leaving her and Isabel, his common-law wife, in Helena at the time. That arrangement seemed to work for the both of them because they were such different people that absence served to keep their marriage alive far longer than if they'd lived together in the same house. In the middle was Cassie.

"When were you there?" Cassie asked.

"Years ago. I let your father convince me to go on a run with him and I regretfully said yes. I remember rolling into Victor in time to see a mob shaving the hair off a Native American outside a bar. They held him down and shaved off

59

his long black hair and let it fall into the street. I told your father to keep driving and I've never been back."

Cassie pursed her lips. "I've never heard that story before." She couldn't imagine that at one time in her parents' union that they'd been close enough that Isabel would actually agree to accompany her dad on the road.

"It was horrible," Isabel said. "I swore I'd never go back."

"Was this the sixties, then?"

"No—early seventies. How old do you think I am?"

Cassie didn't take the bait. "That's a long time ago and a whole different world."

"And I seriously doubt those people have changed." Isabel sniffed.

Then her face softened. "Of course, I'll be here for Ben, but he's getting more difficult. We used to have such a wonderful time together, but now I see how he looks at me."

"He's at that age," Cassie said.

She didn't add, *He looks at me that way, too.*

"I'll leave cash for groceries and I'll call every night," she said. "Maybe you can figure out separate dinners while I'm away so there isn't so much drama."

"He needs to eat healthy foods for his own good," Isabel said.

Cassie smiled. "Did you see him tonight? He ate twice as much as you and I. Wrestling practice after school makes him ravenous when he gets home, and he hasn't gained an ounce of fat. I wish I could eat like that."

"You could, once," Isabel said, taking in Cassie in a way that Cassie didn't like. "It's that cop diet. You cops eat garbage all day."

Cassie didn't want to argue. She recalled a piece of advice

once given to her by her then-mentor Cody Hoyt of the Lewis and Clark County Sheriff's Office, who said of day-to-day law enforcement routine, *Take every possible opportunity you can to eat and take a shit, because this county is 3,500 square miles, a third of it roadless.*

"So, you'll work it out with Ben?" Cassie said as if they'd agreed on something.

"I'll do my best if he will," Isabel said as she looked back to the television. Within seconds, she was shaking her fist at the screen.

CASSIE TAPPED on Ben's closed bedroom door and waited a beat.

"Yeah?"

She was still not used to the deep croak of his adolescent voice.

"Can I come in?"

"I guess."

He lay fully clothed on his bed and as she entered the room and closed the door behind her, Ben shoved his phone under a pillow to obviously hide what was on the screen. To cover the move, he reached out and pulled an open history book closer to him.

He was still wearing his shoes and she fought the urge to tell him to remove them from the coverlet. It was one of those small battles she no longer needed to win because of the overall consternation it would cause.

"Doing some homework?" she asked, knowing he hadn't been.

"I've got a couple of chapters to read."

She sat on the end of his bed. "Then maybe a little more reading and a little less texting."

He rolled his eyes and sighed, but Cassie smiled. She was encouraged by the fact that he *had* been texting with someone. She could only imagine how tough it had been for him to start the ninth grade at Bozeman High School having recently moved there and without knowing anyone. He was at a tough age to be a freshman *anywhere*. And she could only imagine it because Ben didn't talk to her about it.

She glanced around his room because she didn't enter it very much anymore. There were dirty plates on his desk from midnight snacks, a new poster with the MSU Bobcats football schedule, clothes piled on his chair, and an overflowing trash can.

"I know, I know," he said. "I'll clean it up."

She nodded.

Ben's father and Cassie's husband, Army Sergeant Jim Dewell, had died in combat in Afghanistan. Ben had never met him but he'd hung a photo of him in the camo uniform and helmet on his wall back in North Dakota and it was on his bedroom wall now. With every month, Ben resembled his father more and more: dark-haired, wide-spaced eyes, a slouched and ambling gait, a little more of a passive-aggressive attitude than necessary. In Ben's mind, his father had been a hero and Cassie encouraged his perception.

So many years had lapsed that she no longer dwelled on the fact that Jim had enlisted in the military shortly after he learned she was pregnant. If Ben had ever done the math himself, comparing his age and his dad's enlistment date, he'd never brought it up.

"I'm going to be gone for a few days for work," she said.

He moaned and threw his head back.

"It won't be so bad," she said. "I'm asking for you to try and find a way to get along with Isabel."

"She's such an old hippie, Mom. And the stuff she tries to make me eat…"

"She's your grandmother and she loves you."

"I'm trying to gain weight and that brown rice crap she feeds me doesn't help at all."

"Why are you trying to gain weight?"

"So, I can move up a wrestling class. There's this guy, Jason—I can't beat him. He owns the hundred-and-thirteen-pound weight class and as long as he's there I'll never be able to travel with the freshman team. I need to get to one twenty."

"I'm sure you will," she said, trying to remember what it was like when she didn't have to worry about putting on more weight. "Or maybe you'll beat him."

He shook his head as if to say it simply wasn't possible. "Maybe if he died or something."

"Ben."

He shrugged. "Mom, I've really been thinking about the sport of wrestling lately."

She arched her eyebrows but she had an inkling what was coming.

He said, "What would you think if I quit? I don't think I'll ever beat Jason. It's like he's a superhuman monkey or something. And I'm not sure I really love it, you know?"

"I understand what you're saying but you're a Dewell. Dewells don't just quit when things get hard."

"Isabel says I should follow my passion."

"And since when did you listen to Isabel?"

He moaned and rolled his eyes.

"Your dad never quit," she said. "He didn't like quitters. *I* don't quit. Just because something is difficult is not a good reason to run away."

He seemed to be thinking about it. "Did Dad really say that? That he didn't like quitters?"

Although Cassie couldn't actually recall Jim using the words, Cassie nodded in the affirmative.

"I'll tell you what," Cassie said. "Finish out the season. Do your best. If you absolutely don't want to sign up for wrestling next year, we can talk about it then. But you made a commitment and you have to see it through. It wasn't a commitment to me or your coaches—it was a commitment to yourself.

"If you start letting yourself off easy every time things get tough, you'll regret it," she said.

He sighed. "Okay. I'll stick with it this year. But if they kill me or cripple me that's on you."

"I'll take that chance." She smiled.

"Don't forget me here while you're on your trip," he said. "Isabel might try to poison me with that health food crap."

"I'll leave enough money that you can eat out a couple of times if you must."

He moaned again but it wasn't as forceful as the first time.

She caught herself from wondering out loud if maybe he could stay with a friend for a night. It might give him something to look forward to. But she wasn't sure he had any close friends. Back in North Dakota, it would have been Kyle Westergaard.

She patted him on the leg and said, "So how are things going? You don't talk much about school."

"They're fine." Deadpan.

"Are you meeting some people? Making some new friends?"

"Please," he said squirming, "I told you everything is *fine*."

"You can still talk to me about things, you know," Cassie said.

"Yeah, I know."

"So maybe you should."

"Don't say you worry about me, Mom. Okay?"

She knew there was no point going on. She pursed her lips and patted his leg with finality and stood up.

"You can always call or text while I'm gone," she said.

"I know."

"By the way," she asked, trying to make the question sound simply conversational, "You were chatting with someone on your phone when I came in. Do you mind if I ask who it was?"

"Ah, it was nobody," he said but his face flushed. "Just someone I met in English class. She's kind of weird."

"*She?*"

"That's why I didn't tell you," he said adamantly. "I knew you'd blow it up into something I didn't want to talk about."

"I'm not blowing anything up."

"She just moved here, too. That's all."

"Okay, Ben."

"Really," he said, "*That's all*. Jesus, Mom."

Cassie closed the door behind her. In the hallway, she hugged herself and smiled.

Then it was time to get to work.

FIVE

WITH HER LAPTOP OPEN on the kitchen table and glass of Syrah within reach, Cassie flipped to a fresh sheet on her legal pad.

She'd decided to start at thirty thousand feet and zoom in.

Hutterites were communal Anabaptists who traced their roots, like the Amish and Mennonites, to the Radical Reformation of the sixteenth century in Germany. They faced religious persecution in Europe and fled to Russia, which welcomed them to establish farm colonies to help feed the local populace—until the Russians threw them out as well. The Hutterites did what so many persecuted religious sects did: migrated to either Canada or America in the 1870s. Shortly after establishing themselves on the prairies of western Canada and the Rockies, the group branched out into three distinct congregations, called *Leuts*, known as *Schmiedeleut*, *Dariusleut*, and *Lehrerleut*. All three factions lived in colonies, practiced pacifism and socialism (which they described as "the sharing of goods"), dressed in traditional clothing, and spoke English as well as an off-brand Bavarian dialect.

There were nearly fifty thousand Hutterites still in Montana, most of them members of the *Lehrerleut* branch, named after their leader who was a teacher, or *Lehrer* in German.

Hutterites believed in six guiding principles:
Baptism was for adults, not children;
Members should not wield the sword;
The Lord's Supper is symbolic of the suffering of Jesus
    and should be done in remembrance of Him;
Pastors in the church are responsible for teaching,
    disciplining, and other duties;
Oaths are not to be taken;
and the ban should be applied to those baptized members
    who fall into sin repeatedly.

It was the ban Cassie was most interested in, because that was the reason the Kleinsassers had ended up leaving the colony and founding their ranch in Lochsa County in the first place. They'd been banned from the *Lehrerleut*.

She could find no additional information online why Horst Kleinsasser and his wife, Pauline, had been thrown out of the *Lehrerleut* sect. She wasn't really surprised, since the Hutterites online presence seemed to be limited to anodyne website documents and a few video clips from documentaries done on the colonies in Montana. It was obvious that the sects didn't like to speak to the press or issue statements of any kind.

If there were other families banned from the sect, Cassie couldn't find any mention of them. Only the Kleinsassers, and no reason was given. Was it some kind of religious offense, she wondered, or did the grandfather commit other sins, like assaulting young women? Maybe it ran in the family.

On her pad, Cassie sketched the family tree from what little information she could find on Hutterite websites and Lochsa County records and made notes next to each name.

Horst (deceased). *Born 1892, Russia. Patriarch of the family, banned from his sect. Founded the Kleinsasser ranch south of the town of Lolo in 1916 in Lochsa County. Supplied beef to U.S. Government during WWI. Established the Kleinsasser Trust. Married to Pauline. Died 1981.*

Pauline (deceased). *Matriarch. Married to Horst. No info. Died 1983.*

Jakob (deceased). *Firstborn son (1925), inherited and expanded the ranch to 60,000 acres. Officer, Montana Stockgrowers Association. Republican. Ran and lost a bid as lone Montana congressman in 1952. Married to Rita. Died 1972 on the ranch.*

Rita (deceased). *Born 1928. Three children: Horst II, Wilhelmina, Susanna. Married to Jakob. No info. Died 1980 in Great Falls.*

CASSIE SEARCHED in vain on the internet for any records for Wilhelmina or Susanna and gave up after fifteen minutes. It was as if they'd vanished. Horst II, however, had plenty of hits.

Horst II (67). *Born 1952. Inherited and expanded the ranch to present 80,000 acres. Served in U.S. Navy during Vietnam War. Established a small chain of livestock feed stores in western Montana. Found not guilty of second-degree murder*

of a ranch hand. Named Montana Stockgrower of the Year,
1992. Lochsa County Commissioner, 1984–2004. Chairman,
Montana Republican Party Central Committee. Montana
delegate to 1980 and 1984 Republican National Convention.
Married to Margaret. Still on ranch.

Margaret (64). *Born 1955 in Victor. Four children: Blake,*
Cheyenne, John Wayne, Rand. Married to Horst II. Still on
ranch.

Blake (43). *Born 1976. Left Montana in 1995, age 18.*
Graduated Columbia University 1999. Employed Bridgewater
Associates (1999–2002), JPMorgan Asset Management
(2002–2005), D. E. Shaw & Co. (2005–2009), Kleinsasser &
Associates (2009–present). Divorced, no children. Residence:
NYC and Gallatin County Jail.

Cassie snorted at that. His resumé was... discordant.

Next, there was: Cheyenne (39). *Born 1980. Lolo High*
School graduate. Two years, Montana State University.
Married and divorced (three times). Currently single. Daughter
Franny Porché, age fifteen. Lives on ranch.

John Wayne (35). *Born 1984. Graduated University of*
Montana 2006, Agribusiness Degree. Married to Rochelle.
Currently CEO of Kleinsasser Ranch. (Suspected by Blake
to be behind it all.) Two sons, John Wayne Junior, and
Tristan. (Ages?)

Rand (32). *Born 1987. Entered U.S. Army in 2005,*
dishonorably discharged 2006. Divorced, no children. Con-
victed of assault—eighteen months in Deer Lodge. Currently
working on Kleinsasser Ranch. (Said by Blake to worship
John Wayne.)

*

CASSIE SAT BACK and noted a few things that might be of significance.

The Kleinsasser women, from Pauline through the present time, seemed to make no mark. This was unusual in Cassie's experience. On the Montana ranches she grew up around, the women were the heart and soul of the enterprise. While their husbands worked and catted around, the women maintained the family enterprise. The Kleinsasser clan appeared to be an aberration from that.

Second, the journey of the family seemed to follow the pattern she'd discussed with Rachel earlier when it came to so many private ranch holdings. The multigenerational Kleinsassers were an illustration of "the curse of the third generation." Horst and Pauline founded the place, Jakob and Rita expanded it, Horst II and Margaret grew it further, and the third generation of Blake, Cheyenne, John Wayne, and Rand were blowing it all to hell.

The third generation also appeared to be an aberration from the past, which appeared to Cassie to have been fairly stable. The oldest, Blake, had run away at his first opportunity to make a life elsewhere. Cheyenne remained but had multiple husbands and at least one child. John Wayne was married, but Rand seemed to exist in his own dysfunctional world.

What *happened* to them?

She thought of a quote she'd once read by Samuel Butler in *The Way of All Flesh*: "If there are one or two good ones in a very large family it is as much as can be expected."

Yet the Kleinsassers appeared to have missed even that meager benchmark.

Also, John Wayne seemed to have been the first manager of the ranch not to expand it or create additional enterprises.

Lastly, she thought it was odd that there were only three grandchildren: Franny Porché, John Wayne, Jr., and Tristan. How could that be? Hutterites were known around Montana for large families. The Kleinsassers seemed to be an odd exception to that.

Then Cassie thought about what Blake had told her about the trust and the moral turpitude clause.

With Blake out of the picture, would fifteen-year-old Franny as the oldest grandchild eventually inherit everything?

Cassie made a note to ask Rachel her legal opinion on that the next time she talked with her.

SHE TURNED to the discovery evidence that the prosecution in Lochsa County had turned over to Blake's original attorney and that had since been forwarded to Rachel.

Cassie confirmed that Blake's first lawyer was named Andrew Thomas Johnson. Cassie underlined that name because he was a man she wanted to talk to. Whether Johnson would talk to her remained to be seen.

The arrest report file for Blake Kleinsasser contained a document that was entitled "Statement of Franny Porché."

Cassie read it over.

STATE OF MONTANA
COUNTY OF LOCHSA

The undersigned, FRANNY PORCHÉ, being duly sworn hereby deposes and says:

1. I am under the age of 18 and am a resident of Montana.

I have personal knowledge of the facts herein, and, if called as a witness could testify completely thereto.

2. I suffer no legal disabilities and have personal knowledge of the facts set forth below.

3. I'm accompanied by my mother Cheyenne (Kleinsasser) Porché and my uncle John Wayne Kleinsasser, both of legal age.

Executed this third day of July, 2019.

THE STATEMENT was signed in a loopy, childish script by Franny as well as by her mother and her uncle.

On the evening of July 2 I participated in my church youth group at the First Congregational Church in Lolo. When the youth group concluded I went outside the church to wait for a ride from my mother back to the ranch. I was alone.

I was surprised when instead of my mother waiting for me in the parking lot it was my uncle Blake. He opened the passenger door of his car, which was a blue four-door sedan, I believe. He said he'd drive me home.

I asked him about my mother and he said my mom had given him permission to pick me up. I didn't have any reason not to believe him even though I didn't really know him all that well. Uncle Blake had not been around when I was growing up and I'd heard things about him from my uncles but I'm not one to judge.

I got in the car and we drove out of town in the direction of the ranch. Even though the windows were open (it was a hot evening), I thought I could smell alcohol on his breath when he spoke. His eyes were red and he looked flushed.

Uncle Blake asked me if he could borrow my phone so I gave it to him thinking he was going to call my mother and let her know we were on our way home. But he didn't use the phone and instead placed it in the center console and closed the lid.

He said it was hard to talk to anyone these days because they were always on their phone—especially kids my age.

Then he said he wanted us to get to know each other better so that we could trust each other. He said he really wanted me to get to know him better. I know how that sounds, but it wasn't creepy at the time. I was kind of flattered that he thought of me that way.

He said he wanted to show me where he spent most of his time when he was growing up on the ranch. He said he wanted me to know that even though my uncles told me different, Uncle Blake had spent a lot of years there and he had a real connection to the ranch that I probably wasn't aware of.

I thought that was weird, but most adults are weird. I didn't feel threatened at that time and I was curious to see where he was taking me. I've spent the last few years on the ranch when my mom moved back but I don't know it all that well. I didn't grow up on the ranch like everyone else. I knew there were old buildings scattered around but because I can't drive yet I've never been to them.

We went down a kind of rough dirt road up into the trees. It was in a part of the ranch I've never seen before. Uncle Blake said it used to belong to some neighbors before my grandfather bought it from them. He seemed to know where he was going but it was farther from the ranch headquarters than I thought it would be.

We arrived at a two-story old house on the side of a meadow. The house was kind of dumpy, I thought. Some of the windows were broken out and the cattle had been on the porch and collapsed it. There was old cow manure everywhere. It was outside the house and inside the front door. The place smelled like cows. I'm not fond of cows. I'm a vegan, you know.

I thought we'd look at the place and then go home, but Uncle Blake said he wanted to show the inside of it to me. He said he used to spend so much time there and he was curious what it looked like now.

I asked him if he used to live in the old house and he said no, that ranch hands used to live there. He said the ranch hands were friendly to him and let him hang around.

We stopped the car in front of the porch and Uncle Blake got out and asked me to follow him. The door to the house was unlocked and he went in first. It wasn't dark outside yet because it was summer but it was dark inside the house.

I know you aren't supposed to go somewhere with a stranger. But Uncle Blake wasn't a stranger. He was my uncle.

Uncle Blake lit a candle thing called a kerosene lamp and put it on the table. He said he wanted me to see all the old rooms but I said I was kind of scared. I was afraid the floor would collapse and there were all kinds of rat turds and stuff all over it. Uncle Blake took my hand and sort of gave me a tour. He knew who used to stay in which room. He showed me a room with bunk beds in it where ranch hands used to stay together.

When we were done with the tour, he poured two glasses of whiskey from a bottle he must have brought from the car. We were back at the table in the dining room. I'm not a drinking girl like some of my friends at school and church, and I told him I didn't want any. He said it was a special occasion and I should try it. I took one sip and thought I was going to throw up. He drank his whole glass and poured another one. I recognized the smell from inside the car.

He did a "toast" to me and we clinked glasses and he made me drink. I didn't really like it but I did like the way he was treating me, like an adult. Then he started to tell me how my uncles had him all wrong and that he'd come back to try and reconnect with all of us. He said he wanted to talk to me because I hadn't been around long enough to be poisoned against him.

I guess at that point I was getting drunk, which is something I never want to do again. My head was really fuzzy.

Then Uncle Blake came around to my side of the table and lifted me up. He was strong. He sat me on top of the table and started kissing me. He has really fast hands and he was touching me everywhere. He stood there between my legs and held me in place.

I told him I didn't want to do anything with him. He said not to think of it that way, but to think of it as a way to get closer to each other. He said he really liked my eyes, which is weird because I don't think they're anything special.

I didn't scream because I didn't know what to do and there was no one to hear me. I thought if I fought him with my fists, he might beat me up.

It happened really fast. He pushed me back and pulled

my panties down and put his penis inside me. I'm not a virgin but it really hurt.

I didn't know what to do so I just let him finish. When he was done, he said, "That's what I think of this family," and he just walked out. He said it really mean.

I stayed inside and cried because I didn't want to go anywhere with him. He drove away just as it got dark, and I realized he still had my phone so I couldn't call anyone for help.

I walked down the road in the moonlight until I could see lights in the distance.

That's when I knocked on my uncle J. W.'s door and I told him what happened and he brought me here.

"YOU BASTARD," Cassie said aloud. "I hope you rot in Deer Lodge."

Before Cassie could reread Franny's statement and start a fresh page with her observations, her phone lit up on the table with an incoming call.

The screen read BRYAN. She snatched it up and punched the icon to refuse the call.

"Another bastard," she whispered while she reached for her glass of wine. "This place is full of them."

Bryan Pederson was the sheriff of Park County and she'd known him—and known of him—for years. He'd been there for her after the shooting of the trooper and he'd been there for the final act of the Lizard King. She'd noted that some time between the two encounters that he no longer wore his wedding band.

He was a good man, an honest cop as far as sheriffs went,

and she let herself start to feel comfortable around him off the job. And he was certainly attractive in a laconic cowboy kind of way.

Cassie became suspicious of him after the first night she stayed over at his house. She'd opened a closet door by mistake instead of the bathroom door and saw that it was filled with his ex-wife's clothing. When she brought it up to Pederson he explained it away by saying his ex-wife had never come to retrieve her clothes and he'd forgotten about them since he never used that closet. He bolstered his case by saying she was such a spendthrift that she'd likely already replaced her old wardrobe. Bryan said by the next time Cassie came to stay for the night the closet would be cleaned out and all of the clothes donated to charity.

Cassie had let herself believe that, but there was a kernel of doubt in the back of her mind that remained there for months, waiting for another shoe to drop.

It dropped on that afternoon in June when she opened his office door and saw Bryan and his ex-wife grunting on the carpet behind his desk. He looked over his naked shoulder at the sound of the intrusion and their eyes locked. There was panic in his face but Cassie didn't say a word. She had stepped back, closed the door, and walked straight out of the building to her car without looking back.

And she still hadn't.

There was nothing that needed to be said after that, and Bryan hadn't even attempted to make contact with her.

Until tonight.

Cassie muted her phone and placed it screen down on the table in case he called back. She didn't even want to see his name again.

He was out of her life, whatever the reason for the call. It was likely, she speculated, that his ex had thrown him out again so he was reaching out to her to try and mend fences. Men thought that way. Cassie didn't. Betrayal was betrayal.

She was grateful she'd not brought him to her house to meet Ben last summer. Ben would have likely been in awe of Bryan, and that would have made the split even more bitter and complicated.

Her instincts had been right on that count, even if they'd been a little skewed when it came to going out with Bryan in the first place. But she'd been lonely, and she still was. It had almost been worth it—at least for a few months.

She refilled her wineglass and tried to shove Bryan and his call out of her mind while she turned back to the affidavit and her observations about it.

ON THE EVENING OF JULY 2 wasn't something a fifteen-year-old would lead with, Cassie observed. It was legal language, and likely prompted by the prosecutor in the room. Neither was Franny's description of the "blue four-door sedan." What teenager used a phrase like that? It was cop language, not teenager talk.

Those phrases weren't disqualifying at all, but they indicated to Cassie that at least some of the language in the document wasn't as free and natural as it could have been. The heavy hand of the prosecutor was present in the affidavit. Cassie was sure Rachel had picked up on that as well and she'd likely use it in court to taint the evidence.

Cassie knew from her years in law enforcement that of course prosecutors "improved" witness statements. A literal transcript of witness recollections was filled with unclear sentences, incomplete thoughts, and dozens of "ums" and "you knows." A literal transcript was often a mess. Editing was necessary for clarity.

At the same time, editing allowed for a prosecutor to create a document more damning to the accused than what was actually said. It wasn't supposed to be done, but Cassie knew it happened all the time.

Cody Hoyt had once told her, *You'll find, Cassie, that it's us against the world. We do our damnedest to put away degenerates and douchebags so innocent people won't be hurt by them, but all the forces out there are set up to make us fail. We've got county attorneys that won't take on a case unless it's airtight, judges who want to invent the law instead of enforce what's there, defense attorneys who want to show publicly how fucking incompetent we are, and juries who want to stick it to the man. So, when we've figured out that someone is guilty as sin, sometimes we need to stack the deck a little. You know what I'm saying?*

She did.

CASSIE READ FURTHER and scrawled more notes.

Cheyenne gave permission to her brother Blake to pick up Franny at church? Why would she do that if Blake was a non-person within the family? There was more to that story.

I'm not one to judge also struck Cassie as a phrase unlikely to be used by a fifteen-year-old. It sounded paraphrased or coerced, unless Franny was exceptionally mature. But the rest of the document didn't indicate that. There was a flippant undercurrent in the statement Cassie thought odd and misplaced for a traumatized girl, including the lines about not liking cows and being a vegan. But Cassie also knew that victims sometimes focused on strange recollections.

Where was Franny's phone now? Back with her or missing? The phone wasn't listed on the impound sheet, which could be a clerical error or possible proof that the prosecution was withholding evidence. Cassie knew that *everything* was on a teenager's phone: photos, texts, contacts, and call records. Having the phone in custody was like having Franny's brain in custody. Would the prosecution withhold an item so vital and important, and if so, why?

That's what I think of this family also didn't ring true to Cassie as something Blake Kleinsasser would say. It came across to her as too melodramatic for the man she'd met that day. It seemed more like something Franny thought he might have said due to his heinous crime and demeanor. Maybe she'd misheard him, or it was a line fed to her by her mother, her uncle, or the prosecutor taking the affidavit.

Finally, Cassie found it interesting that Franny went first to her uncle John Wayne's house and not her own. Of course, there could be a simple explanation. Maybe John Wayne's house was closer. Or was there another reason?

FOR THE SECOND TIME that day, Cassie felt dirty. She didn't like finding questions and inconsistencies in the statement of a girl who was likely traumatized and emotional at the time she gave it. Cassie knew that's what defense lawyers had to do, but it bothered her once again that she was on the wrong side of the crime.

She reviewed the arrest report ("subject appeared inebriated and disoriented"), the witness list made up primarily of youth group participants as well as the youth pastor of the Congregational church who would all vouch that Blake picked her up that night.

There were printouts of digital photos: the interior and exterior photos of the old ranch house that looked as described by Franny, and shots of Blake's tire tracks on the dirt road that led to the abandoned home next to comparison photos of the tire tread marks on his rental car.

The statement from the medical examiner from Ravalli County confirming a match of the semen found on Franny's underwear with Blake Kleinsasser's DNA was the killer, though, as far as Cassie was concerned. Ravalli County bordered Lochsa County, and Cassie assumed that law enforcement in the region shared resources, including the medical examiner himself. Even without the affidavit and all of the other available evidence, the DNA match was enough to put Blake away.

Seeing the additional documentation tamped down the doubts Cassie had from the affidavit. No case was ever perfect. There were always nits to pick, which is what defense lawyers did as a matter of course.

Overall, though, she thought it was a pretty clean and straightforward case. All of the history she'd read earlier about Hutterites in Montana and the Kleinsasser family tree was irrelevant when it came to the cold hard facts of the arrest. She'd taken much weaker cases to county attorneys that had resulted in guilty verdicts.

Blake Kleinsasser was going to prison and he deserved it. His trip home to Montana had turned out much different than he'd thought.

SHE WAS so focused on her thoughts that it took a moment to realize that her house was shaking. Her first thought was, *It's a mild earthquake.*

The wine in her glass rippled and she could feel a low rumbling through the soles of her slippers from the floor. She pushed back from the table and looked around. She could hear the tinkling of glasses from inside her kitchen cupboards.

Cassie pushed back from the table. The source of the disturbance, she realized, wasn't from beneath her. It was coming from outside on the street.

She retrieved her Glock from where she stashed it every evening on the top of the refrigerator and she gripped it muzzle-down as she padded through the living room toward the front door. The vibration and rumbling increased in volume the closer she got to the front of the house.

The gun was out of view along her right leg when she opened the door and stepped out onto her porch.

What she saw chilled her to the bone.

A massive eighteen-wheel tractor-trailer idled right in front of her taking up the entire suburban street. It was a black Peterbilt tractor: the boxy shape of the cab and long nose were unmistakable. There was no reflection from chrome that had apparently been removed or from the exhaust stacks, which were blacked out. The cab was high and she couldn't see who was behind the wheel due to her angle and the dark tinted windows. Dim amber lights ran down the length of the trailer and their glow reflected on the windshields of parked cars as far as three houses away.

The semi was so huge, so dark, and so out of place in her neighborhood. It was a replica of the Lizard King's unit or the truck itself.

She was frozen in place. Her heart raced. She couldn't walk toward the truck or back up into her house. She could feel the rumbling of the diesel engine not only through the concrete but from within her chest.

When the driver released the air brake and there was a sharp hydraulic squeal she gasped for a moment and couldn't get air.

Then it slowly rumbled forward. She stood on the porch trembling, unable to move or act until it was gone. She'd tried to get a license plate number from the rear of the trailer but the light back there was broken—or disabled. She couldn't even see the state of origin.

Cassie peered at the houses on the block on both sides of the street, expecting to see her neighbors with their faces pressed to their windows to determine the cause of the disturbance.

There were a few lights on, but most of the curtains and blinds remained closed. It was as if they'd heard nothing at all.

FINALLY BACK INSIDE, Cassie closed and locked her front door. She couldn't stop trembling.

She *knew* it couldn't have been the Lizard King. She *knew* he was dead.

Was it a sick copycat driver who knew where she lived?

Or was there a more innocent explanation, like a confused freight driver lost within the circuitous labyrinth of Bozeman's suburban streets?

Isabel opened her bedroom door and stumbled out toward the bathroom with her sleep mask pushed up on her forehead. When she saw Cassie, she stopped.

"What are you doing standing there with your gun?" her mother asked.

"Didn't you hear that?"

"Hear what?"

"The truck outside our house?"

Isabel gestured to the earplugs she wore, shook her head, and went into the bathroom and closed the door.

CASSIE QUIETLY OPENED the door to Ben's room. He was asleep with his phone next to his head on the pillow.

He'd obviously slept through it as well.

SHE PLACED her Glock in the nightstand next to her bed and climbed under the covers. Her mind was swirling: an unholy mix of Kleinsassers, Franny's statement, what she'd need to pack for her trip to Lochsa County in the morning, and that eighteen-wheeler parked outside her home in the middle of the night with its engine running.

And there *had* been a truck out there.

Right?

SIX

A FEW BLOCKS AWAY, the driver parked his truck on a side street near the high school and turned his engine off.

He sat and waited, rotating his head from the windshield and side windows to the mirrors outside his doors. There was no one out on the sidewalks and no headlights in front or behind him. Nevertheless, he gave it fifteen minutes. For cover, he opened a map across his lap. If a patrolman knocked on his door he would say that he had gotten lost and was trying to find his way back to the highway. He'd have the map handy to bolster his argument.

Plus, there was no law against parking on a public street, even in the People's Republic of Bozeman.

THE DRIVER leaned back in his seat. With the heat off he could feel a few small tendrils of fall cold enter the cab, but it wasn't uncomfortable. Winter was still a couple of months away, even though there could be a cold front or even snow at any time in Montana.

There was very little wind in the air, and smoke from the distant forest fires seemed to catch and hold on the streetlights. Each one looked as if it had its own halo. The back of his throat was scratchy from breathing smoke all that day and when his eyes raised above the profile of the school building he could see the jagged line of the flames from distant mountains. And there were no stars. The smoke blocked them out.

THE SCHOOL was as big as he remembered it although it looked like there were a few add-ons near the old brick gym. The grounds were grass turning yellow, cottonwoods shedding leaves, and dark spruce trees standing like sentinels. Hanging wisps of smoke gave it an eerie feel. The light blue glow from overhead lights cast shadows and made the campus look far more serious and formidable than he knew it to be.

Seeing the building again—peaked roof, brick and glass construction, everything unimaginative and institutional— brought back a flood of memories that made him stir in his seat. They weren't good memories.

If it was possible to hate a building, he hated the building in front of him. He hated every brick, every bland tile in the hallways, every locker, every teacher, every administrator, every classroom but one—auto shop.

And he despised nearly every kid that went to the school back then. He doubted they were any different today and they were probably worse.

From what he'd observed, the coming generation was just a bunch of pussies. Coddled, softheaded narcissists, all of them.

They were all heroes in their own minds and in the minds of their parents and the school administration. They all had a shelf stacked with participation trophies.

They were so into their own feelings. Their heads were on swivels to constantly look for offense so that they could be righteously outraged by something. He'd read where the senior class of the school in front of him had gone on strike the previous year because of something a gym teacher said that was construed as racist and homophobic. The students were portrayed in the press as champions of tolerance. The gym teacher was suspended and later let go.

Pussies.

These little snowflakes had no idea what they were going to face when they got out into the real world. They should all have to spend thirty days in prison to find out what the law of the jungle was truly like. They should be assigned to a cell in D Pod with no television, no cell phones, no social media, and no Wi-Fi. They should have to bunk with a Crow Indian from the res who was in there for murdering a seventy-year-old Good Samaritan couple from Missouri who stopped on the highway to help him and his broken-down pickup.

That thought made him smile.

HE'D PROMISED to himself to stay clean for the night. No alcohol, no weed, no meth. He'd kept his promise, although he couldn't stop his left leg from bouncing up and down as he sat.

The driver painted the whole of the school with his eyes. He picked out individual classrooms where he'd once been trapped. He recalled that his only solace was staring out the window toward the mountains and waiting for the final bell of the day.

He was surprised how vivid his memories were and how much they affected him now. He hadn't expected it.

Few knew what it was like to go to a high school in the wake of a legacy—his siblings—and come up short. To be judged not on your own accomplishments or attributes but solely in comparison to those who had gone before. You could see it in the eyes of his teachers once they established his lineage. Sometimes they told him stories about those before him as if that somehow would make him feel better about himself. Instead, though, it drove home the fact time and time again how he paled in comparison. Every damned time.

And he hated the factions: the stoners, the cowkids, the hipsters, the socials, the athletes, the emos, the nerds, the elites. He never belonged to any of them. He was an outcast and he hung around with other outcasts, most of whom he couldn't stand.

He would forever be an outcast.

But it was different now. He was an outcast with a plan.

A plan and a gun.

WITH THE WEAPON tucked into his waistband and his jacket pulled over it, the driver climbed out of his truck and shut the door behind him and walked toward the high school.

He crossed the teacher's parking lot quickly because it was wide open and illuminated by overhead lights, pausing only when he was in the deep shadow of a campus spruce. He looked around again, checked the streets, checked the sidewalk.

He turned his back on the front doors of the school where he knew there were closed-circuit cameras. There had been cameras even when *he* went there, although he wasn't sure they'd actually worked.

The truck driver knew about the cameras from a clip he'd watched on YouTube depicting an act of student bullying that took place inside the entrance vestibule. The cameras clearly identified the perpetrators—they pummeled a kid who looked like he deserved pummeling—and the offending students were later suspended. He didn't care about that. What interested him was the range and quality of the video cameras. It was like a fucking television studio inside the vestibule.

No one could enter the front doors of the school without being clearly seen, and it was a long way inside—past the principal's office, past the guidance counselors, past the school security room—to where the classrooms were located.

There was no need to take that gamble.

FROM TREE TO TREE, shadow to shadow, he progressed the length of the long building toward the back. He paused at the gym building and stood tall to look through a window into the interior. The gym was lit by widely spaced emergency lights but from what he could see it still looked the same. The uncomfortable stands, the gym floor, the stupid paintings of the mascot on the walls under each basket. Looking inside brought back a flood of feelings he didn't like.

He could smell the sour sweat and piss from the locker room and hear the reverberation of sharp sounds inside the gym itself. That place was a special kind of hell and he fought an involuntary shiver when he took it in.

*

HE STAYED close to the exterior brick walls because the angle of the moonlight kept them in complete shadow. The grass ended as he got closer to the farthest building from the front of the school, the auto shop. They didn't bother to keep the grass groomed back there because it couldn't be seen from the street and the students who hung out there were losers anyway.

His boots crunched on gravel mixed with cigarette butts and it nearly made him smile. He used to smoke there, right there in the same place. He was glad the tradition had been upheld.

At the corner of the end of the building the driver paused and reached for his pistol. It was a Browning Buck Mark .22 semi-auto with a homemade suppressor and a ten-round magazine filled with hollow-point rounds. It felt balanced and substantial in his hand.

Then he leaned around the corner and aimed up. Under the high eave was a glass bulge that looked like an upside-down bowl. That's where the closed-circuit camera was housed.

He racked a cartridge into the pistol and caught a glimpse of brass before it was seated. Then he raised the weapon again and steadied it by leaning against the brick. He thumbed the safety off and squeezed the trigger.

Snap-snap-snap-snap-snap-snap.

Shattered glass and pieces of the surveillance camera fell to the driveway. What remained of the camera itself stuck out of the housing like the tongue of a dead animal.

The sound of the shots were high-pitched and, he thought, not loud enough to draw attention.

He targeted what was left of the camera.

Snap-snap-snap-snap.

The unit dropped out of the housing and hung there, held

up by a single electric wire. It twisted in the moonlight like a dead rabbit caught in a snare.

THE DRIVER gathered up all the spent casings and counted them twice to make sure he had them all. They'd all been kicked out the same direction and most of them had been nestled in a crack in the concrete driveway. He dropped them into his pocket along with the empty magazine and shoved an extra ten-shot magazine into the grip.

With the pistol tucked back into his waistband—the barrel was surprisingly hot—he walked around the corner and tried to turn the knob of the outside door. Locked, as he thought it would be.

Then he bent and grasped the handle of the big garage door. If the students were like the ones he'd gone to class with, they sometimes forgot to lock the overhead garage door. He pulled up on it. Locked.

But he knew a trick that used to work.

He grasped the garage door handle with both hands and set his feet. The latch that anchored the folding garage door to the track used to not line up to the locking slot correctly. It had been installed poorly when the building was built.

In the driver's view, maintenance people working for the school system, like the teachers and administrators, did the absolute minimum possible. They did their day-to-day chores, enough to keep them employed. But they rarely took the initiative to fix a fundamental problem like a misaligned garage door unless it was an immediate problem.

Then he jerked the door hard left, putting his weight into it. The latch gave with a *click*.

He thumbed the green button next to the doorjamb and he heard the opener inside growl to life. The door rumbled and began to raise.

He paused it after two feet, just enough to see the shiny concrete floor on the inside and to get a whiff of motor oil and transmission fluid. Then he closed it and rocked the door to the right until the latch reseated.

From the auto shop there was an annex that led to the main classroom building. There were no doors or barriers in between.

He knew there were probably cameras in the hallways but he wasn't concerned with them. They might capture his image, but by the time they did he'd be well inside moving to his destination. It would be too late to stop him.

The driver knew he could get into the school any time he wanted to.

He also knew it might take weeks for the repair order on the outside camera to work its way up through the administration and back down again to a breathing maintenance man, who would then have to order a whole new closed-circuit video assembly and wait for it to get shipped before he could even think about installing it.

THE DRIVER stayed in the pools of shadow as he made his way back to his truck.

He climbed inside the cab, closed the door, and returned the Browning to the center console.

After checking the streets to ensure that no one was watching, he started the engine and rumbled away. His target, he thought, would never see him coming.

PART II

Envy slays itself by its own arrows.

—The Greek Anthology, X 111

You shall not hate your brother in your heart.

—Leviticus 19:17

SEVEN

AS CASSIE DROVE to Lochsa County the next day, she was still unnerved from the encounter the night before with the tractor-trailer outside her house. It had been so unexpected and it had awakened in her a feeling of dread and doom that she thought she had left behind.

Maybe she should see someone, she thought, a counselor of some kind. If simply seeing a semi-truck in a state filled with them on every highway brought out this kind of dread...

She tried to push it aside. Cassie had always thought herself smart and strong enough to deal with her issues and she had secret contempt for people who ran to psychologists as a matter of course to dissect their feelings. But maybe when things slowed down she would see someone, she thought.

The last thing she needed, though, would be for word to leak out that she was undergoing psych treatment. That might discourage current and future clients. She knew from experience how fast rumors could travel within law enforcement and legal circles even among the more enlightened. She knew she'd have to discreetly ask around for a name or two of counselors who could keep their mouths shut.

But first, she had work to do.

Blake Kleinsasser, rapist and moral reprobate that he was, deserved a competent defense. And if he was as guilty as he seemed, Rachel needed to know it so she could negotiate with him on solid ground to cop a plea.

That would be the best route, Cassie knew. Blake would go to prison and Franny would be spared reliving the crime in front of jurors and press coverage.

SMOKE HUNG in every valley and it distorted the view of the mountains in every direction, as if someone had smeared Vaseline on the interior windows of her Jeep. It was so thick she could taste it.

She glimpsed makeshift camps of temporary firefighters as she drove west as well as distant helicopters and aircraft carrying loads of water and fire retardant. The fires were everywhere there was timber, and that meant there were fires throughout the Northern Rockies.

Cassie chose to leave Interstate Highway 90 after Butte and she cut south and west on two-lane state roads. There was no direct route because the Sapphire Range ran north to south between the interstate and Lochsa County. There was one unpaved road that switchbacked over Skalkaho Pass, but she'd seen digital roadside warnings reporting that there was an active fire on top and long delays were likely.

So she took Highway 43 to Wisdom, Montana, with the Pioneer Mountains on her left, the Sapphires and Continental

Divide on her right, and the Big Hole River coursing through the stunning empty valley. She encountered less than a half-dozen cars along the route, although she glimpsed drift boats and fly fishermen at times on the river.

Cassie recalled from her Montana history that the Big Hole Battlefield was where Chief Joseph and his Nez Perce engaged the U.S. Seventh Infantry in a day and a half battle in 1873. It was a sad and depressing story, as well as a typical one.

The American government renounced a treaty they'd signed with the Nez Perce to allow settlers and white miners into their lands, and Chief Joseph—betrayed too many times already—had decided to lead the entire tribe through the mountains to Canada where he hoped to team up with Sitting Bull and his relocated Lakota. The army intercepted them along the Big Hole River and attacked, killing almost a hundred Nez Perce men, women, and children.

With the survivors, Chief Joseph fled east through what was now Yellowstone Park, then cut to the north hoping he could elude the army. Forty miles short of the border and starving, he surrendered.

The valley might be breathtakingly beautiful, she thought, but it cloaked one of the worst episodes from the settling of the state and the country.

SHE WAS SLOWED TWICE by farm machinery inching along the blacktop and at one point by a large herd of black Angus being driven by mounted cowboys. The pavement was covered with wet green manure and the inside of her Jeep smelled of it for fifteen miles. Then she began to climb into the mountains.

Finally, she descended via a sharp set of switchbacks into the Bitterroot Valley on U.S. Highway 93. The route would take her north parallel to the Idaho border into the series of communities and counties in far western Montana.

As she drew closer to Lochsa County, she was reminded of observations she'd made in her high school sports days when the bus she was in ventured to that part of the state. While Montana was made up of mountains, valleys, rivers, and plains, it was as if those massive formations and vistas were pushed together and jammed against a wall the farther one traveled west. Mountain ranges seemed taller and closer together, meadows and hayfields were smaller and steeper. It was as if the terrain of the state was pinched together from the sides up against the sawtooth border of Idaho—which ran along the top of the Continental Divide all the way to Canada—and it was all extreme and mildly claustrophobic.

BECAUSE SHE HADN'T been able to sleep after her encounter with the curbside trucker, Cassie had researched Lochsa County itself and its odd origins.

With Missoula County to the north and Ravalli County to the south, Lochsa was small by Montana standards. It stretched east to west, sandwiched between the two and without a town with more than two thousand residents. The county seat was Horston, population eighteen hundred. She found it striking to study the map and see that between Hamilton and Lolo it was almost a void. And in the center of Lochsa County, hard against the Bitterroot Mountains to the west and the Bitterroot River to the east, was the vast Kleinsasser ranch.

After reviewing Blake Kleinsasser's arrest report and all of the documents Rachel had provided for a second time, Cassie had turned to a fresh page on her legal pad and made a list of what she hoped to accomplish on her trip to Lochsa County: interview Sheriff Ben Wagy and review evidence and charging documents; try to interview Blake's former defense attorney, Andrew Thomas Johnson; find Hawk; find Lindy; Kleinsasser Ranch; try to walk through building where assault took place; write report with conclusions for Rachel.

Of those, the only item she felt good about was talking with the local sheriff. The others could be stymied by non-cooperation (Johnson) or pure shots in the dark (Hawk, Lindy, getting permission to view the crime scene).

Cassie found the website for Lochsa County and composed a brief email introduction of herself and made the request to speak to Sheriff Wagy the next day. She knew that being the sheriff of a rural county was equal parts political, social, and law enforcement. If the sheriff was cooperative with her—and most in her experience were—it was by far the best way to start an investigation and build a time line.

SHE ALSO DID a deeper dive into the founding of the county itself, and the name "Kleinsasser" popped up everywhere. Horst I, Jakob, and Horst II were involved in everything: local politics, county politics, planning commissions, joint powers boards, school boards, weed and pest control boards, on and on. John Wayne and Rand were mentioned on a much smaller scale. Blake's name was nonexistent.

Horston, of course, was named after Horst I.

She also found it interesting that the Kleinsasser Ranch had another name. It was officially registered as the Iron Cross Ranch, and its brand was the German Empire symbol:

AS THE LATE AFTERNOON heated up into the seventies, the heat and dry air fueled the many fires and Cassie had to slow down as visibility decreased. She turned right at Chief Joseph Pass and dropped into the Bitterroot Valley on a steep highway featured with S-curves.

The sharp outline of Trapper Peak, at 10,157 feet, dominated the western wall of mountains, but Cassie had to remind herself that there were 199 peaks in the state that were higher.

Like everywhere in Montana, small white crosses designated highway deaths on the side of the road. Some were decorated with plastic flowers, ribbons, and totems from their loved ones. Others weren't. Cassie always felt sorry for those souls that were bare of remembrance.

Both sides of the road were heavily timbered with ponderosa and spruce. The mountains and the trees kept the highway heavily shadowed, and *this* is what she remembered about the area: that instead of the infinite views and big Montana sky she'd grown up with, it seemed as if the rough villages were linked by narrow tunnels through the forest.

A dead cow elk, freshly killed and abandoned by a motorist, lay sprawled across the northbound lane of the highway. Shards from broken headlights sparkled around the carcass as well as pieces from a shattered front grille.

Cassie winced and drove around it.

★

HAMILTON, LIKE so many small towns in Montana, was in the process of being gentrified. There were espresso bars, clothing stores, brewpubs, hipsters, and more stoplights than she recalled. The timber, hunting, and ranching culture of the valley was being transformed.

As she sat at one traffic light, she noted several men emerge from one of the brewpubs and approach an SUV with California plates. To a man, they wore colorful fly-fishing shirts with lots of pockets, zip-off trousers, floppy hats, and river sandals. It used to be, she thought, that these tourists would no doubt be dedicated fly fishermen. These days, though, it could just as easily mean they were parishioners from the Church of Trout, a religion coined by her mentor, Cody Hoyt.

The Church of Trout, Cody claimed facetiously, was made up of hundreds of thousands of members who looked the part, dressed the part, and never went near a river. Montana was now filled with them.

SHE DROVE PAST a series of custom log home building companies north out of Hamilton, and within several miles she noted that commercial buildings and private homes along the roadside became fewer.

Cassie filled her Jeep with gasoline in Stevensville ("Home of the Fighting Yellowjackets") and breathed in thin mountain air colored by the fragrances of pine and woodsmoke. The border of Lochsa County was ten miles away.

IT WAS AFTER FIVE when she took the highway exit into Horston and she cursed under her breath. She'd hoped to get there at least an hour earlier so she could meet the sheriff of Lochsa County before the close of the county building. She checked her email on her phone to see if he'd replied to her inquiry. He hadn't. She hoped he hadn't been put off by the 3:47 a.m. time stamp on her message and concluded that she was a crazy woman to be avoided.

Downtown Horston consisted of three blocks on Main Street. Unlike Hamilton, the cool people hadn't yet discovered it. The storefronts looked almost deliberately retrograde and there were few people out on the sidewalks. The town, she thought, could serve as the location for a movie set in the 1950s or '60s and she got the distinct feeling that the place was barely hanging on despite the growth north and south of it.

Horston was what Hamilton used to be, she thought. Before the Church of Trout discovered it.

It was notable, she thought, that the only retail businesses that appeared to be open were three saloons that stood shoulder to shoulder. Two other saloons were spaced out on the other side of the street.

She recalled something she'd learned when she visited the tiny town of Ekalaka in eastern Montana, which was six hundred miles and ten and a half hours away: *any location in Montana is a good place for a bar.*

ALTHOUGH THERE WERE TWO ubiquitous brand-name chain motels on the outskirts of Horston, Cassie had made online reservations at an aging motel called the Whispering Pines in the middle of town. It was located on the next block from the small herd of saloons.

The neon tubing on the motel sign out front quivered with electric light but formed three tall pine trees. A red VACANCY notice hummed beneath it. The lot was shaded with mature ponderosas that gave the facility the appearance of a mountain oasis right off Main Street.

For investigative work, Cassie opted for older motels rather than modern facilities. In newer hotels, it was always necessary to enter and exit through the lobby and encounter the employees behind the front desk. Older motels like the Whispering Pines had individual units at street level with no central hallway and separate doors opening out into the parking lot. That way, she could come and go at odd hours and no one could inquire where she was going or why.

She pulled under an overhang next to an attached structure with a sign outside that read OFFICE. There was something familiar about it, she thought. She wondered if perhaps her high school team had stayed there, but she didn't think so.

CASSIE WAS STILL TRYING to recall if and when she'd been there before as a bell sounded when she opened the door to the office and went inside. She was immediately greeted by the smell of cooking meat emanating from an open door behind the worn front desk. The office obviously served as living quarters for the manager as well.

"Coming," a deep male voice said from beyond the door.

"No worries," Cassie replied.

She looked around while she waited. The lobby was dark and close. Faded Charles M. Russell prints were hung on the walls as well as a framed notice that spelled out WE LOVE

OUR GUESTS in what she first thought were small white seashells but on closer inspection turned out to be ivory elk teeth. Since every elk had only two ivory teeth—called "whistlers" or "buglers"—that meant eight animals had died to make the greeting.

"How nice," she grumbled to herself. Cassie had no issue with hunting and she'd grown up with it. But removing the ivory teeth with pliers and displaying them this way repulsed her. Always had.

The manager was a large bald man with a full beard. He wore a flowing open flannel shirt over a green T-shirt that stretched across his belly. He dabbed at the corners of his mouth with a napkin as he approached the counter.

"Sorry," he said. "You caught me at dinnertime."

"Smells good. I'm Cassie Dewell. I have a reservation."

The manager nodded with recognition and lit up the monitor of his ancient computer. He stabbed at the screen with a stubby finger.

"Four nights, right?"

"It may be less than that. I'll keep you posted."

"Not a problem," the man said. "We're between tourists and hunting season. I don't guess there will be a big run on the rooms."

She anticipated his next request and slid her driver's license and credit card across the counter.

While he punched in the numbers on his keyboard, it hit her. She thought she knew why the motel seemed familiar.

FROM THE PHOTOS she'd reviewed the night before she recognized the mature trees in the parking lot and the layout of the individual units in the background. It was the same motel Blake Kleinsasser had been in when he was arrested.

The manager stopped typing. When he looked up his expression was inscrutable.

"UNIT NUMBER ELEVEN," the man said. "That's the one on the far end. It's a little larger than the other units and very comfortable." In fact, she thought, it was the same room Blake had been in. The photos had clearly shown that it was the last unit in the complex.

She hesitated. Staying in the same room as a rapist repelled her at first. She didn't want to say why that was to the manager. Then she thought staying in Blake's room might turn out to be an advantage in her investigation. Being in the same space might give an insight to his state of mind. There could possibly still be evidence of him in it as well.

"Yes, that's fine," she said.

He hesitated for a moment before giving back her company credit card. "Dewell Investigations," he said. "Are you here on business or pleasure?"

"Business."

"Are you investigating something?"

"Nothing you need to worry about," she said, wishing she'd lied.

"And you're from Bozeman?"

She nodded.

"Bozeman ain't how I remember it anymore," he said. "Too many newcomers. It's hardly Montana in my mind anymore. No offense."

"None taken."

"Well, welcome to God's country. I like to think of this place as what Montana used to be before the folks from California moved here to ruin it."

Cassie had heard similar sentiments from Bull Mitchell, Rachel's crusty father.

He said, "Let me know if there's anything I can help you with while you're here."

"I'd like to get a good steak and glass of wine. Is there someplace you'd recommend?"

"France." Then he guffawed. "I'm just kidding. I don't know anything about wine, but if a place doesn't serve good steak it doesn't last around here. I'd suggest the Hayloft up in Lolo."

"Is there any place within walking distance? I've been in my car all day."

"Stumpy's," the manager said. "Right at the end of the block. Tell 'em I sent you."

"And you are?"

"Glen Steele," the man said. "I own this place. It's been in my family for years."

"Nice to meet you, Mr. Steele."

He did a well-rehearsed oration on the location of the ice machine, the Wi-Fi password, and where the bell was outside the office in case she came in late and forgot her key.

As she turned to leave he said, "This doesn't have anything to do with that Kleinsasser thing, does it?"

"Nothing you need to worry about," she said again. She thought Glen Steele asked too many questions for a motel owner.

*

ROOM NUMBER ELEVEN was the corner room, the last one of the wings. She parked in front of the door and noted that there was only one other vehicle in the lot in front of room number three. It was a green Subaru wagon with Oregon plates.

She threw her duffel and gear bag on the bed inside. The room was dark, clean, and stuffy. On the walls were the same Russell prints as in the office. Steele must have bought them in bulk, she thought.

The room was paneled with knotty pine and the heater and air-conditioning unit was mounted under the front window. She turned it on and set the thermostat at sixty-eight degrees. It awoke and filled the room with cool air.

She closed the door and noticed that the wall shook when she did. The room was cheaply constructed, she observed. Thin walls, cheap carpeting, exposed plumbing under the sink counter. She looked around. There was no telling—although Steele could probably figure it out—how many guests had stayed in the room since Blake Kleinsasser had been hauled out of it by the cops. She looked at the bed and envisioned him passed out on it, and she looked at the plastic garbage can under the sink and imagined it overflowing with empty liquor bottles.

Although the room had been cleaned and disinfected, she thought she could even smell him.

Before unpacking, Cassie dropped to her hands and knees and looked under the bed. There were dust balls, a lone balled-up sock, and an empty condom packet. There was no telling how long any of the detritus had been there, and she made a note to herself to tell Steele his housekeeper needed to do a better job as a courtesy for future guests. But she'd save that advice until she was checking out, she decided. No need to antagonize the man.

Because he had offered her that particular unit, she was a little suspicious of him. As she'd done countless times before, Cassie did a thorough sweep of the room for cameras or listening devices. She unscrewed the light fixtures and heating vents using the screwdriver tool on her Swiss army knife, and checked out the table lamps and hardwired phone near the bed. The single overhead light was out of reach and the desk chair looked too rickety to hold her weight, so she made a note to herself to borrow or buy a small stepladder to check it out later.

Cassie keyed the Wi-Fi password into her phone and laptop and sent Rachel a quick message.

She wrote, Made it to Horston and will start tomorrow. I'm staying in Blake's motel room.

A balloon filled with pulsing dots appeared on the screen. Rachel was responding right away.

Rachel: That's interesting and a little creepy. Have you connected with Sheriff Wagy?

Cassie: Tomorrow, I hope.

Rachel: Please ask for a copy of the DNA report and a sample we can test ourselves.

Cassie: Will do.

THEN SHE CHECKED IN by text with Ben and Isabel. She did so separately.

Ben replied that he was fine but completely bored.

Isabel reported that she was already feeling stifled and she looked forward to having her liberty back.

For Cassie, it was good news. They weren't at each other's throats yet.

EIGHT

AT A SMALL TABLE in the corner at Stumpy's, Cassie placed a Denise Mina novel on the table and sat down. The novel, although interesting and well-written, was also a prop she kept handy for work. It meant: *yes, I'm a single woman traveling alone. But I'm busy.*

A young blond waitress with floral tattoos on her neck and forearms seated her and slid a laminated one-page menu on the tabletop.

"Would you like to start with a cocktail?"

"Absolutely."

She ordered a glass of red wine and put her handbag on an empty chair at the table. It clunked as she lowered it due to the weight of the .40 Glock she'd slipped into it before she left Whispering Pines.

Stumpy's was decorated with a Church of Trout motif: fly rods and nets attached to the walls, fly-fishing prints, framed posters with sayings including TIE ONE ON; IF AT FIRST YOU

DON'T SUCCEED, TRY ANOTHER FLY; A TROUT IS A MOMENT OF BEAUTY KNOWN ONLY TO THOSE WHO SEEK IT; and MANY MEN GO FISHING ALL OF THEIR LIVES WITHOUT KNOWING THAT IT IS NOT FISH THEY ARE AFTER—HENRY DAVID THOREAU.

There was a small bar and lounge adjacent to the dining room where several loud men drank craft beers and chided each other about the fish they'd failed to catch that day on the Bitterroot River.

The only other customers in the restaurant itself was an older couple obviously passing through. The man had an aluminum-colored flattop haircut and he wore cargo shorts, a baggy Detroit Lions T-shirt, and sandals with black socks. He was talking loudly on his cell phone.

"Yellowstone's on fire, Glacier's on fire," he complained to someone. "The whole damned place is on fire. It's ridiculous. I'm not sure where the hell we're going to go."

His wife was a tiny woman wearing a surgical mask. Cassie guessed it was because of the smoke in the air. The woman tugged the mask down for each dainty forkful of meat loaf.

CASSIE ORDERED a second glass of wine when her steak arrived. She was cutting into it when she heard a disturbance in the lounge.

A door banged open and an angry male voice said, "Somebody in here blocked my truck outside. That means somebody driving a GMC with Colorado plates has to get off their ass and move their fucking car."

Cassie leaned over in her chair to get a better angle to see into the bar. The three fishermen had gone quiet and had swiveled on their stools toward the angry man.

"I think that's my Yukon," the middle man said.

"Then I'd suggest you move it," the angry man said. "Like right now."

He was wiry and compact and he exuded menace. He wore tight jeans, cowboy boots, and a big hat with the brim folded up tight to the crown. His arms were pressed to his sides and his fists were clenched. His face was flushed red and he reminded Cassie of an aggravated rodent.

"I'll take care of it," the fisherman said.

"Goddamn right you will. Or I'll smash the hell out of it getting out."

"Just calm down, mister."

"Goddamn out-of-state fishermen," the cowboy said, his voice rising. "You come up here and act like you own the goddamn place. Can't you see when you park and block a vehicle from getting out of the goddamn lot?"

"I said I'd take care of it," the fisherman said.

"Calm down, buddy," one of the other fishermen said.

"I am calm," the cowboy said with a bloodless smile. "You should see me when I'm pissed, you asshole."

Cassie flinched. The older man in the dining room threw cash on the table and helped his wife up. They quickly exited Stumpy's.

"You're *all* assholes," the cowboy added.

She noted that rather than intervene, the bartender busied himself looking down and cleaning beer glasses.

The middle fisherman slid off his stool and walked tentatively toward the saloon doorway where the cowboy stood. He was a head taller and broader at the shoulders than the cowboy, but he seemed smaller.

"Excuse me," the fisherman said.

After a beat, the cowboy stepped aside so the man could go out. As the fisherman passed beside him, the cowboy wheeled and kicked the man in the buttocks with enough force to send him flying through the door.

At that moment, the waitress emerged from the kitchen with Cassie's wine. She paused near Cassie's table and shook her head at the scene in the saloon.

"*Oh, no*," she whispered.

"Do any of you other assholes want to make a statement?" the cowboy asked the two remaining fishermen.

"I don't think he meant anything bad," one of them said. "We just parked and got out."

"And you failed to notice a Ford F-250 sitting in the corner of the parking lot?" the cowboy asked. "That's a big damned rig to not even see."

"Sorry," the third fisherman said. "We didn't mean anything by it. We were just ready for a beer after a long day."

"What are you drinking?" the cowboy asked.

Cassie took a deep breath, presuming the confrontation was just about over. She noticed that she'd instinctively placed her hand on her bag with the gun in it just in case.

"I'm having a Bitter Root IPA," the fisherman said. "Tad here's having a Huckleberry Honey. They're both local, I believe."

"Let me try 'em," the cowboy said.

Cassie noticed how the two remaining fishermen drew back a little when the cowboy walked up between them to the bar.

The cowboy took their beer glasses, one in each hand. He tasted the IPA, then the Huckleberry Honey. He seemed to be considering which one to order for a moment, then he turned both mugs upside down and emptied them on the floor.

"Fucking swill," he said. "Fucking hipster beer."

"Hey," the third fisherman said, "that was completely unnecessary."

The cowboy slammed the empty mugs on the counter so hard it sounded like gunshots.

"Get the fuck out of here," the cowboy said. "Go back to Missoula or wherever the hell it is you're staying. Go back to your god-damned little bubbles."

The two fishermen exchanged looks. It was obvious they didn't know what to do.

"We can take this outside if you want," the cowboy said. "I'd like nothing better than to fuck up some Colorado fly fishermen."

Cassie beheld the three men. The cowboy was much smaller than both of them, but he seemed tightly coiled and ready to explode. The body language of the two larger fishermen was of defeat: slumped shoulders, awkward movements, no attempts to engage the cowboy.

One turned toward the door, then the other followed. The cowboy stood at the bar until they were gone. Then he dug a roll of cash out of his jeans pocket and threw several bills on the bar.

The bartender didn't reach for the money until the cowboy was gone. As he did he glanced into the dining room and his eyes locked with Cassie's for a moment. Then he quickly looked away.

CASSIE SAT back when the waitress placed her bill on the table.

"Sorry about that," the waitress said as much to Cassie

as to herself. "That's one of the reasons I just want to get the hell out of this town."

"Who was that?" Cassie asked.

"Ah, he's a pain in the ass," she said. "Rand's always spoiling for a fight."

"Rand?" Cassie asked. "Rand Kleinsasser?"

The waitress looked surprised. "You know him?"

"Not really. But Rand is an odd name."

"Rand is a hothead as you can see. His family has been here since forever. I went to high school with him before he got expelled for fighting. Now I just sort of see him around."

Cassie dug out her credit card. Before she handed it over she asked, "What's your impression of the family?"

The waitress drew back as if stung. "Oh, no," she said. "Honey, I don't know you well enough to say anything. I'm not going there."

She took Cassie's card and spun away on her heel.

CASSIE COULD SEE narrow yellow lines of fire on the sides of the mountains in three directions as she walked back to the Whispering Pines from Stumpy's. Illuminated smoke formed wispy orbs around the streetlights.

She considered what she'd witnessed at the restaurant. She also kept a look out for Rand Kleinsasser's F-250 and wondered if she'd see it on the street.

"Spoiling for a fight," as the waitress had put it in regard to Rand's behavior only partially described what she'd seen. There were also equal parts entitlement and recklessness. Rand was a loose cannon, and he didn't seem to fear any kind of law enforcement intervention. And certainly not from the bartender, who cowardly stayed out of the situation while Rand chased his customers out the door.

The waitress sold her a bottle of wine to go but didn't speak beyond saying, "Thank you for coming in."

She walked past the Lochsa County Sheriff's Department. It was a modest concrete structure set back from the curb. Next to it was an ancient jail constructed of heavy logs. The plaque on the exterior wall said it was the original jail that had been constructed in 1864 and that it was still in use today. Notorious local outlaws Henry Plummer and Kid Curry had spent time there. Rough iron bars covered the windows.

So that's where Blake had been held, she thought. What a journey—from Wall Street to a historic jail cell in a structure older than the state itself.

AS SHE ROUNDED the corner and walked through the motel parking lot she stopped cold.

The lights were on in room number eleven and the drapes had been pulled back. The front door was wide open.

Cassie paused and reached into her bag for her handgun. She kept it there as she closed the distance to the open door.

That's when she noticed the utility cart parked to the left of the door frame and Glen Steele's hulking frame inside with his back to her. He was unmistakable.

She sidled up to the side of the door and peered inside keeping her bag and weapon out of his view.

"What's going on?" she asked.

He jumped, obviously startled. When he turned around she observed a heavy white cloth in one of his hands and a spray bottle of cleaner in the other.

"You scared me," he said. "I thought you were out for the night."

"I'm back."

"I see that," he said. Then he explained, "I got to thinking after you checked in that it's been a while since I inspected this room. The cops had it sealed off for a long time after Blake's arrest because his stuff was still in it, and we just recently put it back on line. I've been having trouble keeping reliable housekeepers because nobody wants to work around here anymore. So I thought since you're staying here a few nights that I'd make sure it was clean for you and there were fresh towels."

That was a lot of information, she thought. She looked around and saw that the dingy towels on the rods near the bathroom had been replaced with higher quality versions. The floor gleamed from the mopping he'd obviously just done.

She glanced at her gear bag on the dresser. It was packed with weapons, electronics, and other tools of the trade. It didn't look disturbed. Her clothes were where she'd hung them in the closet, and her overnight bag was still on the side of the basin.

"Well," she said, "it's just that you startled me."

"You startled *me*," he said with a heavy laugh.

"Do you want me to come back?" she asked.

"Oh, no. I'm done. But I hope you let me know if there's anything else I can do to make your stay a pleasant one."

"Thank you," she said.

She stepped aside as he lumbered out.

"Good night," he said.

"Good night."

When he was gone and she could hear the utility cart being

117

pushed down the sidewalk toward the office, she closed the drapes again and bolted the door. Cassie also attached the chain lock. The room smelled sharply of disinfectant.

She double-checked to make sure nothing had been moved or taken from her belongings. Everything seemed to be exactly how she'd left it. Her briefcase with the Blake Kleinsasser file was still locked on the small worktable.

She wanted to believe that Steele was sincere, that he was in her room to ensure its cleanliness.

Cassie opened the bottle and poured wine into a plastic water cup. She wished she would have thought to bring a proper glass.

Then, before changing into the oversized T-shirt she wore for sleeping, she once again got on her hands and knees and looked under the bed. The dust, the sock, and the condom wrapper were gone.

She placed the Glock on her bedside table and opened up the novel.

She wasn't tired although it had been a long day and she'd been awake most of the night before. She poured another cup of wine with the hope that it would relax her. She hoped sleep would come.

It didn't for a long time.

SEVERAL HOURS LATER, Cassie sat up straight in bed and tried to catch her breath. Her heart raced and there was a sheen of sweat across her breasts.

It took her a few panic-filled moments to figure out what had happened.

She'd had a dream. An extremely vivid dream.

In it, she was in her Jeep along the side of the state highway in heavy timber. An afternoon shadow from the timber cast a dark pall. Her location was somewhere along the road south of Horston—the road she'd taken to get there. Apparently, her vehicle had broken down and she'd just pulled over.

It was hot out and the evening cool had yet to enter the forest. She wished she knew more about cars so she could attempt to fix the problem. Nevertheless, she prepared to pop the hood, open the door, and check the engine to see if she could discern why it had quit on her.

As she reached for the door handle, a massive tractor-trailer rounded the bend behind her and filled her rearview mirror. The semi was matte black, and every bit of chrome on it except the front grille was blacked out as well.

The truck slowed and inched over onto her side of the road with the shrill whistle of pneumatic brakes. The grille filled her back window. It stopped behind her so close that she could see the red Peterbilt logo on the snout in her rearview mirror. Its rumbling diesel engine shook the ground itself. Even the steering wheel of her Jeep vibrated with it.

She tried in vain to start her Jeep, hoping against hope that the engine would start.

No response.

Cassie checked her side mirrors and saw both the driver's-side and passenger door open on the truck. Two men swung out and dropped to the gravel.

For some reason, her gear bag and weapons weren't on the passenger seat where they should be. Her Glock wasn't in her handbag, either. She couldn't explain why her shoes and socks were missing. She *never* drove barefoot.

Two men approached her Jeep from either side and she

froze. She dismissed the idea of leaping outside and running away because she had no shoes.

Where were her shoes? Her weapons?

The driver was the Lizard King, Ronald Pergram himself, although he looked different. His hair was wispy and white, and rolls of skin hung down from his jaws. There were gaping holes where his eyes should have been. He looked partially decomposed.

But his gait was strong and he strode toward her.

On the other side was a young rooster of a man wearing a curled-up cowboy hat. She recognized him as Rand Kleinsasser.

He was grinning. He had a stiff coil of rope in his right hand and he thumped it against his thigh in a jaunty way.

That's when she woke up in a sweat.

BUT ALL WAS QUIET and dark in her room. There was no rumbling semi outside, and the only light was a dim beige frame of it on the borders of her drawn curtains from the streetlight in the parking lot.

She realized in her panic she'd reached for her weapon but had mishandled it and knocked it to the floor. Cassie was grateful it hadn't gone off.

When she stopped shaking, she slipped out from under the covers and padded to the window. There was nothing to see.

She counted out four ibuprofens from her travel kit and swallowed them with a cup of brackish water from the tap. She hoped they would relax her back to sleep.

Cassie ran her fingers through her hair and looked around the dark room. She tried to analyze the nightmare for clues but she gave up.

It was four thirty. Her alarm was set for six.

She stared at the ceiling and memorized the pattern of the ceiling tile. There was still a half a bottle of wine but she knew drinking more would be a bad idea.

It was nights like this when she longed for a man in bed beside her. Even if he was a knucklehead she met at a bar, his presence would be welcome. It would be easier and less messy to make that scenario happen in a strange town away from Ben and Isabel, she thought.

She tried to conjure up men who'd been in her life and will them beside her. The first was Jim, her dead husband and Ben's father. Jim was young, taut and firm, the age he'd been when he went to war. She could smell beer and chewing tobacco on his breath.

The second was Ian, her ex-fiancé from North Dakota. Poor Ian. He lay on his back and his breathing whistled softly through his nose. He had long eyelashes and his profile in the dark was delicate.

The third was Bryan Pederson. He lay on his side with his naked back to her. His skin was white and there was a wash of freckles across the top on his shoulders. He was no doubt dreaming about his ex-wife.

She fell back asleep fifteen minutes before she had to get up.

NINE

WHEN CASSIE SAW Lochsa County Sheriff Ben Wagy arrive at the county building the next morning she threw down the last of her bitterly bad motel-room coffee and tossed the cup to the floorboard. She identified Wagy by where he parked his county SUV: under a sign that said the space was reserved for him.

She caught up with him as he reached for the door handle on the side of the building next to a COUNTY EMPLOYEES ONLY header stenciled on the exterior block wall.

"Sheriff Wagy?"

He paused and turned and his eyes narrowed. He was short but broad-shouldered and his beige and brown uniform was already rumpled. He had wide-set blue eyes, a heavy jaw, and a thick auburn mustache that bristled over his top lip.

"That's me," he said without warmth. Cassie recognized the instant protective shell that went up around him. It was a shield that hardened with every year in law enforcement to fend off attacks from defense lawyers, county commissioners, potential rivals, the press… and private investigators.

Cassie held out her hand. "I'm Cassie Dewell. I'm doing some work on behalf of the law firm hired to defend Blake Kleinsasser. I was hoping I could ask you a few questions about the investigation."

"Blake?" Wagy said, arching his eyebrows. "You're working for Blake?"

"Kind of," she said. She did so in a way that suggested she wasn't very enthusiastic about it, and she hoped he picked up on that.

"Do you have an appointment?"

"No, sir. I tried to make one but I didn't receive a reply."

"You did?"

"I sent your office an email from Bozeman," she said.

"I've got about four hundred emails on my computer. I can't get to them all."

She smiled. "I worked for a sheriff over in Bakkan County, North Dakota, who was the same way. He had over two thousand unanswered emails in his inbox. He told me he was shooting for three thousand by the time he retired."

"Did he make it?" Wagy asked, amused.

"I believe he did, sir."

"Man after my own heart. Do I know him?"

"His name was Sheriff Jon Kirkbride. He was my mentor."

Wagy nodded his head and his eyes softened. "I remember Jon. He was one of the good ones."

"I agree."

"Those bastards forced him out, if I recall correctly."

"Something like that. It was very nasty and political."

"It always is."

"So…"

Wagy shot out his sleeve and checked his wristwatch. "I've got a meeting with the county commissioners at eight thirty. I'll give you a half hour so I hope you're prepared."

"I am."

"Follow me," Wagy said while punching in a code on a keypad near the steel door frame. "I hope you like bad coffee."

"I'm used to it," she said.

"So you're a private investigator?" he asked over his shoulder as he led her down a dark hallway.

"I am. Dewell Investigations."

"I have to admit I don't think a whole lot of PIs," Wagy said. She sensed that his shield, which had been down for a minute due to his acquaintance with Sheriff Kirkbride, was now back up in full.

"I'm used to that, too," she said.

ON THE WAY to his office, Wagy nodded good morning to an administrative assistant about Cassie's age. She was seated behind the front counter. A plaque on the counter said her name was Linda Sue Murdock.

He asked, "Any urgent messages?"

Murdock shook her head. "No, but I wanted to remind you about that county commission meeting at ten."

"I didn't forget," Wagy said. "Bring us a couple of coffees when you get a minute."

"Yes, sir," Murdock said after shooting Cassie a sidelong glance.

Cassie got the message. Murdock didn't like being treated

like a secretary in the 1960s asked to bring coffee to the boss in the morning. Cassie didn't blame her.

Plus, she noted that Murdock said the meeting was two hours away. Either Sheriff Wagy had been confused about the time or he'd lied to Cassie so their interview would be short.

"Have a seat," Wagy said when they entered his office. He didn't acknowledge or address the time discrepancy. Cassie took a hard chair across from the sheriff's desk and placed a file on her lap.

His office was spartan. There were pronghorn antlers, a dusty mounted rainbow trout, and a few photos of the sheriff posing with Governor Monte Schreiner and other politicians.

He said nothing until Murdock brought the two coffees and placed them on his desk.

"Will that be all?" she asked.

"For now," Wagy said to her. "Please close the door on your way out."

Murdock turned and shared another burning look with Cassie.

"Thank you," Cassie said to her as she reached for her cup.

"You're welcome," Murdock said.

No thank-you from the sheriff.

Oblivious to the exchange, Wagy said, "I'll tell you straight out. I'm not in the business of undermining my team, our investigation, or my office. If you're here to screw with me you'll find your time in Lochsa County pretty unpleasant."

Cassie ignored the threat and tried to get in front of the conversation.

"Sheriff Wagy, I'm not your adversary. I approach every case I take from the side of law enforcement. I'm not here to punch holes in your case in regard to Blake Kleinsasser. I'm here to confirm all of the facts so that my employer can make a convincing argument to the accused that he should take a plea deal if one is offered."

Wagy took a sip of his coffee, cringed, and raised his eyebrows. "Forgive me if I'm a little skeptical about that."

"I understand," Cassie said. "I've been where you are many times. I know how defense attorneys can be and I can't guarantee you my employer won't try some of those tactics if this case goes to trial. I can't speak for her.

"But what I can promise," Cassie said, "is that my report on the evidence and investigation will be truthful and honest even if it doesn't help Mr. Kleinsasser's defense. My job here is to cross the t's and dot the i's of the record. I'd like nothing more than to report back to my client that the investigation was sound and by the book and that the evidence is rock-solid."

Wagy looked skeptical. "Can you tell me with a straight face that you're not starting this thing from the standpoint that Blake is innocent?"

"I'm not."

"Good," Wagy said. "Because he's guilty as hell. And he's also an asshole."

"I'm aware of that."

"Your employer—what is her name?"

"Rachel Mitchell of Mitchell-Estrella."

"Ah," Wagy said with a knowing smirk. "The crusading Bozeman female activists. I've heard of them."

Cassie ignored Wagy again. She wondered if he was trying to provoke her into saying something that would prove to him that she wasn't playing it straight.

"I've read the arrest report and it looks very cut-and-dried," she said. "Were there ever any credible suspects in the assault besides Blake Kleinsasser?"

"Nada," Wagy said. "And not because we were out to get him. I know the history of that family in this valley—everybody does. I know there was bad blood between Blake and the rest of the family. But I don't work for the Kleinsassers. I work for the people of Lochsa County, even those who didn't vote for me.

"When Franny was brought in here with her story we didn't jump to conclusions even though she clearly named Blake as the perp. We got her statement and went through proper procedure. Are you familiar with a Christmas tree test?"

"Yes."

It was a fairly simple and accurate DNA test that could be done on-site by law enforcement personnel. Acid phosphatase applied to an alleged semen sample under a microscope made the heads of sperm appear red and the tails green.

"Of course," Wagy said, "the Christmas tree test just confirmed that there was semen in her panties. It doesn't identify who put it there. That came later after we arrested Blake and swabbed him. We drove the samples to the crime lab in Missoula and they came back with a perfect match."

"Did Blake deny it to you?" Cassie asked.

"He sure did. But every part of Franny's story was corroborated. From the witnesses at the church who saw Blake pick her up to the old cabin out on the ranch. If you've read the charging documents you already know all of this."

Cassie nodded. "I don't remember reading who brought Franny in to you. I'm not sure that was in the file."

"Her mother and her uncle brought her in that night," Wagy said. "Franny had to walk all the way back to the ranch headquarters in the dark after being assaulted. She told them what happened and they brought her here."

"Which uncle?"

"John Wayne."

"Thank you."

Cassie entered the new detail into her notebook.

"Was her statement taken that night?" she asked.

"Nah, just a preliminary statement. The official statement was taken the next day. That's the one that you read, I'll guess."

Cassie flipped through her file and noted that the statement was indeed dated the day after the assault.

She said, "So the uncle and mother brought Franny here instead of asking you or your officers to go out to the ranch."

"That's what I said."

Cassie jotted it down and looked up. "Were you working late that night and you just happened to be here?"

Wagy narrowed his eyes. "Dispatch called me at home to meet the reporting parties here so I came in. I don't sit on my ass in this office twenty-four-seven, but when a serious allegation is made I drop everything and show up. That's my job. Are you suggesting something here?"

"Not at all," Cassie said. "I'm just trying to get the time line straight in my notes."

Wagy didn't comment. She could tell she was losing him as a cooperative subject.

"How would you describe Franny's state of mind when she came in?"

"I'm no shrink," Wagy said, "but I'd say she was pretty

upset. Distraught, crying, that kind of thing. I did my best to make her comfortable. Sometimes sexual assault victims blame themselves so I didn't want to add to that in any way. I called in one of my deputies who is a girl to do the test."

Girl.

"How would you describe the state of mind of Fanny's mother and uncle?" Cassie asked. She studied Wagy's face when he answered.

"How do you think?" he said. "Cheyenne was on the edge of hysterical. She's a strange bird, but I thought she might lose it any minute. Imagine having to go through that with your only daughter."

"I understand," Cassie said.

"John Wayne wanted to find Blake and blow his head off," Wagy said. "I was able to calm him down, but I had no doubt he'd do what he said he'd do. That's one reason we moved on Blake right away and found his car at the motel and arrested him in that room. It was for Blake's safety as much as anything."

"Did you contact the press to be there for the arrest?" Cassie asked. "I saw video clips of it on the internet."

Wagy bristled. "Are you accusing me of grandstanding?"

"Not at all," Cassie said again. Wagy was much more thin-skinned than she thought he'd be.

"No, somebody must have tipped them," Wagy said. "There's always a concerned citizen or two listening to their police scanner. That's probably why they were there. My guess is the word was out about the assault even though we were trying to keep it under wraps. This is a small town with lots of gossips in it, and, you know, the Kleinsasser name gets everyone's attention."

"I can imagine it does," Cassie said.

Wagy made a show of looking at his watch. It was a signal to Cassie that the interview was about to conclude.

"Another state of mind question," Cassie said. "What about Blake? How did he react when you arrested him?"

"Are you asking if he proclaimed his innocence?" Wagy asked with a cold grin.

"Yes."

"Of course he did. He said he didn't have any idea why we were there. And then he turned into the asshole that he is. He started throwing his weight around and said his lawyers would have him out of jail by the next morning and that he was going to sue me and the county. He blamed his brothers and his dad for everything."

Wagy said, "He was inebriated. Drunker than hell, and he smelled like he hadn't had a bath in a while. It was a real pleasure throwing him into our vintage slammer. I'm sure you've seen our jail."

"I have."

"It's a real jail," Wagy said. "Not like one of those cushy country club motel rooms some counties have. When you're in there and that steel door closes behind you you know you're actually in *jail*. That was the first time I think Blake actually took it seriously. He sobered up in record time. And he thought he could talk his way out of it all the way up to the preliminary hearing. You've met him, right?"

"Just yesterday," Cassie answered.

"He's a piece of work, isn't he?"

"How do you mean?"

"Such an arrogant prick," the sheriff said. "He thinks he's better than everybody around here—that he can talk his smooth New York bullshit and do whatever he wants. He's always been like that."

"So, you've known him a long time?" Cassie asked.

Wagy caught himself and sat back. He didn't want to respond. Cassie found that interesting.

"I think we're done," he said.

"I'd like to request a copy of the DNA report from Missoula," she said. "We've got the Christmas tree test but not the match. And I'll probably have additional questions. Can I meet with you again before I go back?"

"Set up an appointment," Wagy said.

"What about the DNA match?"

Wagy sighed theatrically and reached for his hat. He was in a hurry to get to his make-believe meeting.

"I'll authorize Linda to pull the documents and make copies," he said. "We do charge for them, though. I hope your employer will reimburse you twenty-five cents a copy."

"Thank you," Cassie said, standing up. "I'd also like to review the physical evidence. You know, so we can compare the items to the list submitted to the court."

Wagy squinted. "You want to handle the evidence? Sorry, no can do."

"Not *handle* it," Cassie said. "Sheriff, I know how this works. I'd never dream of contaminating evidence. I simply want to photograph the items with my cell phone camera so Rachel has a record of everything. I anticipate that she'll show the photos to Blake in an effort to persuade him the case against him is as solid as it appears."

Wagy glared at her, obviously suspicious of her request.

"You can view it," he said finally. "But only with my people standing right there with you. And if you reach for anything

I swear I'll arrest you for tampering with evidence and you'll get to see our jail from the inside out. Just like Blake did."

"I understand," Cassie said.

"We've got nothing to hide from the defense," Wagy said. "My office is totally transparent. We're an open book."

"It was a pleasure to meet you and thank you for your cooperation and time," Cassie said, extending her hand.

"Wish I could say the same," Wagy said with a smile that could be taken either way. "I guess you'll be headed back to Bozeman later today."

"Not quite yet," Cassie said. "I've got to talk to a couple of people."

"And then you'll be gone." It was a statement more than a question. Cassie didn't respond.

Then he ushered Cassie out of his office and with a few words to Murdock en route he went down the hallway toward the parking lot jingling his keys.

That left Cassie and Linda Murdock together in the squad room.

Murdock said, "What he didn't want to tell you is that he has coffee with the city fathers every morning. He rarely misses it."

That accounted for the discrepancy, Cassie thought.

"The sheriff asked me to make some copies for you and escort you to the evidence room," Murdock said.

"Thank you."

"Follow me."

CASSIE HOPED that Murdock would turn out to be a potentially valuable asset within the Lochsa County Sheriff's

Department. Not that she expected Murdock to turn on her boss, but the administrative assistant was a breed Cassie was familiar with from working in other law enforcement departments: the key civilian who knew how things worked and where the bodies were buried.

Murdock was the heart and brains of the organization, the staffer who quietly did her job and observed the goings-on around her while various deputies and sheriffs came and went. She had the institutional memory of the organization and was rarely given credit for it. Cassie had gleaned more inside knowledge and intelligence from stalwarts like Linda Murdock over the years than from elected sheriffs or assigned chiefs of police.

"Is the sheriff hostile to all women or just me?" Cassie asked Murdock as the administrative assistant fed the forensics documents through the copier.

Murdock said, "Oh, you noticed?"

"It was hard not to."

"I don't mind getting coffee for him once in a while. It makes him feel important."

"It rankled me."

"I honestly think he doesn't even realize it," Murdock said.

"That's kind of you," Cassie said with a smile.

"My husband's on disability. I need the job."

"I understand."

Cassie added the DNA reports to her folder. Murdock dutifully copied all of the photos and documents in the case file even though Cassie recognized many of them as items they already had. She was grateful for Murdock's thoroughness.

It was always better to have too much documentation,

including duplicates, than not enough. Plus, from the standpoint of the defense, if exculpatory evidence was withheld *twice* it showed malice on behalf of the prosecution and not simply a procedural error.

"How much do I owe you?" Cassie asked when the task was complete.

Murdock waved her off. "Don't worry about it."

CASSIE FOLLOWED HER down a hallway toward the evidence locker in the back of the building. Over her shoulder, Murdock asked, "Did he give you the line that he doesn't work for the Kleinsassers? That he works for the people of Lochsa County?"

"Yes, he did."

"Don't believe it," Murdock said. "Between you and me, he answers to them. All of the electeds around here do. The school board was independent for a few years but even that's back to the point where every board member owes their office to the family."

Cassie nodded that she understood. Rachel would no doubt find that information intriguing.

A LARGE older man in a deputy uniform sat at a desk in front of the secured evidence locker. He had a sweeping white mustache and jowls and he reminded Cassie of a walrus. He was in the process of hanging up the phone.

"Just talked to the sheriff," he said as Murdock and Cassie approached. "He said you were here to look at the Blake Kleinsasser box but only to photograph the items."

Cassie nodded.

The deputy turned to Murdock. "Are you going to sign it out?"

"Yes."

"Give me a minute," the deputy said as he pulled on a pair of blue latex gloves. "I'll be right out."

Cassie watched as the deputy rose, turned, and used a set of keys attached to his belt to unlock a pair of heavy locks on the chain-link door behind him. He had a pronounced limp and his movements were stiff. Cassie guessed that he was a longtime LEO who'd been assigned to an easy desk job until retirement rolled around. It was one of the remaining perks of every bureaucracy that no longer existed in the private sector, where seniority counted more than usefulness. She'd seen examples of it in every department she'd ever worked for.

The evidence room was crammed with metal shelving. On the shelves were boxes marked with the names of the investigations they corresponded with. Along the back wall was a large cabinet filled with long guns and other weapons including a samurai sword and a chain saw. Every item was tagged and marked.

The deputy emerged and placed a large white legal box on a table beside his desk. It was marked KLEINSASSER, BLAKE.

Before he cut through the sealing tape with a box cutter, he turned to Cassie. She knew that it would be resealed and marked when they were done and the record of it being opened was to be signed by Murdock and date-stamped by the deputy.

"Stand back."

Cassie took a step backwards. As she did she felt the

vibration of an incoming text from her phone in her pocket. She glanced at it quickly. It was from Ben.

Call me when U can.

She pocketed the device.

THE DEPUTY sliced through the tape and removed the items one by one. He made it a point to make sure the evidence number on each tag was clearly visible. Cassie recognized all of the items from the evidence list as she photographed them, including:

- The largest item, a cast of tire tracks found on the dirt road outside the house on the ranch where the assault took place. It allegedly matched the tread from Blake's rental car.
- Individual fingerprint cards in glassine envelopes identifying both Blake's and Franny's prints.
- Empty and half-full liquor bottles that had been found in the rental car, the structure on the ranch, and Blake's motel room were placed in a row on the table.
- Two smudged glasses in Ziploc bags, which the deputy put on the table in front of the bottles. Cassie recognized them as the glasses from the ranch house with both Blake's and Franny's fingerprints and DNA on them. They were heavy cocktail glasses as opposed to drinking glasses.
- Thumb drives of closed-circuit video in clear plastic sleeves placing Blake at the Corvallis and Hayloft bars prior to the assault.

In all, Cassie thought, the accumulation of physical evidence was overwhelming. She took several shots of the entire table to emphasize that fact.

"Got it all?" the deputy asked her.

Cassie nodded but then paused. "Is this all the evidence?"

"How much more do you want?" the deputy said with a laugh.

"I was hoping her phone would be in there."

The deputy checked his sheet again and shrugged. "No phone," he said.

"Where is her underwear?"

Murdock looked up in alarm. The deputy shrugged. "I'm guessing they're still at the lab in Missoula. They probably haven't sent them back yet."

"But you don't know for sure?" Cassie asked.

The deputy reddened, but walked over to his desk to review the list of exhibits associated with the box. It took him minutes to check each item by pointing a stubby fingertip on the list and then visually checking each exhibit on the table.

Finally, he said without confidence, "That has to be what happened. The lab hasn't sent them back yet."

"Could you confirm that and let me know?" Cassie asked. She knew her tone was strident.

"I'll check with the sheriff," the deputy said without meeting her eyes.

When Cassie looked over to Murdock she noted that the woman seemed poised to add something. Instead, she remained silent.

*

"THAT MIGHT BE a problem," Cassie said as she followed Murdock back toward the front of the department.

"It's probably nothing," Murdock said without conviction. "Mistakes happen. Things get misfiled or lost in the mail. I'm sure the evidence will be located. The sheriff is a stickler about that kind of thing."

Cassie nodded. Then asked, "It looked like you were about to say something back there. Is there anything else?"

"No," Murdock said. "Nothing else."

Cassie gave Murdock her card. "My cell phone number is on there and so is my email address. Feel free at any time to contact me."

"About what?"

"Whatever it is you think I should know," Cassie said.

SHE RETRIEVED her phone to speed-dial her son while she walked toward her Jeep in the parking lot. It was 9:15 a.m. and she knew he had an open-study period from nine to ten and she assumed that he wasn't studying.

After she talked to him to find out what the problem was, she planned to touch base with Rachel and give her an update. It roiled her stomach to do so because she knew the missing underwear could be seized upon by the defense, DNA report or not.

While the prosecution had the awesome power and treasury of the state behind them at trial, the defense had the luxury of second-guessing and questioning every move made by law enforcement and spinning simple errors that occurred in every organization into diabolical conspiracies. Cassie had been on the stand on multiple occasions when defense attorneys questioned her motives, ethics, and competence. It was always demoralizing, and it bothered her to think that she could conceivably play a role in a similar effort.

She didn't want to be a party to that in this case, especially given the overwhelming evidence against Blake Kleinsasser.

TEN

BEN DEWELL WAITED for Erin Reese on a cold concrete bench that had yet to warm from the morning sun outside Bozeman High. He kept a close eye on the double doors for her because he planned to spring up and greet her the moment she came outside.

It was pure fortune that Erin's free period occurred the same time as his. They'd started meeting outside and walking the two blocks to the Kum & Go convenience store for a morning snack. But it was more than that. He couldn't wait to see her.

Erin was a new kid to Bozeman and the school, like Ben. And like Ben, she'd arrived with no friends or connections or cliques that immediately welcomed her to join them. Ben had the wrestling team but it was almost as if having no group at all because he was a freshman and he was so lousy at the sport. He wasn't even sure he'd make the freshman team because his only value, it seemed, was to serve as prey for better wrestlers who needed their confidence built up. The coaches made sure of that. As a result, he was a mass of bruises and sore muscles, and the only other wrestlers he'd really bonded with were as inept as he was and most of them had already quit the team.

That Erin hadn't found her place yet was more of a puzzle for Ben because she was attractive, quirky, and exotic. She was also flighty and book-smart, and she seemed to be very comfortable in her own skin, unlike him. There was no doubt she was considered weird and seemed to care not at all about what other kids said about her with her odd clothing, floppy hats, and flowing scarves.

He expected to lose her friendship at any time when, inevitably, she fell in with the right crowd. He'd noticed some of the drama and theater nerds hanging together at lunch and he guessed she might fit right in with them.

But so far, it seemed, he was her only friend. And he thanked God for it twenty times a day.

They shared two classes, the study period, and late-night texting together. She seemed to like his company and she laughed at his attempts at humor. She lifted his spirits when he was down and playfully called him "Eeyore" after the gloomy donkey in the Winnie-the-Pooh books. When he complained to her about Isabel, which he often did, she laughed uncontrollably in person or replied with laughing emojis in her text responses.

When she appeared behind the heavy glass in the vestibule—her sheer lavender scarf flowing behind her and giving her away—he felt a trill that shot up both legs into his groin.

And, of course, at that second his mother called.

"BEN, IS EVERYTHING all right?"

"It's fine," he said quickly. He wanted to get off the phone before Erin saw him talking to his mom.

"But you texted me to call you right away." She sounded rushed and annoyed.

"Isabel went on strike this morning," he said.

"What do you mean, on strike?"

"That's what she said. She said I don't appreciate her and neither do you. She said she was on strike until further notice."

"Ben, what did you do?"

"Nothing."

"Ben?"

"Why do you automatically blame me? You know she's a crazy woman."

"That's no way to talk about your grandmother, Ben. She means well. So, what happened that she decided to go on strike?"

He sighed. "I wouldn't eat granola for breakfast. I told her I need protein, like bacon. I'm a *wrestler*, Mom."

"And she went on strike over that?"

"That's what she said. So, you need to come home."

"I can't right now," his mother said. "Look, I'll call her and try to straighten things out."

"She's not answering her phone. That's part of her strike."

The conversation was becoming time-consuming and it was getting complicated, he thought. Erin was pushing through the doors to come outside. That she seemed to be searching for him made his legs even weaker.

"I've got to go," he said, making eye contact with Erin and leaping up as planned.

"Ben, you need to try to get along with Isabel."

"Mom, I've got to go. I'm in *school*."

He said it as he approached Erin and rolled his eyes for her benefit.

"We'll talk tonight. In the meanwhile, I'll try to talk to your grandmother—"

He disconnected the call and slid his phone in his shirt pocket.

"Was that your mom?"

He tried for a dismissive tone. "Yeah. She's always checking up on me."

"That's nice."

"Not always."

"Believe me," Erin said with a flip of her strawberry blonde hair, "it's better than not caring at all."

Which made him realize he knew nothing at all about her family. Their conversations had been solely about school, other students, movies, music, and things like that. Ben made a mental note to ask her about her situation when the time was right. He'd heard that girls liked it when boys showed a genuine interest in their lives.

He was *so* new to this, he thought. This girl thing.

Erin smiled at him and gestured up the street in the direction of the Kum & Go. She said, "Ice cream for breakfast sounds awesome to me."

"Ice cream it is," he said, taking her backpack and throwing it over his shoulder. She was a few inches taller than him but he was stronger. She'd told him she really liked how polite he was. She'd called him a "true gentleman."

Ben casually reached into his pocket to make sure he had money. He knew at this rate he'd burn through all the cash his mother had given him in a couple of days. And he didn't care.

BEN LISTENED as Erin told him about her English teacher from second period, how they'd gotten into an argument about *The Iliad*. They were side by side down the sidewalk and twice she grasped his hand for emphasis as she made a point. Her touch made his mouth go dry.

"I told him the poem would be much more interesting if it was told from Helen's point of view," she said. "As it is it's no better than a cheap sword-and-sandals B movie. He disagreed."

He loved the way she talked. It was lyrical and sophisticated and nothing ever seemed to bother her. And she had courage taking on a teacher like that.

Ben couldn't stop staring at her naked ankles as she walked. The hem of her pants was short and he didn't know if it was because her family couldn't afford clothes that fit her or if it was her style. He came down firmly on her style.

As she told him about the flaws she found in the narrative of the epic poem, how she thought it was a "cheap trick" to have Zeus suddenly appear and solve the problems of the Greeks versus the Trojans, Ben realized that it was getting harder to hear her because of escalating street noise. A low rumbling filled the air.

Her spell over him temporarily broken, he looked up with annoyance.

It was a clear shot to the parking lot of the Kum & Go and

the street ahead was empty. Then he turned around to see the grille of a huge tractor-trailer rumbling up the street behind them. It was black and dirty and massive, and he couldn't see the driver because the windows were tinted.

Ben couldn't believe it when the semi crossed the center line of the street into the other lane. It kept coming until the front tires were on the sidewalk right behind them.

Then it sped up.

He grasped Erin's arm and pulled her into an alleyway between the corner and the convenience store. As he did so her backpack slipped off of her shoulder and fell to the pavement. He felt a wave of hot exhaust on his back.

They both watched as the Peterbilt rolled over the top of the backpack. Two sets of front wheels and two more sets of dual tires under the trailer.

Thump-thump. Thump-thump.

ONCE THE TRUCK was gone, accelerating loudly as it passed in front of the Kum & Go and turned at the corner, they looked at each other as if to confirm what had just happened.

"That idiot almost ran us over!" she said. "What do you think he was doing?"

"I don't know," Ben said. "He wasn't looking where he was going. Maybe he was texting or something. I hear they do that when they drive."

"He could have squashed us." Then she said, "You saved my life."

Ben flushed red. No one had ever said anything like that to him before, something so dramatic yet clichéd.

"Thank you, Ben Dewell. You're my hero."

He didn't think he could turn any redder, but he was sure he did.

Ben was surprised by what Erin did next when she leaned into him and kissed him on the mouth. He was too surprised to respond.

Then she laughed as she retrieved her backpack from the sidewalk. She peeled it off the concrete and marveled at the fact that it was totally flattened, like the Road Runner in the cartoons.

Ben's heart raced, and not just from the unexpected kiss. The vehicle was just like the truck his mom had chased for years. He knew the description of it by heart. He also knew his mom had been there for the last breath of the Lizard King.

So, who had been behind the wheel? And why had the driver targeted him?

Should he tell Erin about the Lizard King? Would she think he was crazy or paranoid? Or would she really get into the story because it was so lurid and dramatic?

He thought he knew the answer to that question.

ELEVEN

ATTORNEY ANDREW JOHNSON was seated at the defense table in Lochsa County courtroom number one when Cassie entered the room. His back was to her.

She knew his location because she'd called Johnson's law office and asked for him. The secretary said he was in court.

Cassie slipped into an empty bench and placed her bag next to her. The security officer in the outside hallway had kept her phone and keys. She'd known better than to enter the chambers with her weapons or electronics and she'd left them in her Jeep.

The pretrial hearing had already begun, and Johnson sat next to his client. Across the aisle from him was a young woman prosecutor.

The courtroom was virtually empty except for two other defendants and their respective lawyers who sat on opposite sides of the aisle. Both defendants—an unkempt man in his sixties who noticed her and scowled and a stringy-haired thirtysomething with the toothless grin of a meth addict—seemed as if they'd been there before. There was also an older woman knitting a baby blanket. Cassie guessed she was the type who simply enjoyed sitting through courtroom procedures.

Johnson's client wore an orange jumpsuit with LOCHSA COUNTY DETENTION CENTER stenciled in black across the back of it. He had jet-black hair in a ponytail, and when he turned his head toward Johnson she could see he had Native American features.

The judge was a severe woman who had a grating voice. She seemed bored with the proceedings. Cassie assumed the morning was scheduled for multiple hearings and that it was the judge's intent to bang them out as quickly as possible.

"Mr. Johnson," the judge said, "your client"—she glanced down at her notes for a moment—"Mr. Leland Red Star Wolf, has been charged with driving while under the influence of alcohol and resisting arrest. How does he plead?"

Johnson gathered himself and stood up. "He pleads not guilty, Your Honor."

The judge snorted and rolled her eyes. "Lovely."

"Your Honor," Johnson said, "my client is a member of good standing of the Nez Perce nation. In addition to serving on the Salmon Recovery Board, he's a former vice-chairman of the Nez Perce Tribal Executive Committee. Therefore he's not a flight risk. We would ask the court to consider a reasonable bail so that he can resume his duties for the tribe while he awaits trial."

"That's touching," the judge said with sarcasm.

"This is Mr. Red Star Wolf's first offense in Lochsa County," Johnson continued.

The prosecutor stood up quickly. "Your Honor, what Mr. Johnson fails to note is that although this is Mr. Red Star Wolf's first offense in Lochsa County, he's been arrested two times for the same offense—DWUI—in Missoula County and another time in Idaho."

Johnson looked over at her with faux indignation. Cassie had seen it all before.

"Right," the judge said. She glared at the defendant and said, "Let's hope your client sees his way to a plea deal and doesn't take any more valuable time in my courtroom," before setting his bail at twenty-five thousand dollars.

She banged her gavel and said, "Next!"

Cassie found that amount unusually high considering the charges. She thought that they didn't mess around in Lochsa County.

AFTER WHISPERING briefly with his client, Johnson watched as the deputies led Red Star Wolf away. When the defendant was gone, the attorney abruptly loosened up and exchanged pleasantries with the prosecutor and both of them laughed at a shared joke Cassie couldn't hear.

As Johnson gathered papers to clear the table for the next case, Cassie approached the bar that separated the spectator gallery from the well where the lawyers' tables and bench were located.

"Mr. Andrew Johnson?"

He turned around as if startled. He was thin with close-cropped silver hair, a sharp nose, darting blue eyes, and a cautious manner. His suit seemed to be a size too big.

"Can I help you?" Johnson said.

"I'm Cassie Dewell with Dewell Investigations in Bozeman. I'm working on behalf of Mitchell-Estrella and I was hoping I could ask you a few questions in regard to the case against Blake Kleinsasser."

When she said Mitchell-Estrella she noticed a tightening of his jaw.

"As you can see, I'm busy," he said.

"I'm happy to make an appointment for later today."

"Not possible," Johnson said. "I'm on my way right now to do depos in another case. I'll be occupied for the rest of today and tomorrow."

"It won't take long," she said.

"I can't be late."

"Then we can walk and talk."

He sighed and turned his back on her so he could slide his files into his briefcase. When he turned back around she was still there.

"Walk and talk," he said without enthusiasm.

Cassie noted that the prosecutor watched the exchange with a small grin, as if Johnson's sudden predicament amused her.

"I WANT TO GET my facts straight," Cassie said as she trailed Johnson in the hallway. He was a fast walker, and he was determined to get to where he was going.

There were several small knots of people in the hallway; cops, prosecutors, defendants, lawyers, witnesses.

"What is it that you want to know?" he asked sotto voce over his shoulder. It was in the same manner, she noted, he had talked with his client before the defendant was led away.

"Our records show that you were Blake's initial criminal attorney. Is that correct?"

"Blake? He's Blake to you?" As if the accused was her close friend.

"Only because there are so many Kleinsassers in this valley that I want to be clear."

"Ah, got it."

"So that's correct? You were his defense counsel?"

"That's correct."

"You petitioned the court for a change in venue from Lochsa County. May I ask you why?"

"You can ask," Johnson said, his voice rising inexplicably. "But there's such a thing as attorney-client privilege. I can't tell you about our discussions and if you continue to ask about them I may need to notify the sheriff."

Cassie snorted. "Come on, this isn't my first rodeo. I'm not asking you to re-create your discussions with Blake and you don't even represent him anymore. I'm not asking that you be a witness in his defense, either. I'm just trying to verify the facts and the time line."

Johnson paused at the elevator and pushed the down button. Loud enough for everyone milling in the hallway to hear including cops and court personnel, he said, "Ms. Dewell, I've said all I'm going to say about the Blake Kleinsasser case."

The doors opened and he stepped in and turned around to face her. He crossed his arms in a petulant fashion. Nevertheless, she joined him in the elevator car.

As soon as the doors closed, she said, "Our understanding is that you quit the case on account of your health but I have to say you looked pretty spry in the courtroom back there. How are you feeling?"

"I'm making a living," Johnson said softly as if he were concerned about microphones inside. "I do have prostate cancer."

"I'm sorry," she said. "Are you at a critical stage?"

He shrugged. "My urologist says every man either dies with it or dies from it. We're doing what's called 'watchful waiting' or 'active surveillance' to figure out what we're going to do next."

"So, it's really not that bad," Cassie said. "Thank goodness."

"I suppose," Johnson replied. "If there's such a thing as not bad cancer. Is there such a thing as not bad cancer?"

She knew she had a very short time before they reached the ground floor and the doors opened. He'd made it clear in his way that he was much more willing to talk to her when others couldn't overhear their conversation, so she cut to the chase.

"Was there anything about the case that led you to believe that he might not be guilty?" she asked.

"I never allow myself to think that way. My only concern is to provide the best defense possible."

"Well said. But I guess what I'm asking is whether or not you saw flaws in the prosecution's case at that early stage."

"It seemed airtight," Johnson said quickly.

"So is that the reason you stepped away?" she asked.

The car reached ground level. Cassie prepared to lose Johnson and the opportunity to ask any additional questions.

He surprised her by reaching out and pressing the button that prevented the doors from opening.

"Look," he said, again adopting the sotto voce manner. "I already told you. My only concern is to provide the *best defense possible* for my client. In this particular case, given the defendant and the unique situation here in this county, I did the only thing I could do."

Then she got it. "You're saying that he couldn't have received a fair trial in Lochsa County?"

He nodded. His face was animated while he did it.

"Is that because of the Kleinsasser name?"

Another quick nod. He didn't want his words on record.

"So it wasn't about your health?"

"Actually, it was," he said. "I've been married thirty-one years to the long-suffering Kendra Johnson. We have two daughters and five grandchildren. I'm the patriarch of our little clan."

He leaned so close to Cassie she could smell his Axe after-shave. "If I stayed on the case I would have had all kinds of problems in regard to my health and well-being. You have no idea what it's like if you ruffle the wrong feathers around here. Half my cases are as a public defender assigned by the court. That's done arbitrarily, and those cases can vanish if I'm poorly thought of by certain people. As I said earlier, I need to be able to make a living."

"You were threatened?"

"I didn't say that."

"But that's what you're telling me," she said. "If that's the situation it was pretty gutsy to go for a change of venue."

"It was the least I could do," he whispered as he pressed the button to open the doors. "And believe me, it didn't go over well in some quarters."

She wished he wasn't being so vague but he was a lawyer and for lawyers, she knew from experience, words were a kind of currency. And they were of greater value within the pro-fession than outside the legal world.

The doors wheezed open to reveal two uniformed sheriff's deputies waiting to go upstairs to testify.

"That will be enough for today," Johnson said.

"Christ," one of them said to Johnson. "I thought you were going to take all day. I thought I was going to have to take the damned staircase."

"It's all yours," Johnson said, stepping out and ushering them in. Cassie noted that both men's eyes stayed on her a beat longer than necessary, and it wasn't because she was so obviously attractive that they couldn't help it.

"Have a good day, Ms. Dewell," Johnson said as he left her. "I hope you enjoy your stay."

He said it for the benefit of the deputies, she thought.

Then, as the elevator doors began to close, he said, "Those are the last words you and I will have together and if you quote me on anything I'll deny it."

She nodded that she understood.

CASSIE STOPPED BY her motel room to grab a jacket and she found that the room had already been cleaned for the day. Glen Steele was on his game.

Rachel answered on the second ring.

Cassie told her about her investigation thus far. She said Franny's phone wasn't among the items of evidence in the county jail, and Rachel replied with a curse. When she mentioned the missing underwear, it was like tossing a handful of white bark pine seeds to a grizzly bear. Rachel pounced, as Cassie feared she would.

"Honestly," Rachel said, "this is literally the first chink in their armor. Good work."

"They could show up anytime," Cassie cautioned. "And there's still the DNA analysis from the lab even if the actual article goes missing."

"Of course," Rachel said. "But if our experts can't analyze that particular item..."

"I know," Cassie said woodenly.

"It's not enough to derail the prosecution, but it's something," Rachel said.

Cassie sighed. "I thought my purpose here was to give you ammunition to convince Blake to take a plea deal. Now you're talking like you're preparing for trial."

"I have to prepare for every possibility," Rachel said defensively. "You know that."

Cassie let it go. She told Rachel about her brief conversation with Johnson in the elevator.

Rachel said, "He didn't give you names or specifics. Very cagey. But *really* interesting. I'm amazed that he felt such pressure.

"You're a bulldog, Cassie," she continued. "You can make people tell you things."

Cassie shrugged, but it was true.

She recalled the long looks the deputies had given her and she said, "I've been here less than twenty- four hours and it seems like more and more locals know why I'm here. I think I need to accelerate the pace of the investigation before everyone in Lochsa County knows me by name. I feel like I'm under a microscope and the Kleinsassers are watching me through it."

Rachel told her to be less paranoid, but then said, "There's another reason why that's a good idea," she said. "Blake sent me a message this morning. He's heard some rumblings and he thinks he's going to get jumped by some of the other inmates. He even thinks a couple of the guards are in on it."

"He is a child molester," Cassie said. "They don't do well in jail, you know."

"There's that," Rachel conceded, "but he seems to think the order to go after him comes from where you are. The inmates he suspects have Lochsa County connections."

"The Kleinsassers?"

"That's what he thinks. But who knows," Rachel said, "he might be as paranoid as you and there's nothing to it. Besides, I wouldn't put it past him to try and get transferred to a cushier facility. He's not exactly used to hardship.

"So, what's next?" Rachel asked.

Cassie told her.

"Be careful," Rachel said.

"I thought you just said I was paranoid."

"You can be both."

TWELVE

ON HER WAY NORTH to Lolo, back on U.S. Highway 93, Cassie made several stops along the way. The first was at the Corvallis Tavern, then Hayloft Saloon in Darby, and finally the Corvallis Tavern in Hamilton. Blake had drunk at all three of the bars when he went on his bender.

All were dark and desperate and bleak the way saloons were in the daytime. The only customers had the wan and sallow faces of day drinkers. Although they turned on their stools to check her out when she walked in, they turned back once they saw that she was a stranger and not one of their drinking buddies. She felt like she was crashing exclusive club meetings.

Except for the crazy toothless woman at the Rainbow, who swore Cassie was her long-lost sister from Ekalaka.

"I've been to Ekalaka," Cassie told her firmly. "But I'm not your sister."

"You're *her*," the woman insisted. "I knew Daddy was lying when he said you got kicked in the head by a horse."

Cassie backed away.

None of the bartenders or servers knew who Hawk was or where to find him, but Cassie got the impression the afternoon staff encountered an entirely different breed of customer than the night crew who came in later.

THE ATMOSPHERE on the highway was otherworldly. Rising afternoon temperatures and a stiff northwestern breeze fed the fires in the mountains and filled the valley with heavy smoke. It hung thick in the timber and tendrils of it flowed down the sharp draws like molten lava. Oncoming cars kept their headlights on. The bare summits of several mountains appeared to be snowcapped, but with white ash instead of snow.

To kill time before getting to the Hayloft Saloon in Lolo where Lindy, Blake's lover, allegedly worked, Cassie took Highway 12 west toward the Idaho border and Lolo Hot Springs. It was a thirty-one-mile detour each way, but distances were relative in Montana. She'd driven much farther to simply meet someone for lunch.

The highway wound up through a canyon that was torched by fires from several years before. Bright green grass bristled on the blackened meadows, but there were no flames on the mountainsides. There was nothing left to burn.

LOLO HOT SPRINGS, a kind of resort within shouting distance of the Idaho border, was nearly unrecognizable to her when she arrived. What she remembered about it from a brief high school basketball trip to the area was how old, steamy, and decadent it was at the time.

Cassie drove into the parking lot and backed into a space in the very last row. She was virtually alone.

She recalled that on the school bus some of the girls had smuggled bottles of cheap white Zinfandel they'd been able to steal in Missoula. The team, most of them anyway, had passed the bottles from girl to girl in the back while the coaches huddled and gossiped unaware in the front.

By the time they reached Lolo Hot Springs for dinner and a "swim," Cassie was drunk, as were her friends. What she remembered—through fuzz—was that to her Lolo Hot Springs was a torrid combination of hot sulfur-smelling water, alcohol, and leering old cowboys who seemed to occupy every shadowed corner of the pool. She recalled one of them who reached out under the water and jammed his hand between her legs from behind.

When she wheeled on him to slap his face he'd laughed and ducked. She recalled that he was wearing a sweat-stained cowboy hat with a feather. She'd swung with her left hand and connected. The cigarette he'd been smoking fell from his mouth and hissed dead in the water.

The lewd cowboy had rubbed his jaw and he chuckled at the blow and he'd sidled away, leaving a wake.

"Watch out for that one," he'd laughed to his buddies. "She's a pistol."

At the time, the incident wasn't that unusual—or that shocking. She'd dealt with the unwanted grab by taking a swing at him.

The incident didn't scar her. In fact, she'd never mentioned it to her coaches and hadn't even thought about it until the moment she parked in the lot.

Cassie felt very old. Today, she knew, a high school girl

being groped like that would result in arrests, outrage, and recriminations. Goofy old ranch hands would go to prison for what they did.

The place was different now. It had been modernized, revamped, and looked more like a family water park than the seedy place it had once been. She watched as tourist families led children in bathing suits toward the entrance. There were no leering cowboys with roaming hands.

How the world had changed.

IT WAS IMPORTANT, she'd learned from her previous stops, to arrive at the Hayloft in Lolo when the night crew was working. It was the best chance she had of talking to Lindy.

Cassie didn't want to arrive early and stick out like a sore thumb while waiting for Lindy to go on duty. She'd been to enough Montana bars in her life to know that a single woman sitting by herself—unless she was crazy and looking for her long-lost Ekalaka sister—was considered either desperate or suspicious. She wanted to arrive when the night was in full swing and she could move around and blend in with the crowd.

Which meant she had at least an hour more to kill before driving back to Lolo.

She thought about her conversation with Rachel, how they'd both agreed that speed was important. She checked her cell phone to make sure it had a good signal.

Then she placed a call to the headquarters of the Iron Cross Ranch.

*

HER CALL was answered on the second ring.

"This is John Wayne." His voice was gruff with a Southern twang.

"John Wayne Kleinsasser?" she asked, surprised that he'd answered the phone himself.

"Yep."

"My name is Cassie Dewell. I'm in the area verifying evidence in the case against your brother."

"Yeah, I heard something about that," he said but didn't elaborate further. Then added, "He's not my brother. A brother wouldn't do what he did."

"I understand—"

"I've got a real brother and his name is Rand," John Wayne interrupted. "That phony you're talking about is a bad apple that fell a long way from the tree. Landed in New York City, in fact. I don't know him any more than I know any cowardly low-life bum, and he don't know me. Do you get what I'm saying?"

She did. What surprised her was when she realized John Wayne was talking about Blake leaving the ranch and the state. Not about the assault of his niece.

So she brought it back to that.

"I spoke with Sheriff Wagy this morning. He said you and Franny's mother brought her in to the department the night and the day after she was assaulted."

"Yep. She was very upset and distraught by what Blake did to her."

"You were there when Franny gave her statement, correct?"

"Yep."

"It's a terrible thing for an uncle to hear," Cassie said.

"Yep."

"What I was wondering is if I could come out to your ranch tomorrow. I'd like to see the old building where the alleged assault took place. I'm not one to trespass."

"Good thing you aren't," John Wayne said with a harsh laugh. "Trespassers don't get far on our place, and some of 'em wind up injured."

"Will you be around tomorrow? I won't take too much of your time. You can just point the way to the building and I'll not bother you further."

"I'll be around in the morning," he said. "Follow the signs to the Iron Cross HQ."

"Thank you. I'll be there no later than nine."

He paused. He said suspiciously, "Are you trying to prove that Blake didn't do it?"

"Not at all," Cassie said. "I've seen the evidence."

"Then what are you hoping to accomplish on our place?"

"I just want to get it all clear in my mind where it happened."

"You said 'alleged assault,'" John Wayne said. "There was nothing *alleged* about it. He raped his damn niece."

"It was just an expression," she said. "I used to be a cop. That's how we talk."

"What are you now?" he asked.

She didn't like the turn in the conversation. He was getting more and more hostile.

"I'm a private investigator. I've been hired by Blake's attorneys to verify the evidence in the case. I'm not here to try to prove his innocence."

"Have you met the son of a bitch?"

"I have."

"He's an arrogant prick, isn't he? He thinks he's superior to everyone else. Always been that way, too."

"I see." She didn't know what else to say.

"He couldn't wait to get out of here," John Wayne said. "He just couldn't wait to hit the road and pretend he didn't like or know any of us. Then he shows back up and expects us all to say, 'Thank God you're here to solve all of our problems, Blake!' But it ain't like that. He can eat shit as far as I'm concerned. He's no damned brother to me."

Back to that, Cassie thought.

"I'll see you tomorrow then," she said.

"What are you driving so I'll know it's you?"

She described her Jeep.

"Come straight to the house," he said. "Don't take any joyrides. Not everyone on this place is as easygoing as me."

She was glad he couldn't see her roll her eyes at that.

CASSIE DISCONNECTED the call and dropped the phone on her lap. She was shaken by John Wayne's strident tone and she didn't look forward to meeting him.

After checking the time, she placed a call to her mother. Cassie hoped she could talk things out with Isabel on Ben's behalf. Plus, there could very well be another side of the story.

When Isabel didn't answer, Cassie left a message. Then she started her car and headed for Lolo. Smoke undulated in the headlights.

THIRTEEN

THE PARKING LOT of the Hayloft Saloon was vast and unpaved, and Cassie pulled into a space between two four-wheel-drive pickups on the south side of the building. She slid her Glock into her handbag and slipped the strap over her shoulder so that it hung against her right hip.

She walked past the entrance door to the restaurant and glanced up at the façade before pushing through the saloon door. Floodlights lit up the carved figure of a naked cowgirl sitting in a frothy beer mug kicking up her heels.

The lounge was cavernous and the jukebox was playing Hank Williams, Jr., when she stepped inside. It wasn't packed with customers but the room had the roughed-up and lived-in feel of a place that was often shoulder to shoulder on busy nights. A group of drunk fishermen whooped at one table, and a knot of baseball cap– wearing locals shook their heads at them. Glass-covered panels displayed old and new guns and even a small cannon. Fox News was on one television and bull riding on the other.

Cassie shouldered through a group of young men watching the rodeo toward the long bar that stretched the entire length of the southern wall. An old neon sign for Schlitz beer painted the battered bar top with pink. Several geriatric bikers sat side by side on stools, their gray ponytails hanging down their backs over black leather vests.

An attractive redheaded woman about Cassie's age sat alone at the bar. She was looking at her phone and scrolling through the screen with one hand while holding a smoking cigarette aloft with the other. She wore a blue dress and tooled red cowboy boots. One leg was crossed over the other, revealing her slim calves and white skin.

Cassie was struck by how regal she looked in comparison with the other customers, most of whom were men. She seemed to be living in her own bubble and no one appeared to be bothering her.

"Is this seat taken?" Cassie asked before sitting down.

The woman looked up and noticed Cassie for the first time. "By you," she said. It was a neutral statement—not exactly welcoming but not off-putting, either.

"Thank you."

A platinum-haired server in a sparkly black tank top appeared and raised her eyebrows to Cassie.

"What can I get you?"

Cassie looked around. Most of the males were drinking draft beer and shots, and the attractive woman was sipping on what looked like bourbon on the rocks.

"A glass of wine, please."

"Red or white?"

"Red."

"Red we got," the server said.

Cassie watched as the server filled a wineglass to the top from a cardboard box with a spigot.

"I don't think they serve a lot of wine here," she said to the woman.

"Are you surprised?"

"I guess not."

The woman turned slightly away on her stool as if to signal that she found her phone more interesting than Cassie. Cassie got the message, but she couldn't help not doing a quick visual profile on the woman.

Her big diamond ring glinted in the overhead bar lights, and beneath a gold pendant necklace a dime-size ruby hung at the plunge of her breasts. The ruby matched the color of her lipstick and manicured nails.

Cassie felt dowdy sitting next to her. What didn't add up, though, was why an attractive woman in a place like the Hayloft would be sitting alone.

The question was answered a few seconds later when one of the drunk fishermen approached from behind them and leaned on the bar with both elbows and turned to her. "I was wondering if I could buy you a—"

"Fuck off," the woman said quickly and firmly before he could finish.

"Drink," the man finished.

"Maybe you didn't hear me?" the woman asked.

"I heard you loud and clear," the fisherman said.

"Then fuck off," she repeated.

"Okay, I got the message."

RATHER THAN continue to glare at the exchange and watch

the wounded fisherman skulk away, she studied the mirror and the backbar. Above the bar was a long row of ancient beer cans. Cassie recognized some of them from her youth: Great Falls, Schlitz, Hamm's, Grain Belt.

"Would you like to see a menu?" the server asked when she delivered Cassie's wine.

"Sure."

Cassie was careful when she raised the glass to take her first sip. It was so full she didn't want to spill it on her clothes. The wine was better than she would have guessed it would be.

She glanced around the bar. There were three female employees serving drinks and food. One was a severely thin blonde with huge breasts, the other a cowgirl with tight sequined jeans and a massive buckle, and the server who poured Cassie's wine. All wore the tight black tank tops and any of them could be Lindy, she thought.

It was a long menu but several items were highlighted as local favorites, including the patty melt, chicken-fried steak, and fried chicken gizzards. Cassie ordered the patty melt.

"It goes excellent with your wine," the server said unconvincingly.

"Thank you," Cassie said. "Can you tell me—is Lindy working tonight?"

She hoped the server would say, "I'm Lindy." Instead, she frowned at the mention of the name.

"Not tonight, I guess," the girl said.

"When will she be in?"

The server rolled her eyes. "Your guess is as good as mine." Then she left to put in Cassie's order.

An odd thing to say, Cassie thought. Didn't the employees have a schedule posted somewhere of their shifts?

"You're looking for Lindy Glode?" the woman next to Cassie asked.

"Yes."

"Let me guess," the woman said, leaning back to give Cassie the once-over. She did it in a way that was full-on, not in the furtive way Cassie had profiled *her*. "You're either a pissed-off wife out to tell Lindy off for flirting with your husband or you're a cop."

"More the latter," Cassie said. She was impressed but not flattered.

"I know all the cops in this neck of the woods so you're from out of town."

"Bozeman."

"So why is a cop looking for Lindy?"

"I want to ask her some questions. Her name came up in an investigation. She's not in any trouble."

"Ah," the woman said with a sly smile. "You don't want to tell me."

"Do you know her pretty well?" Cassie asked.

The woman continued to smile as if she was in on the conspiracy, whatever it was.

"I'm in here two or three nights a week, honey. I'd say I knew her pretty well."

"Do you know where I can find her?"

The woman turned and sipped the last of her drink. She signaled the server for another, and nodded toward Cassie's wineglass as well.

"Really, I'm okay," Cassie said.

"That's what you think."

Another odd statement, Cassie thought.

"Lindy kind of sets her own hours," the woman said.

"I think she's using again. When she jumps back off that wagon her appearances here can be few and far between."

"Do you know where she lives?" Cassie asked.

"Now why do you think I'd know that?"

"Just asking."

The server delivered another full glass of wine to Cassie and a bourbon on the rocks to the woman. She said, "Do you want me to put both of these on your tab, Cheyenne?"

"Yes."

Cheyenne. Cassie tried not to let her mouth drop open in surprise.

"You're Cheyenne Kleinsasser?"

The woman nodded. "I was three husbands ago. Now I go by Cheyenne Kleinsasser Porché, or Cheyenne K. Porché, which I prefer because of the musical sound it makes. I've been told it sounds more like a brand of perfume or brandy."

She laughed huskily at that and it made Cassie smile.

Then it got quiet between them. It was Cassie's move.

"I'm a private investigator," she said. "I talked with your brother John Wayne just an hour ago."

Cheyenne took a long drag on her cigarette and squinted through the smoke at Cassie.

"You're Franny's mother," Cassie said. "I'm sorry for what happened to her."

"We all are," Cheyenne said. "So you're working for my big brother Blake?"

"His defense attorney," Cassie clarified. "As I told John Wayne, I'm simply here to verify all of the evidence in the case."

"And you're looking to talk to Lindy why?"

Cassie had nearly forgotten about Lindy now that she had

Franny's mother sitting right beside her. Cheyenne was a much bigger fish in the pond as far as the investigation went.

Cassie said, "In the time line we're checking on Blake's movements before the assault"—she deliberately left out the word "alleged" this time—and Blake said he was with Lindy. He was unclear on the details and he couldn't even remember her last name. I got that from the sheriff's report. Anyway, I wanted to verify that her recollection matched his."

Cheyenne did the laugh again. "Blake couldn't remember the last name of the barmaid he was fucking? That's... so *Blake*."

Then she waved her hand as if erasing Cassie's explanation. "You're assuming that Lindy knows what month it is right now, which is quite the stretch. If she can remember details about her and Blake back in July I'd be astounded."

"She gave a statement back then," Cassie said.

"That's before she was using again, I'm sure."

Cassie nodded. She still wanted to talk with Lindy, but she now doubted it would be helpful.

Her patty melt arrived. Cassie was hungry but she didn't want to dive in and lose Cheyenne's attention or company.

"Do you remember when you and John Wayne took Franny to the sheriff's department?"

Cheyenne looked offended. "Of course I remember. She's my daughter."

"Why did John Wayne go with you?"

"He insisted on it," she said. "As soon as he found out Blake was involved, he was all over it. Before that he pretty much ignored Franny. And me, for that matter. See, if Blake is the black sheep in the eyes of the rest of my family, I'm the gray sheep. Or brown sheep. I don't know which. The only reason

I'm tolerated is because of my two X chromosomes. Therefore, I'm no threat to them or the ranch. They haven't approved of me for quite some time. Because of my bloodline, they had no choice but to provide me a house to live in when I moved back here from France with Franny, but they weren't enthusiastic about it. They were pleased I left Mr. Porché behind, however."

She stubbed her cigarette out with more force than necessary.

"I was the only one who was kind of happy to see Blake when he came back," she said. "After all, I spent the most time with him growing up. John Wayne was a squirt when Blake left, and Rand didn't hardly know him at all. Rand knows the stories my father and John Wayne told him. They hated Blake and they despised the fact that he left the ranch. They thought he was the devil himself."

Which might have proved to be true, Cassie thought but didn't say.

CHEYENNE FINISHED HER DRINK quickly and crooked her finger at the server for another. Since Cassie was still sipping her first glass she didn't order another for her, for which Cassie was grateful.

Let her drink, Cassie thought. Let her drink and keep her talking. The scenario playing out was a private investigator's dream.

Cheyenne slipped her phone into a bejeweled handbag on the bar. Cassie hoped that was an indication that she wanted to continue the conversation.

"Were you surprised when you heard Franny's story?" Cassie asked her.

"Fucking shocked is a better description," Cheyenne said. "I knew Blake was a hound dog, but this…" She shook her head in disgust. "And leaving her out there to find her way home. That was so low."

"Prior to the attack," Cassie asked, "what would you say Franny's relationship with Blake was?"

"Cordial," Cheyenne said. "Nothing special, but Blake was nice to her without being over-the-top. I got the impression he was looking for friendlies in hostile territory and he'd be happy with anyone who didn't hate his guts. Why do you ask?"

"I'm just tying up loose ends," Cassie said. "One of the things that kind of puzzles me was the fact that Blake picked her up at the church. That suggests a closer relationship than I would have guessed."

Cheyenne nodded. She said, "What you have to understand is that everything is a long way from everything else here. The ranch is twenty-five minutes from Horston, so nearly an hour round-trip. I was meeting with my lawyer at my house about some changes I wanted to make in my divorce settlement and I knew Blake was somewhere in town. I texted him and asked that he pick her up. Of course, I really regret that now."

Cassie sat back. "That you asked him to pick her up wasn't in any of my documents. Even Blake didn't tell us that."

Cheyenne rolled her eyes. "He probably doesn't remember. From what I understood later, he was in the midst of a blackout drunk at the time. He claims not to remember anything from that night."

"That's true." Cassie glanced at Cheyenne's bag on the bar. "Do you still have that text exchange with Blake on your phone?"

Something passed behind Cheyenne's eyes, and Cassie took it for a second of panic. Then it was gone just as quickly.

"I've replaced my phone since this summer," Cheyenne said. "Not all of the data got moved over to the new one, including my texts. Sorry about that."

"That's okay. Just asking."

"I dropped my old phone in the toilet and it didn't work after that," Cheyenne explained. Cassie wasn't sure why she'd provided the detail.

"Do you mind if I take some notes?" Cassie asked. She wanted to remind herself to do a check on Blake's phone to confirm the text. As far as she knew it hadn't been done.

"Please don't," Cheyenne replied. "If you start to take notes like this is some kind of interrogation I'll leave and you'll never see me again. People in here will notice that you're interviewing me. This is just talk as far as I'm concerned. Woman-to-woman."

"Woman-to-woman," Cassie repeated. She didn't dare reach for her notebook or the digital recorder in her bag.

"Along those same lines," Cassie asked, "did Franny ever get her phone back?"

"Her phone?"

"She said Blake took it and put it in the console of his rental car so she couldn't call for help."

Cheyenne nodded her head. "She's got her phone with her. I guess they gave it back to her. I didn't know it was an issue."

"It isn't. It's just one of the items I had on my list to account for."

Cheyenne looked at her suspiciously, and Cassie knew she needed to soften her line of questioning.

"If you don't mind," Cassie said while taking a sip of wine, "I think I understand the relationship between Blake and the rest of the family to some degree. There's a lot of hate and resentment toward him."

"Envy is a word you might throw in there as well," Cheyenne said. "But don't ever tell my younger brothers or my father I said it."

"They envy Blake?" Cassie asked, surprised.

"They'd never admit to it but they do. At least John Wayne does. He absolutely hates the fact that his brother went out into the world and made something of himself. It's an irrational hatred. John Wayne thinks anyone who leaves the ranch and the family is despicable. Especially if they do well."

She chuckled and said, "Unfortunately, I reinforce his view on that. Every time I leave I end up coming back with my tail between my legs."

"You said Franny and Blake's relationship was cordial," Cassie said. "What about Franny and her other uncles?"

"This is getting very personal," Cheyenne said.

"I'm sorry. I just want to understand the family better."

"You'll *never* understand this family," she said. "*I've* never understood this family. An army of psychologists would never understand this family. Suffice it to say that it's rotten to the core. Lawyers use a term called the fruit of the poisonous tree. Maybe that describes the Kleinsassers."

Blake said a similar thing, she recalled. But she didn't bring that up.

"Franny's relationship with Rand is the same as mine—nonexistent," Cheyenne offered. "I see him strut around town from time to time, but he's usually gone from the ranch. John Wayne uses him to deliver things around the state or pick them up. What Rand actually does is a mystery to me, and I don't ask."

"What about Franny and her grandparents?" Cassie asked.

"She's scared of them, especially my father. He has dementia and he's turning into a nasty, bitter old man. She stays as far away from them as she can get."

Cassie observed that Cheyenne's face tightened and her mouth turned down when she talked about her father.

Cheyenne said, "My parents didn't really raise us like normal parents do. They just sort of threw us out there and observed us for flaws. My father, especially. I think we all spent more time with ranch employees growing up than with our parents.

"We didn't do things together like families do," she said, looking away from Cassie toward something in the middle distance. "We never went on a vacation together, or got together for holidays. We still don't. My mother tried for a while, like insisting that we all go to church together. But that didn't last. My father used my bad behavior or Blake's moodiness as reasons why we couldn't do that anymore.

"I'm close to my mother but I resent that she never stood up to him. I know she saw that as her role. His role was to lecture us about upholding our good name so we wouldn't disappoint him or our legacy in this stupid fucking valley. He instructed us about the Kleinsasser Trust and all of the rules laid down by my creepy grandfather. I've always thought my father disliked Blake because his oldest son had absolutely no interest in the legacy, which is true."

"And John Wayne?" Cassie asked. This was the question she wanted answered most of all, especially since her exchange with him earlier in the evening.

"John Wayne ate that shit up," Cheyenne hissed.

"And you?"

"It doesn't matter," she said. "I'm a girl."

"What about Franny and John Wayne. How do they get on?"

"They're close, I'd say," Cheyenne said with a roll of her eyes. "He loves to school her on the importance of the family name and what goes with it. She eats that stuff up, or at least pretends to. I'm not sure she isn't just kind of shining him on because she's good at that. I've tried to talk to her about it, you know. I tell her not to necessarily treat everything John Wayne tells her as gospel. I think she gets it, but she's her own person. Young people of a certain age are suckers for family lore, I think. Not because they really care about history but because it maybe helps explain who they are, you know? It gives them an anchor as well as an excuse to act badly because they can say it's in their genes. I think she'll eventually figure him out," Cheyenne said. "I certainly hope so."

Me, too, Cassie thought. Little she'd heard about the Kleinsasser legacy thus far seemed like something to aspire to.

"I have to say this about John Wayne, though," Cheyenne said. "When Franny showed up that night saying Blake had attacked her, John Wayne was right there. I know some of it was his animus toward Blake, maybe most of it. But he was there when both Franny and I were a mess. He took charge and thank God he did.

"Oh, my," Cheyenne said with a laugh. "Did I just say something kind about my brother?"

"You did," Cassie said, smiling.

"I need another drink," Cheyenne said. And she ordered one.

"Are you going to be okay to drive?"

Cheyenne turned on a full-force grin. It was dazzling. It was her way of saying, *I never have trouble getting a ride home*.

"What about Franny?" Cassie asked. "Is there any chance I could talk with her? I promise to be very gentle and you can be in the room—"

"Fuck off," Cheyenne said. It was just as harsh as the tone she'd used with the drunk fisherman. Her entire demeanor had changed.

"Look, I'm sorry if I—"

"I said *fuck off*. Can you even imagine what she's gone through? And you want to bring it all back up to her?"

"Really," Cassie said, "I just thought she might want to tell me her story."

"She's told it enough. What she needs is peace and normalcy. That's why you'll never find her."

What did that mean? Cassie wondered.

Cheyenne leaned into Cassie so closely Cassie could smell the bourbon on her breath.

"We're done here," she said. "Leave Franny and me alone."

FOURTEEN

DISTURBED AND SHAKEN by how the conversation with Cheyenne had turned, Cassie walked out into the cool and smoke-filled night air. Her hands were trembling and she shook her head as if to confirm what had just happened.

She sat in her Jeep for a moment and replayed the entire exchange over in her head. She'd rarely encountered a woman who could shut down and lash out so suddenly. Maybe it was the cumulative effect of all of those glasses of bourbon, she thought. But Cheyenne's tone and demeanor absolutely changed when Cassie brought up the subject of her daughter.

Cassie would still need to try and find Lindy Glode although it sounded like Lindy's condition and credibility might be dicey. She wondered if Cheyenne would ever talk to her again. And she dismissed the possibility of meeting Franny.

*

CASSIE CHECKED her phone to see that Ben had tried to call her while she was talking with Cheyenne. As usual, he didn't leave a message. Isabel had not returned her call.

Cassie checked her mirrors and eased out of the parking lot onto Highway 93. There was no traffic.

When she reached cruising speed she punched the button on the steering wheel that activated the Bluetooth system.

"Hi, Mom." He sounded jaunty, which pleased her.

"I see that you called. Did you get things worked out with Isabel? I tried to talk with her earlier but she didn't pick up."

"She's still on strike," Ben said. "That's part of her strike, you know. She only takes calls from her weird hippie friends."

"Ben, please don't call your grandmother's friends 'weird hippies.'"

"That's what they are and you know it," he said. He still sounded happy.

"You seem to be in a good mood."

"I am. I can do what I want now. I cooked a cheeseburger for dinner and I liked it so much I cooked another one. I hope she stays on strike forever."

"Ben..."

"Oh, and something really wild happened today. It was *crazy*."

Cassie braced herself for what would come next.

"I was walking to the Kum and Go..."

As she crossed the Lochsa County line, red and blue wig-wag lights filled her vehicle and a siren whooped from behind.

"What was *that?*" Ben asked. "Was that a cop car? Are the cops after you?"

Cassie squinted into the rearview mirror to see the cruiser just a few feet from her bumper.

She glanced at her dashboard. Her lights were on and she was going four miles under the sixty-five-mile-an-hour speed limit.

"I'm being pulled over," Cassie said.

"By the cops? What did you do?"

"I have no idea but I need to call you back."

"Keep the phone on so I can hear," he said. Ben seemed to be enjoying the situation a bit too much, she thought.

"Ben, I said I'd call you back," she repeated.

"Don't get thrown in the slammer, Mom! But if you do I'll bring you a file in a cake so you can break out."

She disconnected the call.

CASSIE EASED OVER to the shoulder of the highway until her passenger-side tires sunk into the loam. The cruiser stayed just a few feet from her Jeep, which went against her training as a young deputy sheriff. She'd been taught that when pulling over a driver she should maintain at least a car length distance away from the citizen. That way, the officer could clearly see the plates and call them in to find out if the vehicle was stolen or if she had any outstanding warrants. Also, if the offender decided to reverse his vehicle and ram her unit she'd have enough warning to take evasive action.

This cop, however, had apparently not received the same training. Or he'd chosen to disregard it.

She'd never been on the wrong side of a roadside situation before. It was embarrassing and intimidating. She also hoped that the reason she'd been pulled over was innocuous, that the officer had noted that her taillight was out or he was simply warning her that the fire had jumped the road ahead on the highway.

Cassie placed both of her hands on top of the steering wheel so they'd be in plain view. She didn't want to give the cop any reason whatsoever to suspect her of anything.

So many things could go wrong, she knew. But she'd always experienced a situation like this from the viewpoint of the cop pulling someone over, not the other way around. Would the driver be belligerent? Would the subject pull a weapon or try to drive away? Was there a body in the trunk?

She could see the officer clearly in her rearview mirror. He was angular and young with a shaved head and eyes that were close together, which gave her the impression—likely undeserved—that he was petty and mean.

He was a sheriff's deputy, she could tell by the uniform. Not a state trooper, not a Lolo city cop. He raised a microphone to his mouth, spoke briefly to someone, and reached onto the passenger seat for his jacket and hat.

Then he walked out of the angle of her rearview mirror as he got out.

She shifted her eyes to her side mirror as he closed his car door and approached. When his belt buckle filled the glass, she turned her head toward him and slowly reached down for the button to lower her window.

Cassie was blinded by his Maglite beam aimed squarely into her face.

"That flashlight wasn't necessary, Officer," she said as she looked away.

"It was if I wanted to see your eyes," he said. "They look kind of glassy and unfocused to me."

"They aren't."

"Here's what you need to do for me," he said. "You need to keep your hands on the wheel where I can see them. Do not make any sudden moves unless I ask you to do so." She thought, *Uh-oh, one of those*. But she complied with his order. All she could see were two bright orange orbs from the beam. She tried to keep her anger in check.

"I saw you drift across the center line back there," he said. "Have you been drinking?"

"I think you might be mistaken, Officer. I've been driving very carefully." She kept her voice neutral and measured. "I had one glass of wine at the Hayloft. One."

"It's usually two," he said. "Most folks say they only had two. Two can equal two or it can equal ten."

"Well, I had one."

"Are you under the influence of any other substances?" the cop asked. "Maybe prescription meds?"

"No."

"Then why were you weaving all over the road, ma'am?"

"I don't believe I was, Officer."

"Then I'm sure you wouldn't object to a Breathalyzer test."

"Correct," she said. "I wouldn't object at all."

Cassie knew she had the right to refuse to take the test because taking it was implied consent. But she also knew that refusal could result in additional charges and consequences such as suspension of her driver's license or possible arrest. Plus, she *knew* she wasn't inebriated or driving recklessly.

Her vision had finally been restored and she took him in. He was from Lochsa County, all right. His name badge said BRYAN "ALF" GRZEGORCZYK.

She asked, "How do I pronounce your name, Officer?"

"Why is that important?" he asked. "Do you plan to contest this?"

"No, sir. It's just an unusual name."

He said, "*Greg-or-check*. My buddies in the service couldn't pronounce my name so they called me 'Alf' like in 'alphabet.' It's Czech."

"So I gathered."

"Now that we've cleared that up," he said, "I need you to stay there and don't move. Keep your hands on the wheel at all times where I can see them."

"Yes, *sir*." She knew that some of the sarcasm she'd tried to hold in check had leaked out.

He paused on his way to his car. "What was that?"

"I said, 'Yes, sir.' I don't object to a Breathalyzer test."

"In the meantime, I need you to get out of your car. Let's see you walk a straight line."

"Really?"

"Do I need to repeat myself? Are you having trouble responding to my requests?"

She knew the tactic. Claim the citizen pulled over didn't comply with official police instructions. Then build from there.

"I'm getting out," she said as she opened her door.

Deputy Grzegorczyk stood near his driver's-side door with his hands on his hips.

"Walk toward me."

She did. She placed one foot in front of the other and she fought the urge to look down at her shoes. A pickup coming from Lolo slowed on the highway as it passed and she saw the driver and his elderly wife looking at her with big eyes. It was humiliating.

As she neared him the officer suddenly shot out his hand. "*Stop*."

She instinctively stepped back.

"Little wobbly there," he said.

"I didn't want your hand in my face."

"Right," he said with a mocking tone.

"Look, Deputy Grzegorczyk," Cassie said, "I used to be a cop myself. I know how these things work. You can claim I was weaving down the road and you can claim I couldn't walk a straight line, but neither is true. I can dispute it, but it's your word against mine. I'm trying to cooperate in every way. So, let's cut the crap and give me the test so I can be on my way."

"You used to be a cop, huh?"

"Yes."

"Then you should know you shouldn't drink and drive," he said with a smirk. "And you know you shouldn't mouth off to a peace officer."

She bit her tongue. As much as she had always despised fellow cops who used their badges to intimidate and harass citizens, she didn't need to tell him that. She'd wait until the morning and file a complaint with Sheriff Wagy.

He opened his door and leaned inside. She waited and seethed.

After less than a minute, he stepped back onto the asphalt. "Looks like I left my Breathalyzer tester back at the department."

She waited for more. Then asked, "What's that mean?"

"I thought you said you used to be a cop. You know exactly what that means. It means I need to take you in so we can do it there."

"Take me in?"

"Yes, ma'am. To that place with lots of desks and cells and prisoners and jail bars and stuff."

He was being clearly provocative and sarcastic. He was, she concluded, trying very hard to bait her into a reaction.

She didn't bite.

"Can I please follow you?" she asked. "I don't want to leave my Jeep out here on the highway."

"In your condition?" he said with a grin. "That's fucking nuts. No wonder the cop shop you worked for let you go."

"My name is Cassie Dewell," she said. "I'm a licensed private investigator with the State of Montana."

"Let's hope you can keep that license after this," he said.

"Believe me, I will. Look, I know Sheriff Wagy. I met with him just this morning. He knows I'm here on legitimate business."

Grzegorczyk rolled his eyes. "You're going to try and play that card on me? Act like you and my boss are best buds? Even if he knows you I doubt he'd approve of you driving drunk in Lochsa County, lady."

Then he opened his back door and signaled for her to get in.

"Now I need you to take a seat in the cruiser. Try not to bump your head getting in."

"Can I at least get my purse and lock up my car?" she asked.

"I'll get it," he said. The deputy placed his left hand on the Taser on his belt and his right hand on the grip of his service weapon.

His voice was chilling. "I need you to get into this car right now, ma'am.

"You'll love our jail," he said, stepping aside so she could crawl into his cruiser. "It's really historic."

★

DEPUTY GRZEGORCZYK turned back onto the highway and Cassie watched her Jeep slide by with its driver's-side window and door closed but unlocked.

"So you're a PI, huh?" he asked, eying her in the rearview mirror.

"Yes. License number seven, seven, seven, five."

"Do you make a good living at it? It's something I might be interested in doing some day is the reason I asked."

"I do okay." She sighed. His change in tone was curious to her.

"Good to know."

As they drove toward Horston, she recalled something John Wayne Kleinsasser had asked her.

What are you driving so I'll know it's you?

Or had Cheyenne called a friend in the sheriff's department known as Deputy Grzegorczyk?

FIFTEEN

THE TRUCK DRIVER chose a different place to park the second time he came to the high school building. There was no need to arouse suspicion, no need to create a situation where a resident could later recall that he or she saw the same vehicle idling in the middle of the night at the same location.

So instead of a side street, he chose a gravel two-track on the far east end of the campus near the football stadium. The driver would have preferred to get closer because of what he was about to do, but he was convinced his logic was solid in choosing another spot. Plus, with the exception of a single pole light on the west end of the stadium that illuminated a closed-up concession stand, he couldn't be seen from the side streets.

He powered down the driver's-side window, killed the engine, and pocketed the keys. He sat silently for ten minutes letting the cold night air envelop him. As he did so he waited and watched. The engine ticked as it cooled.

The stadium itself was no different than it used to be although there were some new guest boxes on the top level and artificial turf had been laid down to replace the old grass field. Unlike the landscape around him of brittle tufts of dried grass and cover, the new plastic field with its perfect white stripes looked phony and cheap to him. Just like the coaches and physical education teachers who used to give him such a hard time.

Being so close to the stadium dredged up uncomfortable recollections of doing laps around the track or running up and down the stairs as punishment. He could recall how his leg muscles burned, and how his lungs ached.

Those sadists.

HE SLIPPED OUT of the cab and slung a heavy duffel bag over his right shoulder by the strap and walked toward the high school building. The chain-link fence gate wasn't locked—it never was during football season because players couldn't be expected to wait for someone to unlock it before running through.

He chose a route between the fence and the cavernous back of the stadium itself. He kept in the shadows and moved from pillar to pillar. As his eyes adjusted to the gloom he could read the crude hand-lettered posters that were hung on the interior walls:

Hawk Power!
Bag the Bengals!
Red and Black—On the Attack!

He snorted and rolled his eyes. The cheerleaders who made the signs hadn't come up with an original thought or slogan in the years since he'd been there. Obviously, they'd be hosting the Helena Bengals on Friday.

The smells from the stadium were still the same as well: stale popcorn, spilled soft drinks, sweat, athletic tape. It jerked him back to a place he didn't want to go.

He remembered being told once that the sense of a familiar smell—called olfaction—could trigger intense recollections. It was true. He felt as if he was being jerked back in time.

He cursed and picked up his pace. As far as he was concerned, he couldn't get away from the stadium fast enough.

THERE WERE TWO vehicles in the teacher's parking lot, but no lights on from inside the building. He puzzled over that for a moment, then thought: *Of course. The cars belonged to coaches or advisors who had accompanied a team or group out of town. They'd left their cars for when they got back.*

THE TRUCK DRIVER paused behind a spruce and surveyed the exterior brick wall of the auto shop. The broken camera still hung by its wires above the closed garage door. They hadn't even removed it yet. Typical.

He lowered the bag to the ground and grasped the door handle and tugged hard to the side. He heard the *click* and the door released.

After raising it two feet, he got on his hands and knees and crawled under it, then pulled the duffel bag inside behind him. He stepped on a steel rail and pushed the bottom of the door down within an inch of the concrete floor.

He turned and took in the room. Again, he was assaulted

with familiar odors. Oil, gasoline, diesel fuel. There was a masking antiseptic sheen of floor-cleaning agent over the top of it, but the basic gearhead smells were still there.

That, he liked. At least some of the students were still learning *something* practical. It would only be a matter of time before the auto shop was replaced with a meditation room or multicultural studies area or overall safe space, he reckoned.

The shop was dimly lit by a row of amber emergency lights just below the high ceiling. It wasn't enough light to throw shadows but it was enough to see where he was going. He had no need for the headlamp he'd brought along.

A half-ton Toyota pickup with its hood up was in one of the bays, and a tricked-out Dodge Challenger was in another. He walked between them toward the heavy metal door that led to the main building.

IT WASN'T like he even needed the emergency lights or his head-lamp. He could have found his way down the hallways and wings with his eyes closed. He impressed himself with his perfect recall of the layout of the building with its banks of lockers and closed classroom doors.

And it was all the same. These people never changed. The teachers who thought they were cool and edgy taped slogans and cartoons on the outside of their doors. The display cases were filled with forgotten trophies and team photos. On the brick walls were posters boasting of "Hawk Pride" and bulletin boards covered with politically correct bullshit about suicide prevention and how to prevent sexually transmitted diseases.

The central hub of the building was the library, and he could see it in the distance long before he got there. The windows glowed light blue from the monitors of a bank of computers within. There had been a few of them before, mostly clunky beige PCs, but now the interior looked like Mission Control at NASA.

Those students could really update their Facebook profiles now, he thought.

But it wasn't the new computers he was interested in. What he wondered was if the maintenance crew had ever fixed the loose ceiling panel above the entry door to the library. That's where he and his buddies used to stash their weed and alcohol so it wouldn't be found in their lockers.

The sound of a human grunt stopped him cold. He froze in place and reached back for the grip of his .22 pistol that he'd tucked into his belt.

Then he heard it again, along with rhythmic flesh-on-flesh slapping.

He turned his head toward the sound and realized he was standing outside the open door of the teacher's lounge. In the ambient glow of the emergency lights inside he saw a purse on a table and a pile of clothing on the floor. And two teachers, a man and a woman, going at it on a couch. They were naked and white and she was on top. Her long dark hair obscured her face.

He assumed they were both doughy and unattractive people. But if he could see them they could see *him*.

He took a breath and stepped back. She didn't look up.

He took another step back, then another until he could no longer see them.

The man groaned again, this time with relief, and he

recognized its meaning. Then they were done and both breathing hard, probably clinging to each other.

The driver was grateful that his trucker's boots had soft, quiet soles. He turned and found a girl's bathroom door that was propped open with a wooden wedge on the floor and he stepped inside. The room was completely dark.

He found a stall and backed into it and closed the door.

LESS THAN TEN minutes later, he heard the two teachers talking softly and he could discern from the sounds of zippers that they were getting dressed. The woman came out of the lounge first, her heels clicking on the linoleum tiles like castanets. The man followed. He said something that made her laugh.

Then there was the wheezing sound of a heavy door being opened and shut.

They were gone.

He closed his eyes and waited long enough to make sure one of them hadn't forgotten something and decided to come back.

There was a brief sweep of headlights across the frosted outside window of the restroom as one of the two cars pulled away. Then another.

They weren't coaches or advisors after all. They were just common fornicators.

He thought, *What sick fucks. Using the teacher's lounge! They were probably both married and they were the type who wouldn't hesitate to judge him or lecture him about his behavior.*

Fucking hypocrites is what they were.
Literally.

THE CEILING TILE gave way just as he'd anticipated it would. He slid it to the side.

The driver stood on an upturned metal trash can and felt around at the opening to make sure the space wasn't still being used to hide drugs and contraband. It wasn't. He wouldn't have been surprised to find a baggie of old dried-up weed that he'd left up there.

But there were only dust bunnies.

He climbed down and unzipped the duffel bag. Into the space went a 12-gauge combat shotgun with a pistol grip, a .40 Charter Arms Pitbull revolver, three boxes of shotgun shells filled with buckshot, a heavy mesh bag of smoke and tear gas grenades, and a military-grade tactical gas mask.

When the tile was seated back into place, he briefly turned his headlamp on and choked the beam down.

Satisfied that he'd left no fingerprints or telltale dust smudges on the edges of the tile, he killed the light and waited for his eyes to readjust to the darkness of the hallway.

Then he retraced his steps through the halls and back into the auto shop. The empty duffel bag was now no heavier than an afterthought.

The driver raised the door again and crawled under it, then rolled it back down until it was secure. He walked toward the stadium and his truck in the cold night air.

Red and Black—On the Attack!

It was set.

PART III

There are inevitably two kinds of slaves: the prisoners of addiction and the prisoners of envy.

—IVAN ILLICH, *Tools for Conviviality*

The Family! Home of all social evils, a charitable institution for Indolent women, a prison workhouse for family breadwinners, and a hell for children!

—AUGUST STRINDBERG, *The Son of a Servant*

SIXTEEN

RACHEL MITCHELL didn't arrive at the Lochsa County Jail the next morning until 11:30 a.m. Cassie could hear her voice—it was loud and angry and it bounced off the walls—in the reception area down the hallway from her cell.

"Is that your girl?" Cassie's cellmate Delores Attao asked.

"Sounds like her," Cassie replied.

"She sounds pissed off. I wish I had a lawyer like that. I've got a public defender named Kendrick who can't pronounce my name. Do you think she'd represent me?"

"You should ask her," Cassie said.

It had been a long night, and Cassie felt dirty, disheveled, and oddly ashamed of herself. She'd never spent a night in jail before. It was more dehumanizing than what she'd imagined it to be, and she felt a pang of guilt for placing so many violators behind bars and not considering how awful it must have been for some of them.

Although she wanted out as quickly as it could happen,

she didn't want anyone she knew to see her in there. And she didn't want Ben to know.

Throughout the night, there had been crazed shouts from other cells in a different wing where males were kept. Putrid odors wafted through the vents and nearly made her retch. They'd barely dimmed the cold fluorescent overhead lights and everything took on a dull blue-gray hue. She'd had nothing to do and no way to communicate with anyone outside. They'd taken her phone, keys, purse, and shoes.

The cell for females was the closest to the door that led to the lobby. Three or four other cells reserved for men were farther away down the hallway. Therefore, as drunks and other miscreants were brought in during the night they were led past Cassie. One of them looked in at her, smirked, and did a lizardlike sexual maneuver with his tongue. Another grabbed his crotch and crab-walked out of view while laughing to himself even though the cop that brought him in told him to "move it along."

It was humiliating. And the worst thing about being behind bars was exposure. There were no doors to close or curtains to pull. Even the stainless-steel toilet was in plain and open view from anyone passing down the hall.

The old stone cell was twelve feet by twelve feet and the walls were cold and damp. She'd taken the top bunk because Delores was already camped out in the bottom.

When Deputy Grzegorczyk had led her inside, Cassie had assumed it would be temporary—that she'd be held until he returned with the Breathalyzer. She hadn't seen a holding cell in the ancient frontier jail, after all. An hour passed, then another. It wasn't until then that she realized he wasn't coming back.

DELORES ATTAO was a Nez Perce who'd been arrested for public intoxication and resisting arrest hours before Cassie showed up. Attao was short and round with close-cropped black hair and she wore a billowy tunic and yoga pants that looked spray-painted on. She didn't have the figure for yoga pants but that didn't seem to bother her.

What set off Delores was finding her husband, Arthur, with another woman at the Corvallis Tavern. Delores freely admitted she'd caused a scene and that she'd thrown a glass of beer in Arthur's face. When the bartender called the sheriff's department and they quickly arrested her she surrendered willingly, she claimed. There was no resistance. But the bastards, she said, had charged her for resisting arrest anyway.

Despite her own situation, Cassie had enjoyed listening to Delores talk most of the night. She could focus on Delores instead of the chaos down the hall or her own dilemma. The county had recently slathered the interior of the cell with pale blue paint so thick Cassie couldn't even make out the scratchings or drawings from previous inmates.

Delores had a musical cadence to her speech that was familiar to Cassie from listening to other Native Americans. That was in addition to being precise with her words and nonchalant when it came to spending a night in jail. Delores didn't seem to care if Cassie was listening closely to her or not. Cassie's only responses were variations of "Hmmmm."

Cassie guessed Delores had been there before because she seemed to know her way around and she gave Cassie good bits of advice like not to eat the meat loaf under any circumstances and to insist on Crocs that fit because the cops enjoyed giving shoes that were either too small or large to their "overnight guests."

Sheriff Wagy had not been in even though Cassie had asked for him. Deputy Grzegorczyk had apparently gone off shift.

The only person Cassie had recognized was Linda Murdock from the front office. Murdock had stuck her head through the outside door and stared dumbstruck at Cassie in the cell. Then she shook her head sadly and vanished without saying a word. Cassie couldn't tell if Murdock was disappointed in her or ashamed of the department.

THAT SAME DOOR blew open moments later and Rachel Mitchell appeared like a force of nature. She was red-faced and furious, and her heels clicked on the cold stone floor like muffled gunshots. The undersheriff, whom Cassie had not seen or met, trailed behind Rachel.

"There she is," Rachel said, pointing at Cassie. "Let her out. *Now.*"

"You are a sight for sore eyes," Cassie said to Rachel.

"And if she spends one more minute in there," Rachel said to the undersheriff, "I'll not only sue your department like I'm planning to do but I'll contact the FBI to charge you with kidnapping."

The undersheriff, who was portly, bald, and shorter than Rachel, mumbled something about the whole thing being a mix-up of some kind as he approached the cell door with his keycard.

"I didn't even get to make a call," Cassie said. "I was starting to think I'd be stuck in here."

Delores responded as if slapped and Cassie felt guilty.

"Sorry, I don't mean you," Cassie said to her. "You got me through the night."

"Tell Arthur," Delores said. "Tell him I'm good company."

Before her cellmate could make her case to Rachel that she should represent her as well, Rachel grasped Cassie's arm and ushered her through the door. The undersheriff had to step back so Rachel wouldn't run him over.

Rachel wheeled on him and waved a painted finger in his face.

"Am I correct that my investigator was held overnight without any charges being filed?"

The undersheriff stammered and looked away. He said, "I just started my shift. I don't know what happened last night, but obviously there was some kind of screwup in booking."

Rachel bent down until her face was inches from his. "You seem to have a lot of screwups in this department. What about the fact that my investigator wasn't given her constitutional right to a phone call?"

The man shrugged as if to say, *same answer.*

"What's your name, Officer?" Rachel asked him.

"I'm undersheriff Richard Hewes."

"Thank you. I'll add your name to the lawsuit I'm going to file against Sheriff Wagy, the arresting officer, and Lochsa County for violating my investigator's civil rights. Not to mention false imprisonment. I'm going to hit you like a hurricane," she said.

Hewes grimaced. "But we're a poor county. We're not like Missoula or someplace like that."

Rachel said, "You should have thought of that before you locked up my investigator for no reason. When will the sheriff be here?"

"I don't know," Hewes stammered. "I called his cell when you got here but he didn't pick up."

"He '*didn't pick up*'?" Rachel mocked. "The sheriff didn't pick up?"

Hewes shrugged and looked away.

"Let's get the hell out of here, Cassie," Rachel said.

"Gladly."

Cassie was happy to let Rachel take charge. She was too numb and exhausted to do otherwise. Plus, there was no doubt Rachel thrived in these kinds of situations.

"Return her possessions," Rachel ordered the under-sheriff.

"Linda has them," he said.

"Then tell Linda to get her ass in gear," Rachel said while pushing through the metal doors to the lobby.

AN UNMARKED plastic grocery bag with Cassie's phone and other items was on Linda Murdock's desktop. Linda had already gathered them and she instinctively stepped back as Rachel strode toward her and snatched up the bag and handed it back to Cassie.

"Check and make sure everything is there," she said. "Sometimes these people have sticky fingers."

Cassie did a quick inventory. All of her stuff was inside the sack. The gear bag was nowhere to be seen and Cassie assumed it was still in her car.

When she looked up, Murdock mouthed the words, "I'm so sorry."

Cassie nodded. Murdock did indeed act like she was slightly horrified about the incident.

IN RACHEL'S CAR on the way to retrieve Cassie's Jeep, Rachel said, "What a pathetic shitshow back there. Do you think that for one minute it wasn't all orchestrated? Or are they really that fucking incompetent?"

"I was set up," Cassie said. "My only question is who was responsible."

"What if they stuck you in there with some kind of psycho meth head instead of what's-her-name? What if your throat got cut during the night?"

"Delores," Cassie said. "Her name is Delores. She was a sweetheart, actually. And I'd appreciate it if you'd consider taking her on as a client. From what she told me, the department overcharged her as well."

"I'll talk with her," Rachel said.

"You were magnificent back there," Cassie said. "Thank you."

"*This* is why I do what I do," Rachel shouted. She smacked the top of the dashboard three times for emphasis while she said, "*This, this, this!* Picking up an innocent person and throwing them in that shithole for the night without filing charges or allowing a phone call to me. It's pure intimidation. Everybody despises defense lawyers," Rachel continued. "Especially you cops. But when something like this happens aren't you glad we exist?"

"Yes."

"Did you ever think you'd say that?"

"No."

"Keep it in mind when you hear your brothers in law enforcement bitch about us. That's all I ask."

"How did you know where to find me?" Cassie asked.

Rachel took a deep breath but she was still clearly angry. "I called your cell five times and left messages," she said. "You *always* call me back within a few minutes. When you didn't call I tracked down Ben."

"My son?"

"Of course your son. He said that you were on the phone with him last night when a cop pulled you over. Otherwise, I wouldn't have had a clue what happened to you. I left first thing this morning and sped all the way. They could have held you there for days or worse."

Cassie recalled that Ben had something he wanted to tell her about the previous day, but they hadn't gotten that far before she had to terminate the call.

"How much farther is it?" Rachel asked. Cassie noted that she was going eighty—fifteen miles an hour over the speed limit.

"A couple of miles. And you might want to slow down."

"Fuck it," Rachel said. "Let them try to arrest me now. Let them try."

Cassie smiled. It felt like her face was cracking because it had been so long since she'd done it.

"Why were you trying to reach me?" she asked.

Rachel's face got grim. "Blake Kleinsasser was attacked by at least four inmates in jail. They stove his head in and they pounded a footlong length of steel rebar into his ear. He's in intensive care in the Bozeman hospital. Even if he makes it he might have permanent brain damage."

Cassie sat back, stunned. "My God."

"I should have believed him about the threats," Rachel said. "But he's such an asshole."

"Do they know who did it?"

"Not yet. I'm waiting to hear. But I'd bet you five dollars the bad guys have connections to Lochsa County."

"No bet," Cassie said.

WHEN RACHEL shot around a shadowed corner in the wall of trees, Cassie gasped for the second time in five minutes.

Her Jeep was a smoldering black box of steel and melted tires. The windows had all been smashed in or blown out by the heat and force of the internal fire. A yellow tag was affixed to the front door handle by state troopers who had found the vehicle and marked it to be towed away.

"Oh, no," Rachel said. "Oh, *no*."

"The files and my notes on the case were on the front seat," Cassie said, closing her eyes tightly.

THEY CIRCLED the blackened Jeep. It was a cool morning and Cassie could feel the heat emanate from the still-hot metal. The seat cushions were burned through to the spring coils. She couldn't discern if the ash in the passenger seat was from her burned-up files or from the fabric itself. Her gear bag had either been taken by passersby or had burned so completely it no longer existed.

Cassie studied the pine trees on both sides of the highway. The tops of many of them had been recently blackened and several were still smoldering. She knew enough about unchecked forest fires (everybody in Montana did these days) to know what had happened was called a "crown fire"—when flames leaped from treetop to treetop in a strong wind. Often, the fire didn't drop down to lower branches.

Was it possible that a crown fire had passed through during the night and sparks or burning embers had somehow dropped through the air via the open windows of her Jeep and ignited the contents? It was possible if highly unlikely, she concluded. Yet a potential case could be made...

She fought a surge of emotion that brought tears to her eyes that she quickly turned and wiped away. Although Rachel would likely understand and empathize, Cassie didn't want to give her the opening.

It wasn't the loss of the Jeep or her possessions—both could eventually be replaced. There were hours and days ahead of filling out insurance forms and making phone calls to banks and other entities to replace her credit cards and other lost items.

What overwhelmed Cassie was her sense of sudden helplessness fueled by exhaustion from the lack of sleep the night before. If someone were to design a scenario to make her simply want to go home and forget she'd ever come—they'd succeeded.

WHILE RACHEL pulled out her cell phone to call the highway patrol, Cassie shed her jacket and wrapped her right hand in it and reached down through the passenger window. She fished around in what was left of the car seat until she grasped something solid. It was her Glock .40. The plastic grip had melted onto the frame itself.

"They're coming," Rachel said of the highway patrol. "I don't know what they can do except tow it away, but I don't want the filthy paws of the sheriff's department anywhere near it."

"My PI identification is in my purse," Cassie said. "But my notes and my credit cards... everything was in the car."

"Do you think it was the same cops?" Rachel asked. "Do you think they threw you in jail and drove back here to torch your Jeep?"

"I don't know," Cassie said. "This is unbelievable. I do know that the guy who arrested me named Grzegorczyk never came back last night after putting me in the cell. I can't swear he left the building but I never saw him again."

"I think we know where he went," Rachel said. "I doubt he did this on his own, though. They're sending you a message, Cassie."

Cassie agreed.

"This will all be part of the lawsuit," Rachel said. "I'll depose Sheriff Wagy, this deputy who followed you and pulled you over—anyone who was involved. I'll make their lives a living hell for what they did to you."

"That will take time we don't have," Cassie said.

"Everything takes time," Rachel replied. "Sometimes the time it takes them to fight a lawsuit like this is almost winning in itself. This is the kind of corrupt crap that makes sheriffs lose elections and makes county commissioners question who actually runs this place."

It took Cassie a moment to figure out where Rachel was going.

"The Kleinsassers?" she said.

"At least the ones who were aware of this," Rachel said. "Starting with good ole John Wayne."

Or maybe Cheyenne, Cassie thought but didn't say.

Rachel said, "After the troopers get here for your car,

you and I are driving back to Bozeman together. You need to be gone from this county for your own safety, especially when they find out I'm going to hit them with a ton of bricks. Besides, we've probably got as much as we're going to get from this wretched hellhole."

Cassie dropped her chin to her chest and placed her hands on her hips. She didn't like feeling so defeated.

Rachel continued, "Who even knows if there will be a trial for Blake now? I wouldn't put odds on it. If my client is deceased or mentally incapacitated, this will all be over.

"What these idiots don't realize," Rachel said, "is even if there's no rape trial it doesn't end things for them. Nothing is tied up in a neat little bow. Not when they find out I'm coming after them for kidnapping, false imprisonment, civil rights violations, and the destruction of your car."

Her eyes gleamed for a moment. Cassie realized Rachel was not only outraged by what had happened, but almost thrilled at the prospect of suing Lochsa County for a large settlement. Blake Kleinsasser was almost an afterthought.

Rachel said, "Come on. Let's get the hell out of here while *we're* still among the living."

Cassie looked up at Rachel. "No."

"What do you mean, no?"

"You gave me a job and I'm going to finish it. I won't let them chase me out of here before I complete the investigation."

Rachel shook her head, puzzled. "But I'm the one who gave you the assignment. I can take it away just as easily. They threw you in jail and burned up your car and all your property. You don't owe me a thing."

Cassie set her jaw. "I've never achieved a thing by giving up. I'm not going to start now."

"Don't be ridiculous," Rachel said. "Even if Blake somehow recovers, we're still working for a guilty, rich asshole. Why risk your life for him?"

"He's an asshole, all right," Cassie said, "But until all of this happened I was convinced he was guilty. Now I'm not so sure. Why would they go to the lengths they've gone if they thought the conviction was a slam dunk? Wouldn't they do everything they could to help me confirm the case against Blake instead of stonewalling me at every opportunity?"

She pointed at her ruined Jeep. "Why would they do *this* if they didn't think I was getting too close to something?"

"Too close to what?" Rachel asked.

"I don't know."

"And I don't, either. But whatever it is it isn't worth Blake Kleinsasser. It isn't worth your life. Think of Ben."

Cassie nodded. She said, "I always think of Ben. What's important here is what he thinks about me."

Rachel didn't have a quick response although she was still flustered.

Cassie said, "We had a discussion about responsibility just a couple of nights ago. His father was a soldier and even though Ben never even knew him he thinks of his dad as strong and brave. Ben thinks of Jim as someone who would never retreat from a fight, because that's what I've always told him. Ben *needs* to feel that way about his dad, even though his dad was flawed in ways Ben will never know. Ben looks up to a man who never was, but that doesn't matter. I need to fill that role instead. I need to be that person.

"Let's go back into Horston," Cassie said. "We'll rent a car with your credit card and I'll stroll through the hardware store and restock. Then I'll continue working."

Rachel said, "As your lawyer I strongly advise you to come back home with me."

"You're not my lawyer," Cassie said. "You're my client."

SEVENTEEN

THE AFTERNOON was dark and overcast when Cassie drove her rented Ford Explorer out of town north on Highway 93. She, like every other local in the area and throughout the state, watched her windshield glass with anticipatory glances hoping to see droplets of moisture.

Although hundreds of firefighters and dozens of aircraft did their best, nothing stanched mountain fires like a long, soaking rain—a phenomenon that hadn't occurred in western Montana in thirty-one days.

Lower temperatures and the heavy clouds had pressed a godly open hand over the whole valley, tamping down the rage of the many fires as well as the rising smoke. It was as if the western wall of the Bitterroot Mountains didn't exist.

After she'd left the rental car company in Horston she saw a sign on the marquee of an ancient movie theater that read:

EVEN IF YOU'RE AN ATHEIST—PRAY FOR RAIN.

FOR EIGHT MILES she'd noted the stout buck-and-rail fence that ran parallel to the highway. It looked serious and impregnable, as if built not only to dissuade casual visitors but to retard the advance of an army column. She'd passed by the barrier the previous day but not given it much thought other than *Whoever owns this place isn't friendly.*

The fence eventually led to a high archway constructed of massive ponderosa pine poles and a sign that hung from black iron chains that indicated it was the entrance to the Iron Cross Ranch.

Although the Explorer was a full-sized SUV, it seemed tiny beneath the height and width of the entrance arch, which seemed to have been built for a caravan to pass through. As she did, she glimpsed a small closed-circuit camera mounted on the right-hand pole and a wire leading to a boxy solar panel.

The heavy steel gates had been swung inward. She was grateful that she could drive right through without seeking permission via a microphone and speaker attached to a vertical post.

This was the Kleinsassers' ranch, and they obviously cared about who went in and who drove out.

SHE'D BEEN ABLE to assemble a makeshift PI kit in Horston. With Rachel trailing her with a credit card and a worried expression, Cassie had purchased a secondhand .40 Glock 27 and a Smith & Wesson Ladysmith chambered in .22 long at a pawn shop. She didn't like or appreciate the pink rubber grip on the Ladysmith, but the five-shot revolver was slim and hammerless and it fit into the shaft of her cowboy boot.

At a sporting goods store she'd purchased two boxes of .40 cartridges and a plastic container of a hundred hollow-point .22 rounds. A large can of bear spray replaced the pepper spray that had burned up.

She'd found commercial wire cable ties at a hardware store that would serve as zip ties if she needed them. She also bought a heavy Maglite flashlight and a good pair of binoculars.

To replicate her lost Taser, Cassie bought a 10,000-volt hot shot at the feed store that was designed for cattle. It would do in a pinch, so to speak.

She doubted she would need any of the equipment. She never had. But replacing her lost gear with serviceable replacements seemed to restore her confidence and make her almost whole again.

BEN HADN'T picked up when she called, and she really hadn't expected him to. Cassie knew she'd called in the middle of wrestling practice when his clothes and phone were secured in a locker.

She'd left a voice mail, "Ben, call me the minute you can."

Not that he ever listened to messages, but he'd surely see that she had tried to reach him.

Her call to Isabel went straight to voice mail as well.

"Mom," Cassie had said after a long sigh, "Enough is enough with the strike. I need to check in with you about when I'm coming back."

THE WELL-MAINTAINED gravel road to the Iron Cross Ranch headquarters passed through several treeless miles of close-cropped cattle pasture. She noted thousands of dark piles of manure on the flat but not a single cow.

That puzzled her until the answer became clear. A semitractor pulling a long aluminum livestock hauler emerged from the smoke and fog headed right toward her on the road. Then it made sense. It was fall, and time for cattle ranchers to gather up their herds to sell or move to better pasture.

She eased off the track to give the truck plenty of room. As it passed she glimpsed the panicked white eyes of bald-faced Angus peering out at her through portal-like openings in the trailer. Twenty to twenty-four cattle cried out from each of the double decks of the transport hauler. The bawling of the cows punctuated the afternoon stillness as they passed.

Cassie recalled her childhood on her uncles' much smaller ranch near Helena. After the shifty cattle buyers had arrived and made their deals, after her uncles always swore they got screwed, the big trucks and trailers lined up on the county road that led to their ranch and it was time to ship.

Shipping day was a loud, wild, and exhausting day with all hands on deck. In addition to the single hired hand and her father and uncles, neighbors pitched in as well. Isabel didn't participate.

Penned cattle were sorted and driven through chutes into the trailers. Dust and the screeching of air brakes filled the air. Cows didn't meekly walk into the long boxes single file, either. They bawled, they bolted, they panicked, and sometimes they backed up on the ramps when they were expected to proceed.

Following the last shipment of cattle would be a huge feast of elk roast, mashed potatoes, and gravy prepared by her aunts in the dining room of the main house. Cassie remembered digging in with a knot in her stomach, still bothered by the events of the day. She tried not to cry knowing all those creatures were headed to their deaths. The silence outside following the cacophony of bawls and sounds was nearly overwhelming. She wasn't sentimental about the fate of the cows, but she couldn't deny their plight, either.

THE TRUCK Cassie pulled over for was followed by another, and then another. The heavy vehicles rocked her Explorer each time. She didn't ease back onto the road until six cattle haulers had passed by.

As she turned the wheel she saw a seventh truck coming and she paused for it. It was much smaller than the cattle haulers. Rather than an eighteen-wheeler, the last vehicle was some kind of utility pickup with a boxy shape and instrumentation built into the bed walls. Two men were inside and they nodded to her as they passed. The muddy white new model GMC had a graphic on the passenger-side door that read:

REMR
HOUSTON, TEXAS

The company was unfamiliar to her, although she doubted that the utility pickup was associated with the cattle haulers. The pickup, like the tractor-trailers, eventually vanished into the fog and smoke.

CASSIE KNEW that if it was loading day she was likely to find every member of the family—perhaps with the exception of

Cheyenne—at the ranch compound. The knot in her stomach had as much to do with the passing of the cattle haulers and the fate of the animals as it did with what was coming next.

She took in a long breath and slowly expelled it. The confidence she'd gained from replacing her equipment waned, and she felt very much alone.

CASSIE TOPPED a rise marked with a large sign that read:

TURN AROUND NOW IF YOU DON'T
HAVE AN APPOINTMENT
—*Iron Cross Ranch*

and immediately took in the layout of the Kleinsasser ranch headquarters below.

Beyond a vast and complicated labyrinth of outbuildings, pens, barns, corrals, and loafing sheds was a massive and foreboding three-story stone home with gables and high turrets on each flank. The roofs of several additional stone houses showed through the high fall-bronzed cottonwoods on either side.

The Bitterroots that rose to the west and served as the backdrop to the scene were obscured by layers of clouds and smoke halfway up, making the range look like truncated buttes instead of mountains.

To the north of the huge compound was an ancient traditional red barn as well as a series of metal buildings and Quonset huts housing vehicles, tractors, ATVs, and other farm equipment. Several ranch employees, she assumed, milled outside the outbuildings and turned toward her as she got closer.

She slowed down as the ground leveled and she maneuvered her rental car through the stockyards toward the stone house. The pungent smell of manure and panicked cattle hung thick in the air.

Cassie pulled up to a knee-high barrier fence in front of the house and turned off her engine. As she did so, a half-dozen long-legged dogs boiled out from beneath Russian olive trees on the side of the small yard and circled her car, barking with percussive fury.

She wasn't surprised by the sudden appearance of a pack of dogs. She was used to it. Cassie knew it was impossible to sneak up on a ranch house.

Then she waited. There was no reason to open her door and go outside to challenge the dogs, which were particularly sleek and rangy and of mottled color. One dog had placed its paws on the glass of the passenger window in order to stare at her inside. It had remarkable green eyes.

Finally, the heavy timber front door of the stone house opened and a compact man with a thick mustache came out and glared at her. He was in his stocking feet and there was a fine delineation between the reddish tan of his face and the bald white crown of his head where his cowboy hat usually was.

He shouted at the dogs and they melted away.

She knew it was John Wayne from photos she'd seen of him online. Cassie studied him carefully as he took in her car and then squinted to see her through the windshield. She realized that the reflection of the rolling clouds above on the glass partially obscured her face at first.

Then she saw it: a tell. He'd identified her. At the second

he did his mouth twitched involuntarily and he almost rocked back on his heels. But he recovered quickly and the puzzled look on his face softened.

He motioned for her to get out and she did.

"Are those Catahoulas?" she asked, referring to the breed of dogs. "I hear they're good herd dogs."

"Some of 'em are," he said with a low Southern drawl that was unlike anything she'd heard from a native in Montana. "Some of 'em are just a pain in the ass.

"What can I do for you? I wasn't expecting any visitors."

He said it in a way that told Cassie he was misleading her, that he knew exactly who she was. And she recognized his odd drawl as inauthentic, a way of speaking sometimes adopted by western men to make them seem more like the character they wanted to be perceived as.

"I'm Cassie Dewell," she said. "I talked with you last night."

He made a show of shooting out his sleeve so he could look at his wristwatch. Unlike his flannel western shirt, prominent rodeo buckle, and Wranglers still dusty from moving cattle onto the haulers, his large gold Rolex stood out.

"I'm John Wayne Kleinsasser. I thought you were coming out this morning," he said.

"Are you surprised to see me now?" she asked.

He lowered his wrist and looked at her from the top of her head to her boots. It wasn't a kind assessment, she thought.

"Why would I be surprised, other than you're seven hours late?" he asked.

But she'd noted the tell and filed it away.

"We've been moving cows all day," he said. "Now we're getting something to eat. It's tradition for hauling day."

"I'm not hungry," she lied.

"I don't believe I asked you if you were."

She said, "I'm happy to sit in my car and wait. I don't want to rush you. But if you'll recall, I was hoping to walk through the building where your niece was assaulted, as I said. I'm sorry I'm so late but I was... detained. Is there still a chance I could do that?"

"*Today?*"

"Either that or I could come out tomorrow," she said. "Or the day after that, or the day after that," Cassie added. Her clear meaning, *I'm not going away.*

Again, he looked her over. She strained a smile.

He sighed, and said, "Come on in. I'll finish up and drive you out there. When you're through you can go back to Bozeman and leave us alone."

"Thank you," she said. "I appreciate it. I know what a busy time this must be."

"Making a living," he said. "How'd you get here, anyway?"

"The gate was open."

It took him a moment, then he nodded. "We opened them for the cattle haulers and you slipped right through," he said as much to himself as to her.

He stood aside as she mounted the steps to the porch, then took another step back when she shouldered past him to enter the house.

He hadn't asked about the new car, she thought. Even though he'd made a point of getting her vehicle description the night before.

*

JOHN WAYNE closed the door behind them and Cassie paused near a tangle of cowboy boots on a rug to the side. He padded up behind her in his socks.

"Take your shoes off. It's something we do," he said.

"Okay."

Cassie was grateful that he walked around her as she bent over to pull off her boots. She was able to slip the .22 from her boot shaft into her purse without him noticing.

Then she stood and beheld the great room. High ceilings, heavy beams, dark furniture, mounts of deer and elk heads on the walls. Shafts of light from narrow windows on two exterior walls and a single skylight high above crisscrossed in the gloom.

"An iron cross," she said to John Wayne.

"My grandfather's design," he replied.

Warm odors from the dining room filled the house, and she could hear low chatter and the clinking of silverware and glasses from somewhere down a hallway.

"Please," she said, stepping aside toward a dark floral ottoman, "go finish your meal. I'll sit here and wait."

There was an unworldly squawk from the direction of the dining room that sounded to Cassie like part falcon, part hog. The sound stopped and started again until it ended abruptly.

She looked to John Wayne for an explanation.

"My father would like to meet you," he said. Then he shrugged, as if that wouldn't have been his choice.

"Horst?" she asked, trying to recall the given names of the Kleinsasser clan.

"Horst the second," John Wayne corrected.

She followed him across the polished dark wood floor of the great room and into the hallway. Over his shoulder, in a soft voice, he said, "He had a stroke recently. A pretty bad one. He's slowly getting his speech back, but right now I'm the only one who can understand him. I'm kind of his translator."

She nodded as if she understood. "Really, I don't mind waiting."

"If the old man wants to meet you he wants to meet you," John Wayne said with a shrug.

They took a sharp turn to the right and entered a narrow dining room paneled with light pine. The walls featured old sporting paintings from nineteenth-century Europe.

The table was stocked with a huge platter of roast beef, a bowl of quartered potatoes, a tureen of brown gravy, and trays of green beans, carrots, and sauerkraut.

A square-faced woman in her fifties wearing a full apron hovered briefly at the back of the room. No doubt the cook, Cassie thought. The woman scuttled away through a door at the end of the dining room without looking back.

That left only the family and Cassie.

Seven pairs of eyes greeted her. It was absolutely silent. The absence of Cheyenne and Franny were glaring, and Cassie noted that no place settings had been set for them.

Horst II, John Wayne's father, slumped in a wheelchair at the head of the table. His head rested on his left shoulder and his mouth gaped. His large hands rested on the arms of his wheelchair. He was unshaven and wearing sloppy sweat clothes that looked two sizes too big. Someone had tied a bib around his neck. Horst II looked nothing like the photos Cassie had seen of him in the internet. Only his eyes seemed alive, and they were fixed on her face.

Next to Horst II on the far side of the table was Margaret, Cassie guessed. She had metal-framed glasses and her head was covered with tight curls. Margaret had a fork in her hand with a square of roast beef on it poised to feed to her husband. She had a fleshy porcine face and she wore an out-of-fashion dark dress of thick material that looked like it would rustle when she walked. The expression she aimed at Cassie was equal parts dislike and suspicion.

Cassie didn't blame her. What kind of person crashed a family get-together?

Rand, seated next to his mother, didn't even try to disguise his contempt for her. He tossed his silverware to the tablecloth and sat back and glared at her in disgust. While casually refreshing an ice-filled cocktail glass with more bourbon from a decanter, he arched his eyebrows at her as if to say, *Get the hell out.*

Next to Rand was a young female who looked like she didn't belong, Cassie thought. At least in *this* family. She was thin and wore too much makeup and a multicolored tattoo snaked up the side of her neck from her very tight top. Cassie knew Rand wasn't married and she surmised the girl was either his live-in or somebody he'd picked up and invited to the hauling day meal. The girl nervously drank from an oversized goblet of red wine.

On the near side of the table were two boys aged probably eight and ten. John Wayne's sons, she guessed. They were duded up in cowboy clothes and the roast beef and vegetables on their plates looked virtually untouched. They looked at her like they enjoyed the distraction she'd brought.

Rochelle, John Wayne's wife and the boys' mother, was a wispy and featureless woman with mousy brown hair and an inoffensive manner. She was the first in the room to look away when Cassie found her eyes.

"Everybody," John Wayne announced, "this is Cassie Dewell. She's working for Blake's lawyer to get him off. She wants to walk through the old crew shack to see if the police missed anything."

No one said hello. No one said anything.

"Not necessarily," Cassie said softly.

Rochelle turned her attention to her boys and urged them to eat or they wouldn't get apple pie for dessert. Reluctantly, both John Wayne Jr., and Tristan proceeded to push their vegetables around on their plates as if the activity alone would fool their mother.

Cassie watched as Horst II took in a big wet breath as if loading up, then squawked a staccato series of bursts. She couldn't make out a single word. Then he did it again.

"Dad wants to know why you picked this moment to interrupt our hauling day feast," John Wayne said to Cassie with a bit of a smirk. "He wonders if it's because you don't look like a woman who misses many meals."

Margaret shot her husband a reproachful look. Apparently, Cassie thought, she couldn't understand him, either.

Horst II squawked again.

"He said he was joking," John Wayne said.

Cassie tried to summon up confidence. Her mouth was suddenly dry. She said, "I remember the hauling day feast. We used to have them when I was a girl. Everybody who helped out was invited...."

She trailed off when she realized that unlike her uncles and aunts, who invited in all of the neighbors and friends who assisted in the work no matter who they were, the Kleinsassers had sent all their employees elsewhere. This meal was only for the immediate family.

Rand said to Cassie, "It's a little hard to enjoy my meal with you standing there staring at us like we're fuckin' zoo animals."

"I'm sorry," Cassie replied. She looked to John Wayne for some kind of guidance to stay or go.

Horst II said something that sounded to Cassie like, "Don't shit."

"Pardon me?" Cassie asked. She was rattled.

"He said, 'Don't sit,'" John Wayne said with a grin.

Before Cassie could reply, Horst II rattled out a long string of invective. While he did, Margaret fixed her eyes on the side of his face as if trying to silence him without succeeding. It was not a kind or sympathetic look, Cassie thought.

Finally, John Wayne said, "He says Blake means nothing more to him than any hopeless loser he passes on the highway or cow shit on the bottom of his boot. He says Blake is no more part of his family than you are and if you're trying to get him off you're just as evil as he is."

Cassie didn't respond. She couldn't.

"He also said this might be his last hauling day feast on this earth with his loving family and he'd like you to leave."

"Gladly."

"Now, *git*," Rand said, using his hands to shoo her away as if she were a dog.

"I'll be outside," Cassie said over her shoulder to John Wayne as she turned on her heel. He took a beat to move aside so she could go.

Red-faced and humiliated, she strode down the hallway in her stocking feet. There was a peal of laughter from Rand as the tinkling of silverware resumed.

She fought the urge to run.

*

CASSIE FELT the presence of someone approaching from the hallway while she pulled on her boots. Then she heard the rustle of clothing.

Margaret eyed her coolly. Her bearing was more serious than what Cassie had observed inside the dining room, as if Margaret had shed the costume she wore around her family. She carried the empty tureen as if she'd used it as an excuse to leave the table.

"You should really go home," Margaret warned. Cassie was unclear if it was friendly advice or a threat.

"Everyone in this county seems to agree with you. And I will—just as soon as I can."

Margaret fixed her gray eyes on Cassie. "You have no idea what you've stepped into."

"Your son Blake said the same thing to me."

Cassie watched carefully for Margaret's reaction. But the woman didn't even flinch.

"You don't understand," Margaret said. "Blake no longer exists on this ranch."

"I get that. But he's still your firstborn son. And you probably don't know this but he was attacked in jail. From what I understand he may not make it."

Again, not even a tic. Cassie couldn't discern if Margaret had heard about Blake before she brought it up. Or if she simply didn't care.

Margaret sighed and shook her head. "He's just as bad as the others."

Before Cassie could respond, Margaret turned and walked away, cradling the empty tureen in her slender hands.

EIGHTEEN

A LONG HOUR LATER, John Wayne emerged from the house at the same moment Cassie's phone lit up with a call from Ben. John Wayne pulled on a barn coat, clamped on a black cowboy hat, and chinned toward his pickup to indicate she should follow him. He looked annoyed.

Cassie nodded that she understood his instructions. The man swung into the cab of his truck and it leaped forward, the rear tires raining gravel on her rental car as it turned in the yard and shot over a cattle guard. She gave pursuit and raised the phone to her mouth because she hadn't synched it to the rental's Bluetooth system yet.

"Hello, Ben."

"Hey, Mom. I just got done with practice and I saw that you called."

"Thank you. Yes, we got cut off last night after you started telling me that something crazy happened...."

"Did you really get *arrested*?" he asked.

"Not officially. But a cop pulled me over and took me into the station. I couldn't call you because they took my cell phone."

"Mom?"

"What, Ben?"

"You're breaking up."

Although she was following John Wayne's vehicle on the gravel road at bone-rattling speed, she glanced at her phone to see there was only a single bar of reception. The farther she got from the ranch headquarters, the poorer it got.

The screen indicator changed to NO SERVICE.

"Oh, crap," she said aloud. She cursed and tossed the phone aside where it landed on the passenger seat.

JOHN WAYNE either didn't care that she could barely keep up with him as he raced through his ranch or he wanted to humiliate her further when she lost him and had to find her own way out.

Cassie was fortunate, though, in that the few times he vanished over a hilltop or took a sharp turn he left a telltale cloud of dust hanging in the air to follow. And she did.

She hoped when they got to the crew shack that she'd have the opportunity to question him. The gloves were off as far as she was concerned. John Wayne was no more than a cheap bully, and she'd dealt over the years with plenty of those. He'd been minimally accommodating when they first met when it was just the two of them, but he'd shown his true colors when he tossed her to his family to be demeaned like that.

So many questions. And if he didn't answer them or lied

again, that very fact would be an answer in itself that he was hiding something. She created a mental list of topics:

- Did he or Rand order the sheriff's department to pick her up and detain her?
- Did any of them at the table know that her car had been torched?
- Had the news of Blake's assault reached them prior to her arrival? And if so, how?
- Did any of them order the jailhouse attack? Did they have a connection to the perpetrators?
- Was Horst II capable of communicating with anyone in the outside world, or did he require John Wayne's "translating" ability to convey his wishes?
- Where were Cheyenne and Franny? Why didn't they come to the vaunted family hauling day feast?

And most of all, why did the family and their proxies in the sheriff's department do everything they could to make her investigation difficult if they were confident the allegations against Blake would land him in Deer Lodge for a very long time?

THE TWO-TRACK ROAD paralleled a dry creek bed choked with rust-colored willows. It wound around an old copse of river cottonwood trees with dry leaves quivering on the branches like so many baby rattles. Suddenly the old crew shack appeared.

Cassie glanced down at her odometer to note that the journey was four-point-two miles from the ranch headquarters. That was a long walk for Franny that night, she thought.

John Wayne pulled off the road and motioned for Cassie to proceed. Instead, she stopped next to him. He quickly got out.

"**THIS IS THE PLACE** my brother raped my niece," he said. "Have at it."

"Are you going to show me around?"

"No. I'm going home to take a nap."

"Will you be available to answer some questions?"

"I already did that. Ask the sheriff. Now please step back. I wouldn't want to run over your cowboy boots with my tires."

"I have a lot of questions. Some things just don't add up to me."

He looked at her for half a minute before rolling his eyes and throwing the transmission into reverse.

"Be off the property by sundown, lady," he said. She stepped back toward her car so the open pickup door wouldn't knock her over as he backed up.

She watched as he did a three-point turn and accelerated so rapidly back down the old road that the velocity of the maneuver slammed shut the passenger door on its own.

CASSIE TURNED SLOWLY and observed the crew shack. It was grander than she thought it would be: two levels, peaked roof, old shutters on the windows on both floors. It had obviously been built by people with ambition who later, for whatever reason, abandoned it.

Montana was filled with such houses and they could be found in dying small towns and within vast landholdings. They'd been built when the world was larger, when transportation was poorer. And because Montana was settled late in comparison to other parts of the country, many of the old ghost houses were originals. They'd once been attractive, well-appointed homes but they'd been left to rot. The low humidity and lack of subsequent development were two contributors to why the old structures still existed. Trees and bushes the original inhabitants had planted were dead or wild and untrimmed.

Cassie was always curious about what happened that resulted in the families who lived there to find the need to just walk away. Housing ranch hands was *not* the original purpose for the faded old house. That had come later.

She wondered if this house had been on an adjoining ranch to the Kleinsassers' original holdings, and when Horst I bought it he forced the former inhabitants to flee. She would likely never know.

Although Franny's affidavit had been in the file that either vanished or was burned up in her car, Cassie could recall many of the passages with clarity.

He said he wanted to show me where he spent most of his time when he was growing up on the ranch. He said he wanted me to know that even though my uncles told me different, Uncle Blake had spent a lot of years there and he had a real connection to the ranch that I probably wasn't aware of....

We arrived at a two-story old house on the side of a meadow. The house was kind of dumpy, I thought. Some of the windows were broken out and the cattle had been on the porch and collapsed it. There was old cow manure everywhere. It was outside the house and inside the front door. The place smelled like cows. I'm not fond of cows. I'm a vegan, you know....

Now, though, the structure was probably beyond repair and in the process of collapsing in on itself. The wide front porch sagged and the rail on the hitching post was missing. Most of the windows were broken out and the door hung open at an angle. Old wood shake shingles were missing from the bowed roof and they littered the grass of the hard ground near the cracking foundation. Cattle had obviously used it for shelter although she didn't see any now. There were manure piles on the porch and in the grass.

A warped picnic table in the front yard had been upended and rubbed on by cows until the wooden slats had become fuzzy with hair.

She didn't like the feeling she got from the old house, and she wondered if it was somehow more welcoming to Franny during a sultry summer evening than it was now. Cassie couldn't understand why Franny would want to go inside, even if it was with an uncle who she seemed to like. Unless Franny had a dark side Cassie wasn't aware of.

She reached in and turned off her engine and pocketed the key fob. Not that she was worried about someone stealing her rental car, but she didn't want to run the risk of a "smart" feature locking the vehicle with the keys in it. Cassie didn't want to be stuck on the Iron Cross Ranch at night by herself.

*

AFTER PHOTOGRAPHING the structure from the front and sides, she climbed the steps to the front porch. Cassie was startled when several rabbits shot out from beneath the porch in different directions. Then she was embarrassed for being so jumpy.

Before entering, Cassie carefully observed the open front door. The top and middle hinges were broken off and it hung precariously open and to the side by the bottom one. It looked like it had been open for many months, maybe even years.

> We stopped the car in front of the porch and Uncle Blake got out and asked me to follow him. The door to the house was unlocked and he went in first...

THAT WAS a discrepancy in Franny's account, she thought. Franny indicated the door was closed but unlocked. She'd made a point of saying that.

But careful examination of the doorjamb indicated the hinges weren't recently pulled away from the wood. The indentations where the screws had been were the same barn wood gray as the rest of the frame.

She took several photographs of the open door and door frame, but she really didn't think the discrepancy would turn out to be significant. Franny was fifteen, a little confused by what her uncle had in mind, and her recollection of that night was following a very traumatic experience. If she got the door wrong it probably didn't mean much.

*

CASSIE CLICKED ON the Maglite and opened the beam up wide before stepping across the threshold. Although the scene had no doubt been photographed, dusted, and examined by local crime scene techs, she stayed close to the interior walls rather than to walk into the center of the room.

Although crime scene tape had been removed (if it had ever been there at all), the floor of the dining room told a story in itself. The thick carpet of dust mixed with manure was a maelstrom of footprints and drag marks from law enforcement. A thin layer of new dust since the summer added a veneer, but the prints were numerous. She thought that within the many tracks were prints that could be matched with Blake's and Franny's shoes.

She took dozens of shots of the floor from several angles, although she doubted they'd be of any value.

Uncle Blake lit a candle thing called a kerosene lamp and put it on the table. He said he wanted me to see all the old rooms but I said I was kind of scared....

Then Uncle Blake came around to my side of the table and lifted me up. He was strong. He sat me on top of the table and started kissing me. He has really fast hands and he was touching me everywhere. He stood there between my legs and held me in place.

There was the table Fanny had described, right in the middle of the room. It was old and stout, and unlike the counters and furniture it wasn't covered in a quarter-inch of dust and grime. That's because, she reasoned, Franny's clothes had wiped it clean as Blake molested her. The thought made Cassie cringe.

The vintage kerosene lamp Franny had mentioned was on the kitchen counter next to a dented metal tin of kerosene fuel. Cassie didn't know if Blake had moved it before the assault or the investigators had put it aside. It didn't matter other than to further corroborate Franny's account.

The liquor bottle and drinking glasses Blake had used had been taken away and were now in the evidence locker of the sheriff's department. She'd seen them. But she'd also wondered if Blake had brought the glasses with him or found them in the structure. When she opened the dusty cupboard she found a slew of glassware—mismatched plates, fast-food cups, even several martini glasses. No doubt, she thought, the ranch hands acquired glasses from all over the place and brought them back. The cocktail glasses Blake had used could have easily come from the cupboard.

LONG TONGUES of flocked wallpaper hung from the interior walls exposing wooden slats behind it. There was a cowboy cartoon calendar from 1968 and the last page displayed was December. Cast-iron cookware was in the sink as if the last ranch hand to leave the place had forgotten to wash it.

She took more photos of the interior with her phone, and remembered to close her eyes prior to each shot so the flash wouldn't blind her.

He showed me a room with bunk beds in it where ranch hands used to stay together.

Franny hadn't mentioned following Blake up the rickety staircase to the second floor so Cassie didn't go there.

Besides, the stairs sagged away from the wall and looked dangerous to try to climb. So she worked her way around the main room and through a doorway at the back of the house past the kitchen.

Inside were four sets of old metal-framed bunk beds, as described. Mice and rats had eaten through the thin mattresses and left balls of the insides throughout the room and in each of the corners. As Cassie moved the beam she caught glimpses of rodents before they scattered.

A *Playboy* pinup, circa-1960s because the blond model kept her legs together, hung above one of the bunk beds. A pair of cowboy boots, black with age, were under one of the box springs as if waiting for their owner to get up and pull them on.

She raised the beam to the rafters and was greeted by two dozen yellow eyes reflected in the light. *Bats.*

When they spooked and flew en masse she ducked down so they'd fly out the doorway and not get tangled in her hair or clothes.

FRANNY HAD BEEN THERE, Cassie concluded. She'd actually described the old crew shack with remarkable accuracy, given the circumstances.

Cassie jumped when a blast of lightning lit up the room followed by a near instantaneous thunderclap. It had been very close.

She paused and waited for the patter of rain on the old roof that should have followed. But it didn't.

When she backed out of the old house and turned around she saw that a jacked-up ranch vehicle was now parked directly behind her Ford. With all of the noise in the house—the rats, the bats, her own beating heart—she hadn't heard it drive up. There was no one behind the wheel.

"Hey there," Rand said from where he sat on a bench at the righted picnic table, "I thought when them bats came pouring out of there you'd be right behind them."

"Bats don't scare me," Cassie said. "What do you want?"

There was a half-empty bottle of Wild Turkey on the table in front of him. Rand's face was flushed by alcohol. His smile was more of a leer.

He gasped the edges of the table and leaned way back as if to get a better view of her.

"Oh, Dad sent me out here to make sure you got what you needed. Did you?"

She nodded. She wished her Glock wasn't in her handbag in the Explorer. But she had the .22 in her boot top if necessary.

"I'm done. It all checks out."

"What were you looking for in there? What did you expect to find?"

She shrugged. "I don't know."

"And someone is actually paying you for your mad skills, Inspector Clouseau?"

He snorted at his joke. He said, "So you didn't believe the sheriff's department report?"

"It's not that. I'm just tailing up to make sure the investigation is solid."

"And is it?"

She thought, *He really doesn't want my opinion. He just wants to engage.*

"Pretty much."

"Good to hear, good to hear," Rand said with a smug nod, as if he knew her conclusion long before she did. "Did you see that old *Playboy* centerfold on the wall?"

"I did."

"The image is seared into my mind. I saw it as a kid and jerked off to it for years."

She thought his intention was to shock her. She didn't respond.

"Think about it," he said. "That girl is probably sixty-five years old now. Maybe older."

"So, you spent a lot of time here," Cassie said. "Like Blake."

That seemed to throw him for a minute. He started to answer but then reached for the bottle instead and took a long drink.

"I guess now you'll be headed back to Bozeman."

"Soon."

"That's one fucked-up place," he said. "Full of hipsters and goddam bark-beetles. I have to go there quite a bit on ranch business and once I get there I can't wait to get out. And don't think I haven't heard of you and your defense lawyer."

Again, she didn't respond.

He said, "I didn't spend three years of my life defending this country so the fuckin' green phonies and out-of-staters could move here from California to take over my state, you know? It just pisses me off."

She didn't think it was a good time to bring up his dishonorable discharge or his prison time later. She said, "Why is it that every member of the Kleinsasser family feels the need to give me a hard time? It's getting really old. And it isn't working."

Although deep in her mind she knew she was lying.

He looked up and squinted at her as if seeing her for the first time. Then he grinned.

"You're feisty," he said.

"And I need to get going. Your brother told me to get off the ranch by dark and I intend to do just that."

"Yes," he said, "you're feisty, aren't you?"

She wished at that moment that he would rise up to come after her or fumble for a weapon. She was ready for him.

But he just sat there with that goblinlike leer on his face.

She gave Rand a wide berth as she strode around him toward her car. She could feel his eyes on her the whole time.

"If you lost twenty you might be okay," he said.

"Isn't your girlfriend about due for her meth about now?" Cassie said. "She was looking a little strung out."

He laughed but it sounded false. She was past him now and it was a straight shot to her car.

"Where the *hell* are you going?" he called after her. "Don't you want to stay and chat? Tell me more about my girlfriend? Read me the riot act?"

She reached for the door handle.

"That guy you're trying to save is a fucking limp-dick monster. He ain't nobody. Why don't you come back here and explain why you want to save his sorry ass?"

CASSIE THREW HERSELF in the car and started it up. She was furious.

When she turned on the headlights they bathed Rand in white light and he raised his hand in front of his eyes to block the beams.

Then she accelerated into a U-turn that spun the rear of the vehicle around and threw dirt from the rear tires all over him and drove away. Her last glimpse of Rand was in the rear-view mirror.

He stood beside his truck with both middle fingers extended into the sky. He was laughing.

NINETEEN

BEN DEWELL LAY fully clothed on top of his bed with his phone in his lap and a Ziploc bag of ice cubes on the top of his head like a hat. He wiped the back of his hand across his face to stanch the dark red blood that oozed out of both nostrils from his swollen nose. Empty fry boxes and hamburger wrappers were at his feet. He was confused and depressed and had a headache and he didn't understand girls.

Especially Erin.

In fact, he'd been thinking about her and how she'd blown him off at break time during their usual foray to the Kum & Go instead of his challenge match against Jason Smithfield at practice. He'd been distracted at the moment when Jason shot across the mat toward Ben, wrapped his right arm around Ben's legs and pinned his left arm tight, then wrenched back with all of his strength to throw Ben face-first to the mat in a violent move known as a fireman's carry.

Ben had been so stunned that he'd lost control of his limbs for a few seconds as Jason rolled him over to his back and pinned him. Several wrestlers who'd seen the move whooped. The challenge match had lasted less than ten seconds, and Ben had what might turn out to be a broken nose, two black eyes, and a lump on the top of his head.

He looked so bad when he got home that Isabel suspended her strike and filled the bag with ice and sent him to bed. Most surprising, she asked Ben to place an order for what he wanted to eat. She even agreed to go out and get it even though, she said, she would hold her own nose while doing so.

He'd jotted down:

Two Big Macs
Two Large Fries
Large Chocolate Milkshake

And he'd eaten it all. As long as Jason Smithfield ruled the 113-pound weight class, Ben had no choice but to either quit or move up to 120. So it was time to start gaining weight. There was a stud in that weight class named Philip Warden. Warden was just as unbeatable as Jason, but Warden was a dumb-ass who might have to leave the team because of his poor grades. Ben had that going for him, maybe.

BUT ABOUT ERIN.

He'd waited for her on his usual bench. After ten minutes, he went inside the building. His insides were churning a little because she'd never not shown up before and he knew she was in school.

He found her near her locker. When she looked up and saw him—he was sure she did—she looked away quickly and walked in the other direction. But he caught up with her and something about her seemed different. She was more serious than usual and she was evasive. She said she "had to go."

Ben had tried to act like it didn't matter, that he had plenty of friends and plenty to do. But he knew his face betrayed his anxiety. They both knew he didn't. It was high school reality, and they'd talked about it before.

He didn't see her for the rest of the day, even though they had a kind of routine where they'd touch base in the halls during class breaks. Which meant to him that she was deliberately avoiding him.

Ben tried to figure out what he'd done to make her want to stay away from him. She wasn't a mean person or a cruel person—she wasn't one of those types. She didn't like those kinds of people. But there was definitely something he'd said— or worse, *not said*. Girls were like that, he thought. He could be in as much trouble for what he didn't do or say or think.

Had Erin met another boy? He thought she probably could have, she was certainly cute, although he couldn't imagine who the boy would be. Maybe she'd finally found her niche of thespians and dreamers who hovered around on the periphery of the rest of the student body and they'd invited her in. That invitation wouldn't include a ninth-grader like Ben. He wasn't sure if there was even a niche for him anywhere on the grounds of the school. He certainly wasn't one of the athletes yet, and especially after his performance against Jason in a challenge match that afternoon. But he wasn't yet ready to surrender himself to the pack of losers who hung around out- side the auto shop smoking cigarettes and weed and hating on everyone else. Yet.

That's what he was thinking about when the assistant coach blew the whistle to start the challenge match against Jason Smith-field.

And that's what he was still contemplating while he lay on his bed with his nose swelling and twin drops of blood slowly creeping down his face.

It was a dilemma and he felt alone and lost. He couldn't ask his mom about it, and he certainly couldn't ask Isabel. In the past, it was the kind of thing he'd text with Erin about because she expressed so many of the same feelings of being new and somewhat lost.

Maybe, he thought, he'd interpreted the incident with the truck the day before completely wrong. He thought it had bonded them in a new and interesting way. After all, she said he'd saved her life. But it was possible she looked at it differently now. Maybe she was spooked.

He stared at the phone in his lap and came up with five or six opening texts to try out on Erin. Should he go nonchalant, like he hadn't noticed her change in behavior and was just checking in?

Or get right to the point? Ask her what was wrong and try to address it since it was likely something he'd done or said? Knowing Erin, he didn't think that would be the right approach. She might tell him he was beneath her or a creep. Or tell him to grow the hell up.

Or maybe, he thought, play it coy. Tell her she seemed to be troubled about something (not him). And was there anything he could do to help her through it?

IN THE END, after twenty minutes of deliberating, he sent a text to Erin Reese.

It said:

Hey.

Then he stared at the screen, willing a response while at the same time fearing the wrong one. A small balloon appeared, meaning she was writing back. Then it went away. He imagined her somewhere trying to come up with the right words. He couldn't recall her ever taking so long to find them.

Finally:

Hey back.

It wasn't hostile. It was sort of friendly, if resigned.

Ben: How are you doing?

He immediately wished he'd written "How is it going?" instead. He sent her a curious face emoji.

Erin: I've been better.

Ben: Are you doing all right?

Erin: Not really. I feel weird. Everything is just weird right now.

Ben: Is there anything I can do?

Erin: The best thing you can do is stay away from me. I'm toxic.
   It's for the best.

He sat back, his mind spinning in a dark swirl. He started to text "What did I do?" and deleted it before he sent it. Finally, he settled on:

Ben: I'm sorry you feel that way. I don't think you're toxic.

He fought the urge to say he found her wonderful and enchanting and really, really hot. But he didn't. He wasn't sure how she'd take it.

Erin: 🖤

Ben: Really. Did something happen today?

There was a long pause. So long, he began to fear that she had moved on.
Then:

Erin: It's best for you if you keep your distance. There are things going on that aren't good.

In the "things I should have asked her about" department, he realized he knew absolutely next to nothing about her family situation. Erin rarely spoke of her parents and he didn't even know if she had siblings. He assumed she didn't. He did remember her once referring to staying with relatives, but he didn't know if that was a temporary or permanent situation.

Ben: Is the situation bad at home?

Erin: Not really. Boring, but not bad.

Ben: Same here. Isabel is in the other room watching a doc on a
    band called Jefferson Airplane.

Erin: 😣

Erin found Ben's stories about his grandmother hilarious,
so he kept her updated on things Isabel did and said. Erin said
she kind of admired Isabel's strike but wasn't sure why other
than it showed she wasn't a pushover.

Erin: I may have to go away for a while.

Ben was stunned.

Ben: Why? Where would you go?

Erin: I don't know.

He wasn't sure if she didn't know about why or didn't
know about where.

Ben: How long would you be gone?

Erin: Maybe a week. Maybe forever.

He tried a different tack.

Ben: My mom is a private investigator. She used to be a cop. Do you
    want me to ask her to help?

Erin: God no. 😳

As if triggered by some psychic cue, Ben's phone lit up with an incoming call. Mom.

He moaned. Her timing was horrible. He refused the call. He'd call her back later.

Ben: Is there anything I can do?

Erin: Probably not.

Ben: Does this have something to do with that truck thing yesterday?

There was a very long pause, and several text balloons that appeared and were then cancelled by her.

Erin: It might.

Ben: What does that mean?

Erin: Please, dude. This doesn't have anything to do with you. It's my problem.

Ben: It doesn't have to be. Did you see that truck again?

Erin: Didn't see it. Heard it outside my house last night.

Ben: You're fucking kidding me.

Erin: Wish I was.

Ben: What time?

Erin: 2

Ben: Maybe we should call the cops.

Erin: And say what? Come on, dude. I've got to go.

Ben: Can I call you now?

Erin: No.

Ben: You're scaring me a little.

Erin: Don't worry. You're fine if you stay away from me. I just want
to be friends.

Ben: What does that mean?

Erin: Good night.

After thrashing around on his bed for a moment, he
punched Erin up on his phone and placed the call. It was the
first time they'd ever talked on the phone instead of texting.

It went straight to voice mail. Erin's dreamy voice said she
wasn't in and to leave a message.

He didn't.

TWENTY

CASSIE TOOK THE EXIT to Corvallis impulsively because she realized she was starving and she needed food. As she turned off the highway into the small town she checked her mirrors to make sure that her quick turn hadn't attracted the attention of Deputy Grzegorczyk or any other of Lochsa County's finest. Since she'd been to the Iron Cross Ranch in her new rental, she assumed the word was out on what kind of vehicle she was now driving.

Yes, she thought, she was getting paranoid. Justifiably so.

The Corvallis Tavern was an aged stand-alone structure lit up with neon beer and liquor signs in the window. Small floodlights lit the hand-painted outside sign that was lettered in orange and blue and mounted on a sheet of plywood above the overhung porch roof. It was the only business open on the short block but the parking places along the street were filled with four-by-fours and pickups. The plates were all from Montana. That was a good indication, she thought.

BEFORE GOING in, she sat in her Ford and breathed deeply, trying to regain her bearings. Every interaction she'd had with a member of the Kleinsasser family had been unpleasant and vaguely threatening, even though it didn't seem they were in cahoots with one another. All indications were they hated one another with the exception of John Wayne and Rand. Rand, as Blake had indicated, seemed to revere John Wayne. But he was also a loose cannon and Cassie didn't want to encounter him again.

Cheyenne was a mystery wrapped in a riddle. Horst II was cruel, damaged, and vindictive. Margaret was either an enemy or a secret ally. Cassie couldn't decide.

And she wouldn't be able to sort it all out until she got some food and rest, she thought. She'd barely slept the night before in jail and she hadn't eaten anything the entire day. She was punchy and not at her best.

There was a text message from Rachel saying she'd arrived back in Bozeman.

> Made it back. Blake is in IC and surgery is tomorrow.
> Be careful and come home.

Cassie thanked her and left it at that. She didn't have the energy to fill Rachel in on her day at the Iron Cross Ranch.

She was frustrated that her call to Ben had gone to voice mail. She texted him that she was at dinner for thirty to forty minutes but she would call after that. She asked him to please pick up.

THE TAVERN was much smaller than the Hayloft, and moderately busy. Local cowboys in hats and boots played eight-ball on the pool table and several locals swiveled on their stools to check her out as she slipped into a chair at a small table. The menu was hand-lettered on a board above the bar and she was grateful there weren't many choices.

She was pleased that the wine list had more options than "red or white" and ordered a glass of Pinot Noir, a CT burger, and a glass of water from a heavyset waitress with a thick helmet of black hair and a raccoon's mask of heavy mascara. None of the staff had been there the previous afternoon when she'd stopped by. Which meant, if she had the gumption, that she should ask them if they knew Hawk.

After some dinner, though.

The place was warm and intimate, and the customers seemed to be locals and they were comfortable with one another. University of Montana Grizzlies posters and paraphernalia were everywhere, and someone had stolen and mounted a street sign for BRETT FAVRE BOULEVARD.

As the waitress delivered her wine an older man with a full white beard and red suspenders over a long underwear top came in and asked her, "Has Jody been in?"

The waitress shook her head. "He usually comes in around eight for his nightly martini."

The man looked at his watch, then seemed to contemplate whether to wait a half hour or come back. He decided to wait. He took a stool at the bar and rotated it toward her.

"Beer and a shot," he said to the waitress.

"*Please*," she corrected.

"May I please have a glass of beer and a shot of Jim Beam

at your lovely establishment?" he asked. Cassie couldn't tell if he was grinning through the beard.

"That's better," the waitress said. Then to Cassie, "Never let 'em treat you like shit."

Cassie toasted her, and fought the urge to ask the waitress if she'd ever met any of the Kleinsassers. Because that's how they treated everyone.

CASSIE WOLFED DOWN the burger and ordered a second glass of wine although she knew she probably shouldn't. The first glass had gone to her head because there was nothing on her stomach to absorb it. She could already feel warm tendrils of alcohol extending through her body.

The old man at the bar kept checking his watch. He was obviously waiting for eight o'clock to come around.

He gestured toward a poster board behind the bar. It was a hand-lettered weekly football pool where patrons could pay a few dollars and guess the sum of the scoring for the University of Montana game, the Montana State game, and either the Seattle Seahawks or Denver Broncos contests.

"Well, look who won," he said to the waitress.

Cassie followed his index finger to the pool results to see that "J. Haak" was circled in red. She guessed the "J" stood for Jody.

"I guess I know who will be buying a round for the house," the man said.

"Yeah," the waitress said. "I think that's two weeks in a row."

"Lucky bastard," the man grumbled.

"Oh, yeah," the waitress said with sarcasm. "Jody is really a lucky guy."

The old man snorted as they shared a joke Cassie wasn't privy to. She looked at the name on the football pool and formed an idea.

When the waitress delivered her second glass of wine and the bill, Cassie asked her, "I heard you two talking about Jody. How do you pronounce 'Haak,' his last name?" Cassie said it like "*Hack*."

The waitress looked at her skeptically. "Hawk. Like the bird. Why?"

Cassie tried not to react. "Just wondering. I've been trying to find a man called Hawk for a couple of days. I need to talk with him. Am I correct that he'll be here at eight?"

"Most nights," the waitress said. "Not all."

"Do you know where I can reach him if he doesn't come in?"

Something passed over the waitress's face, a kind of subtle mask.

"Who's asking?" She was obviously protective of Haak, which Cassie found interesting.

"My name is Cassie Dewell," she said, fishing in her purse for a card and handing it over. "I'm a private investigator."

"I've heard you were around asking questions."

"Really?"

"I work in a bar," the waitress said with a grin. "I hear everything."

"So, about reaching him," Cassie prompted.

"I'm not the one to ask. When he comes in for his martini I serve it to him. He doesn't talk to me a lot and I have no idea where he lives."

"Would the man at the bar know?"

The waitress looked over at the bearded man. "Yeah," she said. "Frank might know where he lives."

"Thank you."

"No problem," the waitress said. She'd been helpful, although Cassie always bristled when a service employee said "no problem" instead of "you're welcome." But it was a thing these days, she recognized.

"HEY, LITTLE LADY," the bearded man said to her as Cassie took her wine and sat down next to him at the bar.

"I'm Frank," the old man said.

She introduced herself again. "I'm looking for Jody Haak. The waitress said you might know where I can find him."

Frank took a long time to draw a pocketwatch out of his jeans and look at it. "He's late. Maybe he's not coming in tonight to collect his winnings."

"But do you know where he lives?"

"Kind of. But I've never been to his place."

"Is it around here?"

Frank chinned vaguely toward the mountains to the southeast. "Jody lives off the grid," he said. "No phone, no internet, nothing like that. He makes a point of it. That's why I'm here trying to run into him. I want to ask him if I can borrow his flatbed trailer so I can take my ATV into the shop in town."

"Are you friends?"

Frank shrugged. "Not really. Jody is a hard guy to get to know. He doesn't talk much. He's not like me—a guy who never knows when to shut up."

She smiled.

"Hell," Frank said, "he left the state a while back. Never said a word to anyone, he just up and vanished. It was when he got kicked off the ranch where he worked, but he's obviously back now. From what I understand, he's got a cabin up there somewhere."

"What's he hiding from?" Cassie asked.

"You'll have to ask Jody. But my guess is he wants to steer clear of his old employers."

"Do you mean the ranch he worked on?"

Frank nodded.

"Let me guess," Cassie said. "He used to work for the Iron Cross."

"For something like twenty years or more," Frank said. "He knows where all the bodies are buried out there on that place, or so I take it. When they run him off it wasn't a pleasant experience for Jody from what I understand. Not that he told me outright. It's just bar gossip. And here at the CT, there's plenty of that. You can probably believe about half of it."

As Frank talked, he took several baleful looks at his empty beer glass. Cassie understood the signal, and ordered him another.

"Thank you kindly," he said.

"Here," she said, giving Frank her card. "If you see him please ask him to give me a call. If I'm not here in Lochsa County I'll be at my office in Bozeman. I'd really like to talk with him."

Frank studied the card as if he's never seen one quite so interesting before.

"Are you working for Blake?" he asked.

"I'm working for his lawyer."

"Blake is a hard man to figure out. I can't say I like him."

"No one does."

"Except maybe Jody," Frank said.

"Did you see them together?"

Frank nodded. "Blake came in here on a toot last summer. The two of them spent a couple of hours having some kind of big discussion right in that booth over there," he said, pointing toward an empty booth near the back. "It was pretty animated and pretty unusual because Jody isn't usually much of a talker. I stopped by to say hello to Jody and he gave me a look like, 'please get the hell out of here,' so I got the message and left. Blake wasn't friendly at all, but I guess he's that way with everyone.

"A couple of days later I heard what happened to Blake's niece. So, I guess I saw them together the night before the, um, incident."

"Interesting," Cassie said. "Do you have any idea what they were talking about?"

"Some kind of secret ranch shit, I imagine. They both were on the outs with John Wayne and Horst, so I figure they had plenty in common."

"Was Blake drunk at the time?" Cassie asked. The story corroborated Blake's telling.

Frank shrugged. "I guess he was, but I couldn't tell at the time. He wasn't falling down or spilling drinks, but there was a real glassy look to his eyes. I've seen it on other big drinkers, where they don't even look like they're three sheets to the wind but they're actually blotto. Blake had that look, I'd say. Like he was there listening to you but he really wasn't there at all."

That also supported Blake's account.

"Was Blake by himself with Mr. Haak?"

"Nah," Frank said. "He came with that barmaid from up in Lolo. Now *she* was drunk as a skunk. She had her head down on the table sawing logs the whole time Blake and Jody were talking."

"Was it Lindy Glode?"

"That's her name," Frank said, snapping his fingers. "I'm pretty sure that's who it was. Cute and busty, but really out of it that night."

"I'm trying to find her, too," Cassie said as much to herself as to Frank. "Any idea where I could?"

Frank's eyes twinkled and she assumed he was smiling again. "Believe it or not, little lady, I don't really run with a crowd that includes cute and busty young women."

"Got it."

Frank's eyes slid from her face to over her shoulder. He said, "Well, speak of the devil."

"Lindy?" Cassie said. She could feel a breath of cool air from the open door on the back of her neck.

"The man himself," Frank said.

CASSIE SPUN AROUND on her stool. Jody Haak was short, solid, and stout. He had a long face with jowls and eyes that looked to have seen it all. He wore a stained cowboy hat with a short brim, a week's worth of silver whiskers, and scuffed cowboy boots.

His eyes shifted from Frank to Cassie and he seemed to know who she was by the tightening of his mouth.

Haak turned on his heel and walked straight out of the bar.

"Jody, can I borrow your trailer?" Frank called after him. Haak never looked back.

"Doesn't seem like he wants to talk with you," Frank said to Cassie.

She thanked Frank, quickly settled the bill, and strode across the Corvallis Tavern and out the door behind Jody Haak.

All she saw of him were the taillights of his pickup headed southeast.

SHE WAS EXHAUSTED when she got to her room at the Whispering Pines. Her plan was to talk with Ben, have a nightcap, and go to sleep early. She closed the door behind her and eyed the bed.

She'd not even kicked off her cowboy boots before there was a gentle knocking on the door. Cassie rose, fetched her handbag with the Glock in it, and peered out through the peephole.

Linda Sue Murdock stood a few feet away in a brown cloth coat. She was looking over her shoulder as if suspicious that someone had followed her.

Cassie slid the bolt and opened the door.

"I've been waiting for you to show up. May I come in?" Murdock asked.

"Of course," Cassie said, stepping aside.

Murdock entered quickly and waited for Cassie to close the door.

Cassie asked, "Is someone following you? You seem nervous."

"I *am* nervous. I shouldn't be here. I need a drink."

"All I have is wine."

"That's fine."

Cassie poured some into two thin plastic motel room glasses.

"Do you have any ice?" Murdock asked.

"It's red wine," Cassie explained.

"I like it with ice and a little Seven-Up. I'm a lightweight."

Cassie nodded. "I can get you both. There are a couple of machines near the lobby."

"Don't tell Glen I'm here."

"The manager?"

"Yes. He's one of them."

"You mean friends of the Kleinsassers?"

Her eyes said yes.

"Okay," Cassie said. "Sit down and get comfortable. I'll go get a Seven-Up and some ice."

Murdock sat down on one of the two plastic chairs at the small table near the window. She kept her coat on and hugged herself.

"I understand you're looking for Lindy Glode."

"I am."

Murdock nodded, then looked away. "I know where she might be. You see, she's my stepdaughter."

CASSIE TRUDGED to the alcove near the manager's office with an empty ice bucket and a handful of change for the soft drink dispenser. The lights were off in the manager's office but she saw the form of Glen Steele lurking behind the counter of the front desk. He retreated back to his quarters as she got close.

Had he seen Murdoch enter her room?

She filled the bucket and fed coins into the vending machine. There wasn't any 7-Up so she chose Mountain Dew. Cassie figured that if Murdock liked sweet drinks it was as good as any.

As she turned to walk back to her room she noticed that the always-present hum of traffic from the main highway seemed to be louder than usual. And it quickly increased in volume.

Something blacked out the illuminated Whispering Pines sign at the curbside and she felt the roar of a big engine as well as a heavy vibration through the soles of her boots.

It was a massive eighteen-wheel tractor-trailer barreling through the parking lot with its headlights and running lights quenched. And it picked up speed.

She screamed and dropped the ice and soft drink as the big truck drove head-on into the front of her corner unit. The crash of broken two-by-fours and imploded wood paneling was tremendous.

The truck never stopped. It rolled into and through the motel room and continued out the other side, leaving a wake of twisted material and furniture and sparking electric wires.

Linda Murdock never had a chance.

Cassie wouldn't have, either.

PART IV

Nothing on earth consumes a man more quickly than the passion of resentment.

—NIETZSCHE, *Ecce Homo*

If you hate a person, you hate something in him that is part of yourself. What isn't part of ourselves doesn't disturb us.

—HERMANN HESSE, *Demian*

TWENTY-ONE

"IT SHOULDN'T BE all that hard to find," Cassie said to Sheriff Wagy, "just look for an eighteen-wheeler with a smashed-up front end."

He said, "I don't really appreciate your sarcasm at the moment. I lost a very valuable member of my team in your room. She's the first fatality the sheriff's office has ever had."

"I'm glad to hear you're worried about your record," Cassie said bitterly.

"You didn't even provide a description of the truck," he said. "Do you know how many eighteen-wheelers are out there on the road?"

They stood in the parking lot of the Whispering Pines. It was still hours before the dawn sun would slide over the top ridges of the eastern mountains. Every sheriff's department vehicle was either parked on the lot to block the entrances or out on the street to turn away gawkers. Word of the incident had apparently spread quickly among the residents of Horston. A photographer from the *Horston Express* had already been shooed away.

Missing was Deputy Grzegorczyk, whom Cassie had seen drive by. When he recognized her in the parking lot he kept going.

The wreckage of unit number eleven was cordoned off with yellow plastic crime scene tape and lit up by a battery of portable spotlights borrowed from a construction company by the sheriff's department. Smoke from the fires in the mountains hung in the beams of light.

The ambulance containing Linda Murdock's mangled body had left the scene two hours before. Cassie had watched in dulled horror as the EMTs lifted beams and debris off her torso and rolled it into a black body bag before lifting it on a gurney. Her body seemed smaller and lighter than when she was alive, and the harsh lighting was cruel to her memory, Cassie thought.

She also watched as several deputies picked through the demolished room. They wore gloves and paper masks and they carried flashlights. Cassie had no idea what they expected to find that could be of any help at all. It's what the sheriff had ordered them to do. One of them found the red wine bottle and lifted it up and shined his beam on it so Wagy could see it.

"So, you two were having a little party?" he asked her.

"Not at all," Cassie said. "I told you exactly what happened."

"Hmm."

"What in the hell is that supposed to mean?"

He shrugged, but the implication was clear.

"The only time I met her was in your office," Cassie said.

"But she was comfortable enough with you to visit you in your hotel room?"

Cassie closed her eyes and tried to keep her anger in check. Her world seemed to be spinning out of control.

She'd told him the sequence of events leading up to the truck taking out the room. He'd listened, but the skeptical look on his face annoyed her.

She told him everything *except* for something she held back. She hadn't told Wagy or any of the deputies that Murdock was there to tell Cassie about Lindy Glode, her stepdaughter. Cassie didn't trust them any more than she trusted Glen Steele, who was on the telephone in his office with his insurance agent.

"We'll find this guy," Wagy said to Cassie. "When we do I wouldn't be surprised to find out he fell asleep at the wheel or was under the influence of drugs and alcohol to cause this accident. He might have taken a wrong turn off the highway and just panicked. Hit the accelerator instead of the brakes— something like that. Once he woke up and realized what he'd done he just kept going."

Wagy had been talking this way since he arrived at the scene, and Cassie was beside herself with rage born of both experience and adrenaline.

Although she fought it, tears filled her eyes.

"It wasn't an accident, I told you that," she said to him. "I watched that truck speed up, not slow down."

"But you didn't see it closely enough to give me a vehicle description," Wagy said.

"He had all of his lights off. I told you that. Look, I was the target. Linda Murdock was just a very unlucky citizen who happened to be in the wrong place at the wrong time."

"A target, huh?" he said. He raised his eyebrows when he said it.

"There's history here," she said. "I once spent several years of my life going after a long-haul trucker who was a serial killer. I know you know the story."

He nodded skeptically. "I've heard," he said. "So, you think this guy came back to life and drove all the way here to target you?"

"I'm not saying it was him. But this was deliberate. It wasn't an accident."

"Then who would do this?" Wagy asked. "Who did you piss off? I mean, besides *everyone* around here?"

"Why won't you do your job?" she asked him. "You don't need every deputy in the department standing around here with nothing to do. Send them out on the road to find that truck. Have you even issued an APB?"

Wagy didn't respond.

She said, "Go talk to your buddy Glen in there. He was spying on my room last night. I saw him. Go ask him why and who he might have talked to about it."

"Glen called it in," Wagy said while he shook his head. "He was very upset. Are you suggesting he knew that some-body would drive into his hotel and wreck it?"

"I don't know. Maybe you should ask him."

"And maybe you should step aside and let us sort this out," Wagy said. "Just because you worked in law enforcement once doesn't mean you have all the answers when it comes to me doing my job."

He reached into the pocket of his uniform trousers and came out with a Kleenex. He offered it to her.

Cassie slapped it out of his hand.

"Easy there," Wagy cooed. "Calm down."

★

ONE OF THE deputies in the debris held up Cassie's gear bag and displayed it for Sheriff Wagy.

"That's mine," she said. "I need that."

She started striding toward what was left of unit number eleven.

"Hold your horses," Wagy warned. "You've got no business entering a crime scene."

"I thought you said it was an accident," she hissed over her shoulder as she lifted the tape and ducked under it.

She stepped through a tangle of wood, broken ceiling tiles, and wires to retrieve her bag. It was covered with drywall dust but it hadn't been crushed. She looked around for her luggage but she didn't see it. The cheapness of the construction of the room was now exposed to all, she thought. It was as if a matchstick house had been kicked apart. No wonder the truck could blow through it and keep going.

"I'll need to ask you to leave," the deputy said. He wasn't as strident as Wagy had been.

"I want what's mine," she said while moving a piece of interior paneling with her boot toe.

"Sheriff?" the deputy asked. He wanted direction.

Wagy motioned for him to kick her out.

"You need to go now, ma'am," the deputy said.

"When I'm good and ready," she said.

"It's for your own safety," he said. She felt his hand grasp her arm.

She glared at him and she suspected that she looked a little insane. "Don't you dare touch me."

He relaxed his grip. She felt guilty for taking all of her anger and frustration out on him. He was simply following orders from Wagy.

"Okay," she said. "I'll leave. But if you find my suitcase and my overnight bag please return them. They aren't evidence of any kind and I'd like them back."

The deputy nodded.

As she carefully stepped around material to return to the parking lot her right boot was held back by a strand of wire. She bent over to remove it and she gave the wire a tug. A broken light fixture on the other end jumped out of the debris and she reeled it in.

The wire led to a small multidirectional microphone that had been embedded in the overhead light fixture. She studied it and her rage returned.

"See this?" she called to Wagy.

"What is it?"

"It's a fucking mic," she said. "Somebody bugged my room."

Which meant, she realized, that her conversations with Rachel about the case and who she planned to interview in the county had likely been overheard. Every move she'd made was known by someone in advance.

"I wonder how long it's been there?" she asked aloud. "I wonder if it was there when Blake Kleinsasser stayed here?"

Wagy gave no response. He appeared to be thinking of what to say.

"Now maybe you'll have your talk with Glen?" she said, nodding toward the manager's office. "And if you don't, I *will*."

CASSIE HAD the microphone in her hand when she pushed through the office door. Sheriff Wagy was a few steps behind her.

Glen Steele was behind the counter and he looked up at her with alarm. He held a handset to his face.

Cassie reached over and pushed down the cradle of the telephone, killing the call.

"Hey," Steele said, "I was talking with my insurance guy."

She slapped the mic down on the counter so he could see it.

"You better have a damned good reason why this was in my room," she said. "Either you're a pervert or you've been keeping tabs on me for other reasons. Which is it?"

Cassie had experienced a similar situation when she was in pursuit of the Lizard King where a gas station owner had installed a secret camera in the women's restroom. She couldn't believe it had happened again.

Steele stepped back and slowly shook his head. He stared at the microphone. "I'm afraid I don't know what you're talking about," he said. She didn't believe him.

"Was there a camera in there, too?"

He continued to shake his head.

"Now I know why you put me in that room," she said.

"It's our best room," he said. Then he added, "It *was* our best room, I mean."

The bell above the door jangled as the sheriff came in behind her.

"Arrest this son of a bitch," Cassie said, pointing at Steele.

"She's a little worked up," Wagy said to Steele.

"I'd say," Steele replied.

"I was almost killed," Cassie said. She jabbed her finger toward the manager. "And this son of a bitch was listening in on my conversations."

"That's crazy," he said.

"Glen," Wagy asked, "Do you know anything about this

device she found?" He asked the question in a very reasonable tone.

Steele quickly denied knowing anything about the mic. While he did Cassie noticed that he was looking over her shoulder to Wagy as if she weren't there. She had the suspicion that some kind of silent compact had passed between them, but when she looked over her shoulder at the sheriff he looked away.

"Hold it," Steele said, smacking his forehead with the heel of his hand. "I just remembered something. I know why it was there."

Cassie narrowed her eyes while waiting for the explanation.

Wagy said, "Sheriff, you'll remember a couple years back? The county attorney suspected that a guest in unit eleven was using it to sell meth?"

"I remember," Wagy said.

"They got a warrant to put a bug in there. They told me all about it and even though I pride myself on maintaining the privacy of my customers, I didn't see where I had much choice in the matter. The attorney's office sent a couple of men out here to install it when the guest was out of his room."

"They never got anything they could use in court," Wagy said helpfully to Steele. "I do know that."

"They must have forgotten it was still out there," Steele said. "It's been there the whole time. I'd completely forgotten about it or I would have asked them to come back and remove it."

"That's a lie," Cassie said. "You're lying."

"The sheriff here will confirm my story," Steele said.

Cassie wheeled on him.

Wagy shrugged and said, "He's telling the truth. We were

trying to build a case against a drug guy and it didn't pan out. I plumb forgot about that bug in there."

Cassie's chest went cold with sudden realization. She looked at Wagy and back to Steele. They'd obviously settled on their story, and they were supporting each other while telling it.

"So it was *you* listening in," she said to Wagy. "It wasn't Steele. You keep the mic there and Glen makes sure which guests get that room. First Blake Kleinsasser, and then me."

Wagy made a face suggesting she was out of her mind.

"Who else knew I was using that room?" she asked. "Somebody told the truck driver which one to aim for."

"That's a really dangerous accusation, Miss Dewell," Wagy said. "I think maybe you ought to just calm down and get some rest. You might want to see somebody at the clinic to help you deal with your trauma. I'm happy to make a call over there and let them know you're coming."

"I'm not going anywhere," Cassie replied. Then she asked, "Which one of the Kleinsassers is your boss? John Wayne? Horst himself? Do you answer to Cheyenne as well?"

"Actually," Wagy said, gripping her arm, "you *are* going somewhere. And if you stay here even a minute longer and continue to make accusations and impede the progress of this accident investigation, I'll arrest you and you can spend another night or two in our fine jail."

"Don't touch me," Cassie warned.

But Wagy was fast and he was strong. He spun her toward the counter and he pinned her arms back. She felt the cold metal of handcuffs tightened on her wrists. Wagy leaned into her until his weight held her in place. Then he bent her over until her face was mashed into the top of the counter.

His whisper in her ear was low and menacing. "You'll regret what you just said, you fucking nutjob. If you ever say anything like that again I'll find you and I'll take you out."

She didn't struggle or scream.

He said, "I'm going to take these cuffs off of you now and you're going to walk out there and get in your car and drive away. Go back to Bozeman and don't show your face ever again in my county. Do you understand?"

She nodded that she did.

The pressure of his full weight eased off. She heard the jangle of keys and the handcuffs were removed.

When she turned to face him, his face was once again a stoic mask. Glen Steele, meanwhile, was frozen to his spot behind the counter.

"I worked for years with good honest men in law enforcement," she said to Wagy as she shouldered around him toward the door and stepped outside. She leaned back in to say, "There's nothing worse than a corrupt cop."

She could feel his eyes burning holes in her back as she walked across the parking lot toward her Ford.

CASSIE CALLED Rachel on her home number and woke her up.

"You won't believe what just happened," she said.

She told her the whole story.

"You need to get out of there now," Rachel said.

TWENTY-TWO

CASSIE AWOKE WHEN her cell phone burred. She thrashed around in bed and for a moment she didn't know where she was. Morning light streamed through the curtains and pooled on the floor and she remembered checking into the Holiday Inn Express in Lolo and paying with cash the night before. She recalled the puzzled expression on the face of the night manager when she said the room needed to be on the top floor or she wouldn't take it.

She finally found her phone buried in the folds of the covers after it had stopped ringing. Ben had called and of course he hadn't left a message.

It was ten thirty in the morning and her head was foggy despite nine hours of sleep. As it cleared, the events of the night before came flooding back and she rubbed at her eyes. It was all still unbelievable and immensely depressing.

The foundation of the case against Blake Kleinsasser was crumbling all around her. The sheriff in charge of the investigation was crooked which meant everything he'd been involved in—the time line, the affidavits, the evidence—was suspect. Witnesses including Jody Haak and Lindy Glode were either avoiding her or hiding out. She'd been spied on by someone. Her car and possessions had been destroyed. The entire Kleinsasser family wanted her gone. The accused was in a coma and might not recover.

And a truck driver had tried to kill her but instead murdered an innocent woman.

You need to get out of there now rang in her ears.

"WHY AREN'T YOU in school?" she asked Ben when he picked up.

"I'm not feeling good today. I'm sick."

He did sound very down and unlike himself, she thought.

"What's wrong?"

"Oh, my stomach. I might have eaten too much."

Despite herself, she smiled.

"Is Isabel okay with you staying home?" Cassie asked.

"I guess. She went to her hot yoga class."

"We've been really missing each other on these calls," Cassie said. "You were going to tell me something the other night and we got cut off."

"By the cops," Ben said.

"Yes, by the cops. So, what was it?"

"It seems like a million years ago now," he said with a sigh.

Cassie sat straight up when he told her about the eighteen-wheeler.

"Did you get a look at the driver?"

"No. He was too high up to see in the window."

"Did you get the license plate number?"

"No, Mom. I didn't even think about it."

"Did you call the police?" she asked.

"Nah. Erin said they'd think we were crazy."

"I don't," Cassie said. "I absolutely believe you."

She debated whether to tell him about the destruction of her motel room and decided against it. She'd tell him later when she returned and they were together. She didn't want to alarm him.

"Have you seen it again?" she asked.

"No."

"Has Erin?"

"She might have. That's what she told me last night."

"Ben," Cassie said, "I'm not really convinced that you're sick enough to stay home. But I'm glad you did."

"Why?"

"I'll explain it all later," she said. "I'm just glad we finally connected. It's been just as crazy here and it's nice to talk with you. It feels so normal."

"Are you coming home?"

"Yes. Probably tonight."

"Good."

She'd just made the decision during the phone call with her son. Cassie would make another attempt to find Lindy Glode and Jody Haak, then return to Bozeman even if she wasn't successful in locating them. It seemed almost pointless now to continue her investigation. All she was really doing was checking off boxes. She'd had enough. She was whipped.

"Is that all that's wrong—that your stomach hurts?" she asked. "I can tell by your voice that something's bothering you."

"You can?"

"I'm your mother. Are you doing all right besides?"

He paused for a long time. "I guess I just don't get girls very well."

"Are you talking about this Erin?"

"Yeah, I guess."

So now she knew who he'd been texting. And who had put him into such a giddy mood for the last week or two.

"Teenage girls are hard to figure out sometimes," she said. "Even mature women are sometimes hard to figure out. Except me, of course."

He laughed weakly at that.

"It's just hard to know what to say," Ben continued. "Or how to know what I should have said, I guess."

"Do you want to tell me about it?"

"Not really. Why would I want to tell my mother about it?"

"Because maybe I can help a little," she said.

He seemed to think about it, then said, "Nah. That's okay."

"You know you can always talk to me," she said.

"Yeah."

"So, rest your stomach and plan to go to school tomorrow. Okay?"

"Okay."

"Don't fight with Isabel."

"That's a little harder to do," he said. She could tell he was smiling.

"And don't worry about Erin," Cassie said. "Girls that age can turn on a dime. You never know why they act a certain way. It may even not have anything at all to do with you."

"Yeah."

She disconnected the call and hugged herself. It was nice to have a hopeful feeling. She loved that boy.

CASSIE DRESSED in the same clothes she'd worn the previous day since her bag was still somewhere under the wreckage of her motel room. Then she made bad coffee in the hotel coffee-maker and opened her laptop on the small table.

She rarely looked at Facebook and never posted anything. Her account was under Dewell Investigations, not her own name. Occasionally, someone would try to contact her there and she had received a couple of pieces of business that way.

Since Jody Haak didn't have a phone or internet, he likely didn't have an account. He didn't look like the type. And he didn't, at least under his own name.

But Lindy Glode of Lolo, Montana, did. She was of the right age. Cassie sent her a friend request. Maybe she'd respond.

Then Cassie checked out Ben's account. She always felt a little guilty when she did so, but not guilty enough to stay away.

She was curious about Erin Reese. She wanted to see a photo of the girl who had broken Ben's heart. She scrolled through Ben's friends and Cassie gasped when she found her.

Erin Reese looked just like Franny Porché. Cassie had seen photos of Franny in the case file. And she recalled Ben saying his new friend had just moved to Bozeman and was new at the school as well.

Erin Reese *was* Franny Porché.

Cassie shared the profile picture to her phone and attached it to an email to Rachel.

Cheyenne had created a new identity for her daughter and moved her to Bozeman. Whether it was to protect Franny by getting her away from Lochsa County and what had happened there, or away from the Kleinsasser family snake pit, Cassie didn't know.

Perhaps, Cassie thought, the reason might be to hide Franny away from people like Cassie and Rachel.

RACHEL CALLED before Cassie left the room. "Is this photo who I think it is?" she asked.

Cassie explained where she'd found it.

"She's been right under our noses the whole time," Rachel said with astonishment. "It does make some sense, though. Cheyenne's stashing Franny away where she can go to school and live a normal life until she's called to testify at trial. Either that, or she's hiding Franny so no one can talk with her about her story."

"My thoughts exactly," Cassie said.

"Does Ben have any idea who she really is?"

"No, and I don't look forward to telling him. He's smitten with her, although he's worried about her right now. He doesn't understand how she's acting or why. It's possible she feels threatened and she's trying to keep him out of it."

Cassie relayed to Rachel what Ben had told her about nearly being mowed down by the semi-truck.

"Do you think it was the same one that went after you?" Rachel asked.

"Who else could it be? It's too hard to conceive of more than one driver doing all this. I think Ben is a target because of *me*. He doesn't know it yet. And Franny might think, given her situation, that the near miss was about her instead of him."

Rachel didn't disagree.

"Where are you now?"

"I'm at the Holiday Inn Express in Lolo."

"Does anyone know you're there?"

"No."

"What about your rental car?"

"I parked it in a safe place and walked," Cassie said. "That's not to say that it hasn't been located by Sheriff Wagy's thugs, but I wouldn't bet on it."

"Good," Rachel said. "Get packed up. Then go get in it and come back."

"There's really nothing to pack. All I've got are the clothes on my back."

"Will you drive straight here?"

"Later today. I promised Ben."

"Thank God you've finally come to your senses," Rachel said. "Look, our firm has good connections with the administration of the school district. Jessica used to represent them and she's personal friends with the superintendent and the principal of the high school. I think we can work through them to make Franny available for an interview."

"Really?"

"I'll take Jessica along to be in the room with me when we talk with her," Rachel said. "You should be there as well."

Cassie said, "That might be a little awkward. Ben's mom interviewing Franny, after all."

"Good point. We don't want to spook her."

"Won't you need permission from Cheyenne?" Cassie asked.

"Who knows? We don't even know Franny's situation here. She might be staying with relatives or friends of the Kleinsassers until she testifies at the trial. I'll try to find out and I'll keep you posted."

THINGS WERE MOVING fast now. Cassie felt a sense of exhilaration that the end of the investigation was in sight. She also hoped that she could make it out of Lochsa County before they closed in on her.

She stepped out of the elevator and walked past the front desk on the way out. It felt odd not having a clothes bag of any kind.

A young woman behind the desk said, "Ma'am, were you in Room 827?"

Cassie looked at her key card because she couldn't remember. The number 827 was written on the sleeve.

"Yes."

"I'm sorry, but the night clerk didn't check you in properly."

"I paid cash."

"Yes, but he didn't get an ID."

"That's okay," Cassie said as she walked out through the double glass doors.

THE MORNING was warm and it was even smokier than it had been. It felt more like dusk than mid-morning as Cassie looked for oncoming cars before crossing the highway. She didn't see any, and she was grateful. Cassie had the feeling there were lots of people looking for her, which is why she hadn't presented her driver's license at the front desk the night before. The extra twenty she'd given the night clerk helped him forget about that step.

There wasn't a sidewalk on the other side of the highway and she followed a trail two blocks south to the used car lot where she'd parked her rental Ford. There had been an opening between two pickups for sale and she'd left it there, thinking that local law enforcement wouldn't cruise a used car lot to look for her rental.

As she passed through a stand of pine trees toward the lot something crashed from within the brush. Cassie jumped back and dug into her handbag for her Glock, her heart whumping in her chest.

Something big and dark pushed through the tangle and she trained her weapon on it.

It was a lone cow elk and the creature's left side was blackened by fire, the hide burned down to cracked black skin. The elk saw Cassie at the same time and froze, her nostrils enlarging and her eyes widening.

"Poor girl," Cassie said, lowering her handgun.

The elk snorted and pivoted on her hind feet and smashed through the cover. Cassie could hear its hooves pounding through the timber until she could no longer see it.

The elk was singed, but still alive. Cassie felt a kinship with her.

CASSIE WALKED through two rows of vehicles and used her key fob to unlock the Expedition from twenty feet away. A salesman in a short-sleeved dress shirt and tie appeared from a low-slung office.

"Is that your car?" he asked her.

"Yes."

"You left it here?"

"I did."

"Well, that solves the mystery of the morning," he said.

"Thanks for not selling it to anyone." She smiled as she climbed in and drove away.

FROM HER CAR, she called the Lochsa County Assessor's office.

Since her arrival, Cassie had played fair and followed the rules. That was over. Rules no longer applied when the people she was up against were venal and corrupt. She could hear the words of her mentor Cody Hoyt in her mind.

You'll find, Cassie, that it's us against the world....

"Hi," she said. "I'm Sandra with UPS. We're trying to deliver a package to a rural resident named Jody Haak. That's spelled HA-A-K. Unfortunately, the address has only a post office box and we need his physical address for delivery. I've tried to reach Mr. Haak with no luck. Is there any way you can help me since he sends his property tax check to you?"

"Well, this is kind of an unusual request," the woman on the other end said. She sounded matronly, Cassie thought.

"The problem is," Cassie said, "I think it's a food delivery of some kind and there's an expiration date on it. We'd hate for it to spoil."

There was a long pause, then a sigh. The woman said, "Just a second and I'll look it up."

"Thank you so much."

Cassie wrote down the address on the back of her rental car folder.

THEN SHE CALLED the Lochsa County Sheriff's Department. A man answered, and Cassie recalled the large jowly deputy she'd met running the evidence room and she thought the voice sounded like his.

She made her own tone high and breathy and she hoped he wouldn't recognize her.

"I just heard that my friend Linda Murdock was involved in a horrible accident last night. I've called around and no one seems to know where her body was taken. Can you please help me out?"

"Hold on," the man said.

He came back in less than a minute. "Ma'am, her body was taken to Hamilton Mortuary and Chapel."

"That's in Hamilton, then?"

"Yes, ma'am. We don't have a funeral home here in Horston or anywhere in the county."

"Thank you. That's very good to know."

She disconnected before he could ask her name.

Hamilton was twenty miles south, just beyond Corvallis on the highway. After trading her rental in for another make and model that wasn't yet known to law enforcement, she'd drive straight through Lochsa County and out the other side.

Hamilton Mortuary and Chapel was a few miles farther south. Jody Haak lived somewhere farther up a mountain road. She had the address.

With luck, she could be on the road back home by late afternoon.

TWENTY-THREE

CASSIE DROVE THROUGH Horston in her new car, a Honda CRV with Nevada plates, wearing sunglasses and a complimentary ball cap from the rental agency. She didn't see any sheriff's department vehicles and no one pulled her over. She didn't begin to breathe easily until she drove past the Lochsa County line. She kept an eye out for the injured cow elk but didn't see her again. The heavy smoke hung in the trees as if being pushed down from above by a giant hand. Her throat was raw from breathing it.

The Hamilton Mortuary was on Main Street a block west of the small downtown. It had a façade made of logs and a sign beneath that read, CARING FOR YOUR LOVED ONES SINCE 1978.

She turned off the engine and checked her face in the rearview mirror. The bags under her eyes were annoying but she no longer had her makeup kit so there was nothing she could do to fix her look. She sighed and climbed out. There were four other cars in the parking lot, all with Montana plates.

The reception area was somber and hushed. Gentle Muzak played at very low volume, although she recognized the song as "Every Breath You Take" by the Police. She thought it was an inappropriate choice for a funeral home, but it was such an anodyne version that it probably didn't draw much notice.

A plump woman in her sixties sat behind a desk. She had glasses with faux tortoiseshell frames and tight curls of silver hair. A kindly smile was part of her ensemble.

"May I help you?" she asked gently.

"I'm here to pay my respects to Linda Murdock. I understand she's here."

The woman nodded that she was. "Are you with the family?"

Cassie couldn't make herself lie or come up with a ruse. The seriousness of the situation almost overwhelmed her, and she felt guilty for being there. After all, she'd thought that if there was any chance to finally meet face-to-face with Lindy Glode, her stepmother's death might smoke her out. But Linda Murdock was a real human being and she deserved respect. She was a wife to a disabled husband and the stepmother of a likely grieving stepdaughter. And she'd died because she came to Cassie to offer information and help.

Cassie was exploiting the situation.

"I'm not with the family," Cassie said. "I was with Linda when she was... killed."

"It was a horrible accident," the woman said. "It was a real tragedy what happened."

It wasn't an accident, Cassie wanted to say but didn't.

"Have they found the driver?" the woman asked.

They aren't even looking for him.

Instead, Cassie asked, "Is the family here?"

The woman nodded. "We have a grieving room. It's a place for the family to gather and mourn the deceased before funeral arrangements are made."

"Is it in the back?"

At that point Cassie envisioned entering a room as a stranger while Murdock's loving family sought comfort from each other. It was as inappropriate as the song being piped through the facility. If the woman behind the desk asked Cassie to leave the premises, Cassie was okay with it.

"Lyle is back there with them in case they need anything," the woman said. "Maybe you can check with him."

"Lyle?"

"Lyle is my husband. We own and manage Hamilton Mortuary and Chapel."

"Thank you."

THE HALLWAY was dark and her footfalls were cushioned by thick pile carpeting that, she guessed, had not been updated since the building had opened.

A man approximately the age of the woman at the receptionist desk sat in a high-backed wooden chair outside of a closed door. He wore a suit and his trouser cuffs were hiked up to reveal bands of white ankle. He quickly pocketed the smartphone he was looking at when Cassie appeared.

"Lyle?" she asked.

"Yes. May I help you?"

His voice was low and preternaturally soothing. It was well-practiced and likely beneficial for his line of work, and

Cassie fought the urge to ask him questions that would require long answers just to hear his voice.

"Is the Murdock family inside?" she asked, gesturing toward the door.

"Yes."

"Is Lindy Glode with them?"

"I'm sorry," he said, "but Lindy is quite bereaved and she asked me to screen any visitors with a couple of questions."

"Go ahead."

"Are you with law enforcement?" he asked.

The question surprised her and it must have showed.

"No."

"Are you here representing the Kleinsasser family?"

"Absolutely not."

She stepped forward and handed Lyle one of her cards.

He read it and asked, "Couldn't this be done at a later time?"

"I wish it could," Cassie said. "If she doesn't want to talk to me there's nothing I can do about it. I'll leave quietly. I know this must be a very difficult time for her.

"But when you give her the card please tell her something for me. I was there last night. Her stepmother came to see me to tell me something important. I was the only eyewitness to what happened and Lindy might have questions about the... incident. Her stepmother seemed like a very nice person who was trying to do the right thing. I might be able to provide some answers to questions she might have."

She deliberately refrained from using the word "closure." She hated that word for a reason. When the military liaison showed up at her door to break the news about the death of Jim overseas, they said they were there to provide "closure."

It was a word they'd been taught to say, she guessed. But Jim's death brought no closure at all. Instead, for a pregnant woman without a job at the time, it opened up a terrifying new world for her.

Lyle looked back at the card, then again at Cassie. Then he gathered himself up without a word and slipped into the grieving room and closed the door.

Cassie had been right about finding Lindy Glode. But she didn't feel good about doing it.

She leaned back against the wall and waited. She couldn't hear the words but Lyle's soothing tone filtered through the paneling.

Cassie expected Lyle to emerge from the room, hand her back her card, and tell her that Lindy was too upset to consent to a meeting. Instead, the door opened and Lindy emerged with Lyle.

Lindy Glode was exactly what Cassie had imagined her to be: blond, thin, and curvy with blue eyes and a hard set to her mouth. She looked like she'd fit right in at the Hayloft. She also seemed frail; either hungover or truly overcome with emotion.

She said to Lyle, "Give us a minute, will you?"

"THANK YOU for seeing me and I'm very sorry about the timing. I'll try to keep this short." Cassie said.

Glode nodded. "I appreciate that. Lyle said you claimed you were there last night."

"I was. I saw it."

Glode looked up and her eyes flashed. "What the fuck happened? It doesn't make sense to me that a big truck just

288

drove off the highway and plowed through a motel and kept going." As she talked Cassie noticed how Glode pounded her right fist into her left palm with pure frustration.

"No, it doesn't make sense if you think of it as an accident. I know that's what the sheriff is claiming, but—"

"I don't trust anything that man says," Glode cut in. "He's bought and paid for."

"So I gather. I'd classify what happened as a homicide. What I can't determine at this point is if the driver was aiming for me or your stepmother or both."

Lindy Glode stopped pounding her fist. The implication of what Cassie just said took her aback.

"Why would someone want to kill Linda?"

"I don't know."

"Why would they want to kill you?"

"I've turned over a lot of rocks since I've been here. No one seems to like that."

"What happened last night?"

Cassie told Lindy Glode the story as briefly as she could, from meeting her stepmother at the sheriff's department to the incident the night before.

Glode listened closely and sadly shook her head while doing so. At the conclusion, she said, "It sounds just like them."

"Them?" Cassie asked.

"You know who I'm talking about."

"The Kleinsassers?"

Glode nodded her head. Then she smiled slightly. "You know that detail about you going to get soda and ice? That sounds just like her. The sweeter the drink the better as far as she was concerned. I used to tell her to learn to drink like a real woman, and she'd just laugh at me. Who knew it would be the death of her?"

Or what saved my life, Cassie thought but didn't say.

"She wanted to quit that job she had," Glode said. "I hope that wasn't the reason they went after her. But it was hard for her to give up the benefits. My dad is disabled."

"I understand. I know it's not much consolation but she died quickly. She didn't suffer."

"That happens when a truck tire rolls over your head," Glode said bitterly.

"Do you have any idea what she wanted to tell me?" Cassie asked. "She led off by saying you two were related."

"Yeah. I think she heard you were looking for me. I heard the same thing. She was worried about me."

"Why was she worried?"

"I think she heard something at her job to make her worried. Maybe she wanted you to find me before the sheriff did. You know, because of that thing I had with Blake."

"They might have found out that I wanted to talk with you because the room was bugged," Cassie said. "I found the device."

"That doesn't surprise me at all. It sounds like something they'd do."

"Did your mom know where you were living?"

"No," Glode said. "I move around a lot. I stay with friends. She didn't know exactly where I was but she knew who to ask. We kept in contact through text messages."

"I do that with my own son," Cassie said. She wasn't sure why she said it.

"Yeah, well. It looks like they got to her before they got to me."

"And all of this was because of Blake?"

"No doubt in my mind."

Cassie studied Glode's face and tried to put things together. She was having trouble understanding what Lindy was telling her.

"What is it they wanted?" Cassie asked. "Do you have information that would benefit Blake's case? Is that why you were hiding?"

Glode shrugged. "They seem to think so. Or at least, that's what I was told by someone who was in the position to know."

"Who would that be?"

"Cheyenne Porché," Glode said. "She was a customer at the bar. She told me her brothers were worried about me and she said I should disappear for a while."

This was information Cheyenne hadn't shared.

"That makes no sense," Cassie said. "Cheyenne should want Blake prosecuted more than anyone else. Do you know why she told you that?"

"No. But I believed her. Especially when Rand and Sheriff Wagy came by the Hayloft the next night and asked about me. Lucky for me, I'd taken the night off. And I haven't been back since."

"And you don't know why they were trying to find you?"

"No," she said. "I don't. I told the prosecutor and Blake's old lawyer everything I remembered. I wasn't with Blake the night it happened. Half of the time we were together I really can't even remember, to be honest. I don't think Blake does, either."

"He doesn't," Cassie said. "He said he was mostly blacked out the time you two were together."

Glode snorted. "That's not exactly what a girl wants to hear—that the man she was with for forty-eight hours straight can't remember a damned thing about it. But Blake is Blake, I guess. I know he's an asshole, but I got along with him. I guess I like ass-holes. My track record is filled with them."

"I've got a few in my past," Cassie conceded. "So you don't recall anything Blake said or did that would be relevant to the charges?"

"Not that I can remember," Glode said. "Like I said, it's all kind of hazy. We drank, we fucked, then we drank some more."

Cassie tried not to react to the bluntness of her statement. She asked, "Did he ever come across to you as someone capable of raping his niece?"

Glode shrugged again. "He didn't seem like that kind of guy, but who knows? I know sometimes I have blind spots. Like, why was I hanging out with the guy in the first place? We both knew it wasn't going to go anywhere. As for Franny, I don't remember him talking about her very much except to say that he liked her more than the others."

"In what way?" Cassie asked while narrowing her eyes.

"Not in that way," Glode said with a shake of her head. "Blake said he liked Franny because she didn't seem to have what he called the Kleinsasser gene."

"What does that mean? The Kleinsasser gene?"

"I think he meant she wasn't toxic."

"Ah."

Glode said, "I do remember getting kind of paranoid when I was with Blake. I'd see a sheriff car parked down the street from the bar, or I'd see John Wayne or Rand out of the corner of my eye. Blake just laughed about it because he said his family suspected he was back to do them some kind of harm, which he said he wasn't. He all but convinced me I was paranoid and losing it."

Cassie urged her to continue.

"I know all about the bad blood between Blake and his family. Everybody does around here. Maybe I was just sort of imagining things. But at the time I had the feeling they were shadowing us as we went from bar to bar and back to the motel."

"Did you tell the prosecutor or lawyer about that feeling?"

"No," she said. "I knew how nuts it sounded. Plus, they weren't asking me about my feelings. They just wanted me to confirm I was with Blake for two full days leading up to the arrest, which I was."

"Obviously," Cassie said, "those feelings you had were strong enough that you listened to Cheyenne when she told you to run and hide."

"Obviously," Glode repeated. "I mean, they must have figured Blake told me something they didn't want me to repeat. I've beaten my head against the wall trying to figure out what that might be but for the life of me I can't come up with anything. We just talked about life and drinking and fucking, like I said."

"Got it," Cassie said. "When you say you knew they were probably following Blake around, what exactly do you mean?"

"I know they were," she said. "I caught them."

Cassie didn't understand.

"After the second night we were together," she said, "I left his room that morning and realized I'd left my cell phone there. I was *really* hungover. I went back to the Whispering Pines in my car because obviously I couldn't call Blake to ask him if he'd found it. But when I got there he'd already left for the day and they were searching his room."

Cassie felt hair prick up on the back of her neck. "Who was searching his room?"

"There was a deputy there inside the room. The manager was standing outside. He must have let the cop in, is what I thought at the time."

"Can you identify the deputy?"

"He has an unpronounceable name," she said. "Gregor-something. I've seen him around. He still works for the sheriff, which means he works for the Kleinsassers."

"The manager was Glen Steele?"

"I guess. I really didn't meet him. Oh, and I saw John Wayne and Rand there, too. They were sitting together in a pickup. They left when I showed up."

"What happened next?" Cassie asked.

"I told the manager I'd left my phone in the room and he told the cop I was coming in."

"Did they say why they were searching the room?"

"No, and I didn't ask. Like I said, I was so hungover. And after spending all that time with Blake, I'd had my fill of Kleinsasser drama. I just wanted to go home and sleep it off."

"Lindy, did you see anything unusual in the room? What was Deputy Grzegorczyk doing?"

"He was on his hands and knees looking under the bed. In fact, he was the one who found my phone. It was on the floor. He handed it to me and I went on my way."

"And this was the morning of the assault, correct?"

"Yeah, but of course I didn't know it at the time," she said.

Cassie observed that Glode was tired and running out of steam. She understood. The girl had been through a lot.

"This is all really interesting," Cassie said. "Thank you. Is there anything else you can recall?"

"Not really. I'm exhausted."

"You have my card," Cassie said. "If you think of anything please give me a call."

Glode sighed. She said, "Honestly, I probably won't. I think I'm hitting the bricks as soon as the funeral is over. I really don't want to stay here anymore. I need a fresh start somewhere—maybe Seattle. I hear it's cool. Don't tell the Kleinsassers."

Cassie grinned and hugged her. "I won't," she said.

CASSIE WAS NEARLY to the lobby when she stopped. She turned back around slowly. Lindy Glode had returned to the grieving room and Lyle was making his way back to his chair.

Cassie suddenly recalled the condition of unit eleven immediately after she'd checked in. Before Glen did a thorough cleaning.

She returned to the alcove in front of the grieving room.

"I need to ask Lindy one more thing," she said to Lyle.

Lyle sighed. "Haven't you taken up enough of her time?"

"Please."

Lyle sighed and stuck his head in the room. Without being asked, he trudged away as Lindy Glode came out.

"I need to ask you a very personal question," Cassie said.

Glode screwed up her face as if expecting anything.

"When you and Blake had sex in the room at the Whispering Pines, did he use a condom?"

Glode's shoulders relaxed and she smiled. Cassie could only guess what the girl had been anticipating.

"Of course he did," she said. "I always insist on it. None of them like to, of course. But it's a deal-breaker for me. I don't want STDs and I sure as hell don't want a baby. Can you imagine me as a mother?"

Cassie ignored the question. "Do you have any idea what Blake did with the condom when you were done?"

"Which time?" she asked with a devilish grin.

"Anytime."

"He got rid of it, I guess."

Cassie said, "Did he go to the bathroom and flush it away? Did he toss it in the waste can? Please try to remember. This is important,"

She shook her head. "I really can't remember. I was probably mixing up a new cocktail at the time."

"Is it possible he dropped one on the floor?" Cassie asked.

"Anything's possible, I guess. He was pretty sloppy by that point as well. Why are you asking me these questions?"

"Because when I checked into that same room there was an old condom wrapper on the floor. Under the bed. Maybe at one point there was a used condom there as well."

Glode winced. "That's kind of gross."

"It is," Cassie agreed, "But it would be a really efficient way of collecting Blake's semen."

Lindy Glode furrowed her brow. She didn't understand what Cassie was getting at.

"Plus," Cassie said, "They'd know what took place in that room between you and Blake. They'd know what to look for because they'd listened to you when you were in there."

"That's really sick," Glode said.

"It's likely even more than that."

TWENTY-FOUR

STILL REELING FROM her conversation with Lindy Glode, Cassie drove south from Hamilton on US-93 into a bank of smoke so thick it triggered the automatic headlights on her rental car. She'd plugged Jody Haak's address—2952 County Road 38—into her phone to find out that it didn't officially exist. The graphic on the screen suggested the closest address to the one she keyed in for Haak was 2800 CR-38. Nevertheless, she planned to follow the route where it took her and hope she'd somehow find his place. It wasn't the first time for Cassie that an obscure rural address didn't produce a satisfactory exact destination from her GPS in Montana.

Because of the smoke, Cassie drove well under the speed limit. She checked her side and rearview mirrors obsessively, hoping not to see a Lochsa County sheriff's department vehicle or a Kleinsasser ranch truck. If either were following her she couldn't see them due to the poor visibility.

She connected with Rachel as she neared her turnoff for

the county road that would take her deep into the mountains and over the top of Skalkhano Pass. Cassie glanced at a notice stapled to a wooden sign ordering residents along the road to evacuate due to the fire ahead.

When Rachel answered on the first ring, Cassie said, "The case against Blake might be falling apart. That's not to say he didn't do it, but the prosecution's case isn't the slam dunk we thought it was."

She relayed what she'd learned from Lindy Glode. Rachel's silence on the other end spoke volumes—she was hanging on to Cassie's every word.

When she was through, Rachel said, "Do you think Lindy would testify to what she told you?"

"I'm not sure. She seems ready to get out of this county as soon as her stepmother's funeral is over. I got the impression she wants to wash her hands of all things Kleinsasser."

"I don't blame her," Rachel said. "But we need to get her someplace safe where no one can get to her. Do you think you could convince her to ride with you here? We can put her up in a nice place."

"I can try."

"Please do," Rachel said. "Her testimony could be dynamite."

"Agreed. Now think about it," Cassie said to Rachel. "There are four foundational pieces of evidence they have to convict him: the semen on her clothes, the whiskey glass in the line shack with his fingerprints on it, the tire tracks from his rental car, and Franny's affidavit.

"So far, we've found out that Franny's clothing is missing but that DNA result is still pretty strong evidence on its own. But if the DNA came from a discarded condom found in the motel room, well, that's a big problem for them. We probably can't prove it unless somebody confesses, but it's big."

"It's unbelievable, is what it is," Rachel said. "I could drive a truck through that hole in their case."

"Then there's the glass," Cassie said. "I have no doubt at all that Blake's fingerprints are all over it. But how many glasses did he use when he went barhopping with Lindy Glode during his blackout drunk period? If he was being followed like Lindy thinks they were, anyone could have collected a glass or two from his table after he left the place.

"Three," Cassie said, "Blake didn't deny ever going to that line shack this summer. In fact, he mentioned to us that he drove to it to see if it was still there after all these years. There wasn't any rain here this summer, which is one of the reasons we have all the fires. His tracks could have been made days or even weeks before the assault accusation.

"What I'm saying," Cassie continued, "is that the whole case looks different if you consider that Blake might have been set up the whole time. And if the Lochsa County sheriff and his thugs were working with the Kleinsassers, which appears to be what happened, the whole scenario the prosecution has laid out falls apart.

"The enmity the family has for Blake is well-documented. That goes to motivation."

"I can see it," Rachel said. "You're sounding more and more like a defense lawyer all the time. This has reasonable doubt written all over it."

Cassie responded as if slapped. The last thing she ever wanted to hear was that she was sounding like a defense lawyer.

Then Rachel said, "This is all important, except for one big fat problem."

"Franny's statement," Cassie replied.

"Exactly."

"Have you set up an interview with her yet?"

"I've run into complications with that, but now they seem to make a little more sense," Rachel said.

Cassie waited for the explanation and she hoped Rachel would get on with it. The county road she was on wound up through the eastern mountains into the teeth of the fire. She wasn't sure how much longer she'd have a strong cell signal.

"Cheyenne didn't hide Franny away like we assumed," Rachel said. "Apparently, according to the school, Franny was taken from her mom by the Montana Child and Family Services Division for her own safety and placed in a foster home. I don't know the circumstances because it's under seal, but she was assigned a guardian ad litem in Bozeman."

"*What?* Why didn't we know about this?"

"It was kept confidential because she's fifteen," Rachel said. "I had to pry that information out of my friends at the school district, and they probably shouldn't have even told me. But in order to talk to Franny, I need permission from the guardian ad litem and I don't have a name yet."

Cassie was puzzled. "For her own safety?" she repeated. "Who did she fear?"

"I don't know."

"My money would be on her uncles or grandfather," Cassie said. This, she thought, might explain Cheyenne's odd reaction to Cassie's request to speak to Franny. But why would Cheyenne want to protect the siblings she despised, especially if they threatened her daughter?

Cassie put her thinking into words to Rachel.

"Again, I don't know," Rachel said. "It doesn't make sense

to me, either, except that there is a lot more going on here than we realized. We seem to be witnessing the Olympics of family dysfunction, right here in Montana."

Rachel went on to say that prior to Cassie's call, she'd had a conversation with the neurosurgeon in the hospital who was overseeing Blake Kleinsasser's injuries.

"They're going to put him into a drug-induced coma until the swelling on his brain goes down," Rachel said. "It may or may not work. The doctor said he gave it a five percent chance that Blake will ever recover."

Cassie shook her head, not sure of what to say or think.

"Are we still working for him?" she asked.

"Unclear at this point," Rachel answered. "I'd say yes, we proceed. Think of it this way: we're working for truth and justice, whether or not Blake comes out of this."

"I like that," Cassie said. "It's better than saying I sound like a defense lawyer."

"I thought you would," Rachel said with a sigh. Cassie could imagine her rolling her eyes as she said it.

"Oh," Rachel said, "I almost forgot. After we talked this morning I called the DCI and made a formal request for an investigation of law enforcement in Lochsa County. I got the strong impression they might have been waiting for someone like me to get the ball rolling."

The Division of Criminal Investigation for the State of Montana was the agency that not only certified law enforcement officers, but it was the one entity that had the mandate and authority to look into malfeasance at a local or county level.

"Good call," Cassie said.

"Which is one more reason why you need to get out of

there as fast as you can," Rachel said. "My guess is that Sheriff Wagy is not going to like it when DCI agents show up."

Then Rachel asked, "What turned it for you? What happened that made you start thinking of this whole case a hundred and eighty degrees differently than when you started?"

"I just followed the evidence," Cassie said. "There's a big difference working with law enforcement when they want to help you and when they want to obstruct what you're doing. Then when that truck drove through my room and killed that poor woman, I knew they thought I was getting too close to the truth—whatever it is.

"The thing is," Cassie said, "they overplayed their hand. If they all would have just cooperated and stepped aside, I think I would have proceeded and concluded that the case was a little sloppy but it was as solid as it looked at first. There were red flags like the missing underwear, but there are *always* red flags. But they had to keep overdoing it, like destroying my car and putting me in jail for the night. They thought they'd chase me off."

"They were messing with the wrong woman," Rachel said.

Cassie blushed and changed the subject. "I still don't know where the truck driver fits, though. I don't know if he's somehow involved or on an entirely separate track."

"I only heard half of that," Rachel said through popping static.

Cassie pulled over to the shoulder of the road and checked her phone. She had only one bar of cell reception.

"Can you hear me?" she asked.

There was no response, followed by a prompt that said NO SERVICE.

"Shit," she cursed.

CASSIE REALIZED she'd been in such intense discussion with Rachel that she hadn't paid enough attention to her surroundings. The paved two-track road had given way to gravel, and it climbed and wound up into the mountains following the curves of a nearly dry creek. The canyon walls on both sides were nearly vertical. Smoke poured down through the canyon from fires on both sides like a current of water through a chute.

The fire was close although she couldn't see it clearly because of the smoke. It produced an eerie orange glow ahead, and ash fell on the hood of her car and the windshield.

She checked her GPS to see that the address she'd settled on was less than two miles farther up the road. She assumed Haak's property would be near it—if it was even his property at all. And if he had remained in his house despite the posted fire evacuation orders.

When her rearview mirror suddenly filled with the headlights of a massive truck coming up the road behind her Cassie's heart pounded with panic. She felt the power and weight of the vehicle vibrating through her rental and she gripped the steering wheel and held her breath. She braced for a violent rear-end collision.

But instead of the eighteen-wheeler she feared, it was a heavy mountain fire truck. It shot past and she got a glimpse of a firefighter in the passenger seat gesturing for her to turn around.

She gave a "will do," wave to him and waited for the truck to vanish into the smoke. When it did, she eased back onto the road with her phone on her lap and continued on.

TWENTY-FIVE

CASSIE DROVE PAST a turn-in for 2800 that was marked only by a dented rural mailbox. She couldn't see a home on the end of the road because of the thick trees and hanging smoke. She decided to go another mile in search of an additional road that might lead to 2952.

The conditions were getting worse the farther she drove up into the canyon. Not only ash but live embers floated through the air.

She nearly drove past it—an unmarked path off the right side of the road that led into a thick wall of trees. There was not even a mailbox, but she noted fresh tire tracks in the ruts. Cassie backed up, dropped the transmission into drive, and took the road.

It curved through two walls of pines on either side of the road and when she saw that the crowns of the trees she was driving under were actively inflamed she accelerated. A short burning branch fell across the hood of her rental and landed with a shower of sparks. She pushed through because she sensed a clearing ahead of her where she hoped she could turn around. The acceleration of the car caused the burning branch to roll off the hood and to the side of the road.

Paint blistered on the hood of her car from the heat of the fire and smoke filled the interior. Taking the two-track had been a mistake, she concluded.

A smudge appeared ahead that became a small log home as she neared it. There were a pair of pickup trucks parked near the front and a flatbed trailer was on the side of the home. She recalled that Frank in the Corvallis Tavern had been there because he wanted to borrow a flatbed from Jody Haak.

And there he was in the flesh: Jody Haak standing in the front lawn of the structure wearing a battered straw cowboy hat and bib overalls. He was arcing a stream of water from a hose at the roof of the house to wet it down. His back was to Cassie as she drove up although she'd seen his profile as he glanced to the side.

She parked and got out. She could hear the roar of the fire up in the canyon. It sounded like a jet engine. Embers floated through the air and landed on the moistened shake shingles of Haak's house, where they extinguished with sharp hissing sounds.

A yellow piece of heavy equipment roared around the side of the house. It was a skid-steer loader and it was plowing up a ditch in the dark loam. She couldn't see who was driving it.

"Jody Haak?" she called out.

The man froze. The stream of water from his hose wavered for a moment. Then he turned and shook his head.

"You found me," he said. "How in the hell did you do that?"

She didn't explain.

"Is there anything I can do to help you save your house?" she asked.

"I appreciate the offer. I could use some help. But for right now, just stay out of the way of that skid steer," Haak said. "We're building a firebreak."

Cassie stepped back and watched as the loader passed between them. The blade churned up dark soil and exposed rocks and lengths of white tree roots that looked like bony fingers. As it went by she got a full look at the driver.

Alf Grzegorczyk, out of uniform and wearing soot-covered jeans and a cowboy shirt, tipped the brim of a ball cap to her as he went by. He had a sly smile on his face and he seemed to enjoy her look of befuddlement.

CASSIE ASSISTED, as directed, by moving heavy plastic containers of fuel from a shed alongside the house and placing them in a creek that snaked through the property. She noted that the water in the creek was warm and murky with ash, but at least the fuel wouldn't ignite and take out the shed and the home. Her clothes and hands were filthy with dirt and soot.

The fire seemed to pass right over them from the top, igniting the crowns of the pines but largely not burning to the lower branches or to the floor of the valley. It created its own environment as it moved, heating up channels of rushing hot air and swirling through the timber. One line of flame did drop to the dry pine needles and yellow grass, and it flew along the surface toward the house until it met with the freshly upturned soil of the firebreak, where it stopped and went out.

Next, she found another spigot and hose behind the home and wetted down a four-foot-high stack of split firewood. The light pine turned dark as she soaked it. But it didn't catch on fire from the floating embers.

In the distance, she could hear the rumble of mountain fire trucks on the road. They were racing down the canyon to try and head off the flames, she guessed.

The worst of it was over for now.

CASSIE FOUND Jody Haak and Alf Grzegorczyk sitting on opposite sides of a splintered picnic table in Haak's front yard. They were drinking cans of Coors beer and there was a small plastic cooler on the tabletop between them.

She approached tentatively. "Why didn't you evacuate?" she asked. "I saw the orders on the way up."

Haak shrugged. "Where would I go? If you didn't already figure it out, I prefer to keep a real low profile since I got back. Showing up at the high school gym with a bunch of locals who know me didn't seem like a very smart move. Word gets around here pretty fast, you know."

"I've learned," she said. "Who are you hiding from?"

"I think we saved the place," Haak said, ignoring her question. "Thank you for pitching in like that."

She nodded. Her eyes were on Grzegorczyk. He didn't seem hostile.

"Join us and have a beer," Haak said. "You deserve it."

"I think I'll pass on the beer."

"That's right," Haak said. "If you're a wine gal. I might have a bottle or two in the house."

He started to get up but Cassie said, "Really, I'm fine."

"Suit yourself." He settled back down.

"I was hoping I could ask you a few questions," she said.

"I figured as much."

Haak and Grzegorczyk exchanged a look. Whatever was conveyed resulted in Grzegorczyk rising from the table and turning back toward the skid steer.

"Guess I'll churn up some more ground," he said while snatching another beer from the cooler.

She waited for him to go, then took his place at the table.

"We have a little history," she said.

"I'm aware of it," Haak said with a slight smile. "But Alf's a good guy. You may have him all wrong."

"Maybe not."

Haak shrugged. Oddly enough, she thought, the man looked more bemused and relaxed—even with the forest fire all around him—than she remembered from seeing him at the bar. It was as if he was resigned to her being there. She thought that she might be able to use his resignation to her benefit.

"He quit, you know," Haak said as he nodded toward Grzegorczyk's back.

"The sheriff's department?"

"Yes."

"Because of what he did to me?" she asked.

Haak looked long and hard at her. "No," he said, "because of what he didn't do to you."

She narrowed his eyes at him, not understanding.

"You spent the night in jail," Haak said. "You weren't supposed to ever get there."

"What does that mean?"

"You were supposed to disappear, never to be heard from

again. Alf couldn't go through with it. He's the reason you're here today."

"What do you mean—disappear?"

Haak took a long drink from his can of beer, then opened another. "Lochsa County has more than its share of missing persons. If you did a deep dive in the records over the years you'd find that out. I'd guess that more people go missing per capita in Lochsa County than anyplace else in Montana, including the reservations. It's been happening for years."

"My God," Cassie said. "It's the Kleinsassers?"

"They run everything," Haak said. "It would be hard to prove, but that's the way things work around here. That's the way they've *always* worked."

"How can you be so sure?"

"Because I used to be one of 'em," Jody Haak said.

"Tell me about it," Cassie said. "And I just might have a beer."

He nodded his approval.

JODY HAAK worked for the Iron Cross Ranch as the foreman for twenty-six years, he said. He was hired by Horst II when he returned to the valley after serving in the U.S. Navy, and for most of those years he was the only permanent employee on the ranch. Horst II preferred that Haak use transients when he needed manpower rather than full-time employees for tax reasons—they were paid in cash—and because transients could be cut loose quickly and without process if they got too familiar with the operation or started asking too many questions. It was the standard operating procedure on the ranch since it had been founded.

"That's something you might find a little hard to believe," Haak said, "but the Iron Cross has never been a prosperous ranch. They're land-rich but cash-poor. The only way they could stay in operation was to shoestring it and do everything they could to have their fingers in everything that happened in the county. Jakob learned early on that if it was a level playing field his whole ranch would go under in a hurry. So, they had to control things: the county government, the school system, the adjuster's office—everything."

"The sheriff's department," Cassie added.

"Oh, yes," he said. "There hasn't been a sheriff in that county that wasn't handpicked by the family in years. Same goes with the county attorney, Horston's mayor, the bankers, and most of the business owners. People who don't like it move out or they disappear. It's just the way it goes around here. Jakob and Horst would rather control everything than let the free market work. That's why this whole valley is booming except for Lochsa. You can see it as you drive from south to north."

Cassie nodded for him to go on.

"When I got married to Cindy Lou we moved out on the ranch to a damned fine house," he said. "Horst made sure I was happy and we had a hell of a deal. I had a free house, free beef, free transportation, and enough cash to live pretty good. I kind of felt privileged. I'll admit that I liked it when I was younger. Everybody in Horston knew I was the man from the Iron Cross, and they treated me with the same kind of respect they treated Horst or Margaret or the kids. I kind of let it go to my head, which is something I feel like shit about now."

"Why you?" Cassie asked.

Haak nodded. "I sometimes wondered the same thing myself. Cindy Lou, too. I mean, I *was* a good ranch manager. I was a tough negotiator when the cattle buyers showed up, and I maximized profits on every sale. I learned to hire folks who wouldn't stir up the family, and I cut them loose fast if they screwed up. I protected the interests of the Kleinsassers in every way, and I was rewarded for it."

As he spoke, Cassie could see that his thoughts were wandering off a little. She wondered if there was something he was trying to say but steering clear of it.

"I'd do stuff for 'em I really regret," Haak said, shaking his head. "It's too late now, but I wish I could take many of the things I did back."

"Like what?" Cassie asked.

He broke eye contact with her and stared over the top of her head. He said, "I'm going to miss that view of the mountain. Now all I can see is a bunch of burned trees."

She waited.

Finally, he said, "I'm not going to tell you everything but I'll give you one example."

"Okay."

"Cheyenne was a beauty growing up. If you met her you'd see what I mean. The boys buzzed around her like she was honey. And she didn't exactly discourage them."

Cassie saw no need to interject that she'd met Cheyenne and her effect on men was still the same.

Haak said, "There was a local kid named Steve Bishop. He was a big handsome kid, quarterback on the high school team. Anyone would tell you he was destined for great things. Montana State was looking at him for a football scholarship. His dad was a Lutheran pastor and they moved here from

Oregon. The Bishops hadn't been here long enough to learn about the Kleinsassers and the hold they have on everything. Either that or Steve just didn't care. He liked Cheyenne and she liked him. Too much.

"Horst didn't like the way things were going. He didn't want anyone encroaching on his family, especially some dumb preacher's kid who'd likely want to get married. Horst didn't like Lutherans, either, which was some old German Hutterite thing. He didn't want them polluting his line, you know?

"Well," Haak said, still refusing to look at Cassie, "it turns out that Steve picks up a little extra money babysitting in town. I know it sounds crazy that a high school athlete babysits, but it was a different time and that's what was going on. And I find out he's baby-sitting the kids of one of the guys I'd hired temporarily out on the ranch. This guy was deep in debt and hurting for money. So I had a little talk with him."

Haak shifted uncomfortably and turned his head. He spoke softly and Cassie watched his lips carefully so she could pick up every word.

"So this nine-year-old girl says Steve Bishop exposed himself to her and asked her to put it in her mouth. Then the sheriff finds her panties in Steve's old car. It was a hell of a scandal. The pastor and his family picked up and moved."

He turned to Cassie. His face was haunted. "Situation resolved."

"Horst paid off the father of the girl?"

Haak nodded.

"They've been at this kind of thing a long time," she said.

"That they have. It's the main reason Cindy Lou left me. She didn't like the man I'd become. I don't blame her for it."

"Why are you telling me all of this?" Cassie asked.

"Because I see in you an instrument to bring them down even quicker," he said.

"Which brings us to Blake."

"I figured that's where this was headed," Haak said.

ALTHOUGH BLAKE WAS bright and accomplished, Haak told Cassie that he was a major disappointment to his father because his oldest son had little interest in the family's history, legacy, or staying on the ranch.

"I've never seen anything quite like it," Haak said. "Most parents I know would be proud as hell that their boy got all kinds of honors and awards. But not Horst. It just made him angry that Blake was able to accomplish all these things on his own. Horst thought Blake made him and the rest of the family look like second-class citizens, and I heard him say it more than once. Of course, Blake heard it, too, and it drove him even further away from the Kleinsasser clan.

"I remember Cindy Lou telling me she thought the Kleinsassers reminded her more of a cult than a family. She was right about that, and Blake wanted out."

Haak sighed. "I really did like that kid and he stayed over at our bunk shack with my guys quite a bit when he was growing up. I think he preferred the company of stinky hired cowboys to being with his own family. Horst knew it, too, and he was always asking me to tell him what Blake said about him and his mom. He wanted dirt on his own son."

"Did you tell him?"

"I probably would have because I wasn't a good man back then," Haak said. "But the fact is Blake kept that kind of thing to himself. Even then, he kept his own counsel. He knew he was headed out of here the first chance he got, so he didn't try to stir things up to make that more difficult than it had to be, you know?"

Haak shook his head. "Horst is just like his dad. He's mean and vindictive as hell. And the way he treated his kids—all those years, I looked the other way. I wish now I would have stepped in or called social services or something."

"He treated the other kids poorly?" Cassie asked.

"He turned them into dependents instead of independent people. Horst was so pissed off at his oldest son for going his own way that he drilled Cheyenne, John Wayne, and Rand on what he called the Kleinsasser way. Those kids grew up thinking they were some kind of entitled royalty in this valley and they would always be like that as long as their dad favored them. He made them hate Blake as much as he did. It's what bonded them all together: envy, resentment, and hate. No wonder that they all turned out to be monsters."

"Do you include Blake in that description?"

Haak hesitated. "No," he said. "Blake got out in time. But he's still screwed up. I spent some time with him this summer. I'll admit I told him some things I probably shouldn't have about his dad and the rest of them. None of it surprised him, though."

"Like what?"

"Blake didn't realize what a hold he has on the rest of them," Haak said. "He thought by going his own way they'd forget about him. But it was just the opposite. The more he did, the more he accomplished on his own, the more they resented him for it. So when he showed up here it was like lighting a fuse on a stick of dynamite. He never really got that."

"Do you think he was set up?" Cassie asked.

"No doubt in my mind," Haak said. "It was the same MO as what we did to Steve Bishop. Only this time, I think John Wayne and Rand were behind it all, along with the sheriff. They learned plenty from Horst before he had his stroke."

Cassie simply nodded.

"I can't prove any of that," Haak said.

"That's my job," Cassie said. Then she asked, "Where do Cheyenne and Margaret play in all of this? Do you think they bought into the Kleinsasser way to the same degree John Wayne and Rand did?"

"I could never really tell about Margaret," Haak said. "She didn't say much and I don't think she holds any sway over Horst or her sons. They just ignore her and I don't think they respect her at all. As for Cheyenne—who knows? She tried to make it on her own when she moved overseas and married that French guy. But she came back with her tail between her legs, so to speak. She's headstrong, for sure, but I don't think the rest of them pay any attention to her."

"Even though she's the second oldest in the litter?" Cassie asked.

Haak shook his head. "It doesn't matter to them. After all, she tried to get away. In the mind of the males, that revealed her weakness. She'll never get back in even though they let her live there."

"You've thought a lot about the Kleinsassers," Cassie said.

"I have. I spent years watching that slow-motion car wreck."

"So why did you leave the Iron Cross?"

Haak flinched. "John Wayne fired me after Horst became incapacitated. Twenty-six years and boom—I'm out the door."

"Did he say why?"

"He didn't need to. John Wayne never liked the fact that I

got along with his brother. As long as I was around I would remind him of Blake. Plus, he wanted to clear the deck and consolidate his power. Cheyenne's too flaky to be a threat to him and Rand worships the ground he walks on. He really believes that Kleinsasser way shit. Especially now that Blake's out of the way.

"But there's another reason he fired me," Haak said.

Cassie urged him to go on.

"Have you ever heard of rare earth minerals?"

"No, I don't think so."

"I didn't know much about them until recently, either, but John Wayne is convinced that the Iron Cross is sitting on tons of 'em. He thinks he's going to get rich real soon."

"*What?*"

Haak labored to his feet and chinned toward his house. "Let me show you something inside," he said.

PART V

Mother died today. Or maybe yesterday, I don't know.
—ALBERT CAMUS, *The Stranger*

Three generations of imbeciles are enough.
—OLIVER WENDELL HOLMES, *Buck v. Bell*

TWENTY-SIX

"IT'S CALLED NEODYMIUM," Jody Haak told Cassie as he spread a sheaf of papers across his rough-hewn table. "It's a chemical element that's widely distributed across the globe but really rare to find in concentrated form."

Cassie looked at photos and graphics of the mineral on several printouts Haak had gathered. Neodymium was silver-white in color and displayed on the sheets in either powder or crystalline form.

"I'm no expert at all," he said, "But I've read a lot about it. Most of it in the world today is mined in China and it's used in the manufacture of all sorts of high-tech gadgets like lasers, computer hard disks, glass for high-tech lightbulbs— all sorts of things. Its big selling point is that it's used to make really powerful magnets for hybrid motors for cars— so it's increasing in price every year. It's gone as high as five hundred bucks per kilogram recently."

Cassie made the leap. "Horst and John Wayne think there are supplies of it on the Iron Cross Ranch."

"John Wayne does," Haak corrected. "I don't think Horst has any idea. Maybe Rand knows, but I doubt anyone else has a clue."

"Hold it," Cassie said. "I remember seeing a utility pickup coming out of the Iron Cross when I went there. It didn't quite fit because it was in a line of cattle haulers. But I remember it said 'REMR, Houston, Texas' on the door of the truck."

Haak nodded. "Real Earth Mineral Recovery. I looked them up. John Wayne hired them to do survey work after Horst had his stroke, and I'd seen them sniffing around well before that. John Wayne has spent every nickel the ranch has on retaining REMR. They've already started filing environmental impact statements, from what I understand. And he's gotten a bunch of loans from his friendly bankers in town to do the preliminary work. He's deep into debt to them. I don't think the old man is even aware of what's going on."

Cassie sat back. If what Jody Haak told her was true, things were starting to fall into place.

"The Iron Cross Ranch has always just kind of limped along financially," Haak said. "I know that for a fact. It's damned hard to make money off of cows, and there is too much timber for growing much of anything. There were years when it all looked so bleak I thought Horst might have to sell pieces of it off or even get rid of the whole operation. The Kleinsassers have always gotten by by the skin of their teeth. But John Wayne thinks he's figured out a way to make himself a multimillionaire. He's banking everything on a neodymium mine located in the foothills of the mountains."

"What do you think?" Cassie asked. "Is he right?"

Haak nodded his head yes. "The mineral is there. It may not be in the quantities John Wayne is hoping for, but there's enough of it to create the biggest mine in North America. I know it to be true because I talked to an REMR employee about it one night in the Corvallis Tavern. He confirmed everything I've told you. Those guys are supposed to keep everything confidential, but it's surprising what a man will tell you if you're buying."

Cassie felt electrified. "Talk about motivation for getting Blake out of the picture," she said. "Did you tell Blake about it?"

"I didn't." Haak said. "I probably should have. That would have really made things interesting, wouldn't it? But you can see now why John Wayne and Rand didn't want to talk about selling or diversifying the ranch and all the other ideas Blake had. They just wanted him to go away."

"I know about the Kleinsasser Trust," Cassie said. "They wanted him not only to go away but to be ineligible to make decisions or share in the windfall. So, they settled on a plan that would trigger the moral turpitude clause."

"They were successful," Haak said. "But what John Wayne doesn't know is that he's basing everything on air."

Cassie cocked her head, not sure what Haak meant.

"That's why I came back," he said. "That's why I've been hanging around in the background. I want to be here when the Kleinsassers go down once and for all. I want to see it happen. That'll be the sweetest thing I've ever witnessed when it happens, and one of the best things that ever happened to Lochsa County."

"What are you talking about?" Cassie asked.

Haak sat down. His eyes were animated, as were his

gestures. "I was with Horst twenty years ago in his office when he signed away his mineral rights."

"*What?*"

"It was a really bad year," Haak said. "Beef prices were in the toilet, and Horst had overextended himself paying bribes and payoffs to keep afloat. He couldn't see any way out of it so he took a meeting with some land men representing an energy company. Horst knew there was no coal or oil on the Iron Cross because he's had several surveys done. But the land men didn't know that and Horst didn't disclose the information. He signed away his surface and subsurface mineral rights for cash. I saw him sign the contract."

"*John Wayne doesn't know,*" Cassie whispered.

"No one does except me," Haak said. "Horst made me promise to keep my mouth shut. But he really gloated about that deal—how he'd duped the land men into paying him for nothing. He always thought it was one of the best deals he ever did."

"Who has the mineral rights?" Cassie asked.

"Some conglomerate," Haak said. "That energy company sold out to a bigger outfit, and that one sold to an international conglomerate. It's hard to keep track. But I do know that they'll show up to claim their rights as soon as the word gets out about the neodymium deposits. And there's nothing John Wayne can do about it. With the debt he's racked up on his bet, they'll probably take the ranch away from him as well."

"My God," Cassie said.

"I've got a ringside seat to watch the fall of the Kleinsasser way," Haak said. "Would you like to pull up a chair and watch it with me?"

"THIS IS A LOT to take in," Cassie said to Haak, pushing away from the table. "But it works in a sick way. John Wayne had his scheme going when Blake just showed up out of the blue. John Wayne *had* to take Blake off the table in a way that would remove him from the trust."

Haak agreed.

"But what I don't yet understand is why Cheyenne cooperated with the fake assault and why she brought her daughter along with her? Why would Cheyenne suddenly decide to help out John Wayne and Rand when she obviously despises them?"

Haak said, "I don't have a theory on that. It doesn't make sense. Maybe the brothers had something on the two of them?"

Cassie shook her head. "Cheyenne doesn't seem like the type to meekly go along. I don't know her daughter, but this just doesn't make sense to me."

"Here," Haak said, sliding the information on neodymium across the table to her. "Take this with you. I've got copies. Maybe you can speed things along when you show this to the lawyer you work for."

Cassie gathered up the paperwork. Her head was pounding. Her mouth was dry.

"Thank you for all of this," she said.

"My pleasure," he grinned. He gave Cassie the number to a cell phone he rarely used. "Call me when it all goes down," he said. "I want to be there for it. I want to see the look on John Wayne's face."

"This *family*..." she said. She couldn't finish her thought.

"They need to go away for good," Haak said. "Are you going back to the ranch at some point?"

"I don't know," Cassie said. "I'm not sure I can get through the gate. It just happened to be open the last time."

Haak scratched out a series of numbers on a scrap of paper he'd torn from the documents. "Here," he said, handing her the scrap. "It's the key code for the front gate. They never changed it after I left."

"Remind me to never fire someone after twenty-six years of dedicated service," she said to Haak.

He laughed and slapped his knee.

AS SHE STEPPED over the firebreak on the way to her car, the skid steer zoomed up behind her. Cassie paused and turned around.

Alf Grzegorczyk leaned out of the metal cage. "Sorry about what happened to your car," he said. "That wasn't me."

She acknowledged him with a curt nod.

"I don't know who did it for sure," he said. "But I think we both have our suspicions."

He seemed to be waiting for her to thank him, she thought. But thanking a man for arresting her for no reason and not driving her into the timber and putting a bullet into her head didn't sit well with her.

She turned and strode to her car.

TWO MILES DOWN the road, her phone chimed with a series of texts and messages once she was back in cell phone range. They were all from Rachel.

When she had a strong signal Cassie speed-dialed Rachel's cell phone.

"You're alive!" Rachel answered. "I was starting to get really worried again."

"I'm more than alive," Cassie said. "I think the case has broken wide open."

"It absolutely has," Rachel said breathlessly. "How did you know?"

Cassie frowned. "How did I know what?"

"Franny recanted. I wasn't in the room with her two minutes before she said it was all a lie about the assault. She said her uncles put her up to it and she couldn't wait to tell someone."

"You're kidding," Cassie said.

"No. She agreed to give a new affidavit spelling it all out. She's coming into the office with her guardian ad litem tomorrow after school to do it."

Rachel went on to detail how the meeting had gone, how Franny had broken into hysterical tears and said how sorry she was for getting her uncle Blake into trouble.

"Why did she do it, then?" Cassie asked, suddenly filled with anger.

"She said John Wayne threatened to throw her and her mother out on the street if she didn't cooperate," Rachel said. "Franny said she did it to help out her mom."

"Do you believe her?"

"I don't know what to believe," Rachel said. "Franny does come across as quite the drama queen. But it's not my job to believe her or not. Let a judge or jury make that decision."

That grated on Cassie. "I thought you said we were doing this to discover the truth."

"We are," Rachel said, "but sometimes the truth is really complicated. We can only go on what we've got, and as of tomorrow we'll have a recantation of the assault taking place. Since you've got information to knock down the rest of their evidence, I think we're looking at an acquittal."

Cassie thought for a moment, then asked, "Who besides you knows about Franny's new statement?"

"Well, Jessica. Jessica was there with me. Oh, and Franny's guardian here in Bozeman."

"What do you know about the guardian?"

Rachel hesitated. "I don't know anything about her, really. Her name is Deb Rangold."

"Do a deep dive on her," Cassie said. "I can't do it myself at the moment. Find out everything you can about Deb Rangold and call me back."

"Why? I don't get it."

"Nothing in this investigation has turned out to be what it seems," Cassie said. "This whole social services thing seems fishy to me."

"I'll find out what I can," Rachel said. "Are you headed back now?"

"Not yet."

"*Cassie...*"

"I need to pay a visit to Cheyenne first."

TWENTY-SEVEN

CASSIE WAS WITHIN a half mile of the headquarters to the Iron Cross Ranch when she realized she didn't know where Cheyenne's house was located. She'd never been there before, and no one had pointed it out. The smoke was hanging so thick on the valley floor she couldn't clearly see the layout of the grounds. She wondered if the flames moving down from the mountains would destroy the ranch before she could find Cheyenne.

As Haak had indicated, the key code he'd written out opened up the entrance gates and she drove right through.

She parked out front and knocked on the heavy front door. When there was no response, she tried the latch. It was unlocked. She opened it a few inches and called inside. Silence.

This time, she didn't take off her boots. As she passed by an ancient mirror she was shocked at her appearance: sunken, red-rimmed eyes, dirt and soot-covered clothes, a tangle of hair, muddy boots from traipsing around Jody Haak's property.

"Margaret?"

Cassie thought she heard a chair leg scrape linoleum down the hallway in the direction of the dining room. She called out again.

"What do you want?" Margaret responded. Her voice was soft.

Cassie went down the hallway to find Margaret sitting at the table with a cup of coffee in front of her. To her right, two spots away, Horst slumped to the side in his wheelchair with his mouth gaped and a string of saliva that strung from his bottom lip to his left forearm. His eyes were open but opaque. He was gasping for air.

"Oh, dear. Do you want me to call 9-1-1?" Cassie asked.

"No need," Margaret said. "There's nothing they can do."

Cassie studied Margaret. She seemed oddly passive, even relieved. She seemed to be enjoying her coffee and the serenity of the silent room. She seemed younger than before, and lighter than air. Was she in shock?

"I think we forgot his medication this morning," Margaret said. Horst seemed to hear it and he emitted a low moan.

"It's his time," Margaret said. "We'll bury him up on the hill next to his father and his grandfather. They all like to be together. Other family members are buried farther down the hill."

Cassie wasn't sure what to make of that but the horror of the situation started to fill her up. She said, "We should probably call somebody. We can't just leave him here to suffer like this."

Margaret shrugged and sipped her coffee. "He's fairly quiet right now," she said. "No more of that horrible moaning. Can't you at least let me savor the moment?"

Cassie could hear a hundred-year-old clock tick in the next room. She asked, "Has it always been bad for you, or just since he had a stroke?"

"The stroke was a godsend," Margaret said calmly. She glanced over at Horst but he couldn't turn his head toward her. She was speaking for his benefit, and Cassie shuddered.

Margaret said, "It was like all of the pressure lifted off of my shoulders. I could just move him around the house to where I wanted him. I could feed him what *I* wanted to eat. I could leave him in the bathroom for hours with the door closed until he stopped bellowing, and he had no choice but to watch the television programs I favor. I could dress him in clothes he didn't like. For the last few months he's found out what it's like to be controlled by someone else."

Cassie shook her head. She had no words. Margaret's demeanor was absolutely calm.

Finally, Cassie was able to ask: "Can you please tell me where I can find Cheyenne?"

"Oh," Margaret said, "She's not here today. She went into town."

"Do you know where?"

"I never know where." She sighed.

"Thank you, Margaret. I'm leaving now. Are you sure you don't want me to call the sheriff or the ambulance?"

"Not now," she said. "Not yet."

Margaret turned to her husband and addressed him. "Horst, just sit there and be still. And don't give me that look, or I'll turn you toward the wall."

Horst's eyes widened and his lungs rattled out his last breath.

"There," Margaret said. "It's finally over."

Margaret closed her eyes and let out a deep sigh. A smile tugged at the corners of her mouth.

Cassie backed out of the room. She'd never seen anyone as cold-blooded.

THE REMR PICKUP emerged from the bank of smoke as Cassie reached for the door latch of her rental car. It pulled into the ranch yard and parked next to her. She didn't know the driver, who was obviously an employee of the company, but she nodded at John Wayne in the passenger seat.

The windows of the pickup powered down but neither man got out.

"What are you doing back here?" John Wayne asked her. His face was dark with anger, but he seemed to be trying to keep his emotions in check from the REMR man.

"You need to go inside," Cassie said. "Your mother needs you right now."

John Wayne cocked his head, then dismissed Cassie's suggestion. "I asked you what you were doing here."

"I'm here to pay my respects to the Kleinsasser family," Cassie said after a beat. "It's over, John Wayne. I know everything."

His face twitched. The color drained out of it.

"What in the hell are you talking about?" he asked.

"I know about your mine," she said. "I know how you framed Blake. I know enough to put you into Deer Lodge prison for a very long time."

"You're crazy," he said. He forced a laugh for the sake of the REMR man who was now looking back and forth from John Wayne to Cassie as if watching a tennis match.

"You don't own the mineral rights," she said. "Somebody else is going to make all the money."

John Wayne reacted as if he'd been slapped. The REMR man looked over at him accusingly.

"I knew you were crazy," John Wayne said to Cassie. Then to the REMR man, "She's crazy. Don't listen to a word she says."

Cassie said, "We'll see. What did you have on Cheyenne and Franny to convince the girl to make up that story?"

"It wasn't a story," he said. "It was the truth. My brother did it."

Cassie shrugged. "I'm sick of talking to Kleinsassers."

"You don't know anything," John Wayne hissed.

"Where's Rand?" she asked before opening her car door. She gestured toward the house. "He might want to be here for this."

"He's on a run," John Wayne said. Then: "Be here for *what*?"

"Go inside."

With that, she swung into her Honda and backed out of the ranch yard. She hoped it was for the last time ever.

SHE DROVE TO LOLO as darkness overtook the valley and the fires in the mountains zigzagged across the slopes.

CHEYENNE WAS ON the same stool in the Hayloft she'd been on when Cassie first met her. She sat alone within a cloud of cigarette smoke that was lit up pink from the neon beer signs behind the bar. When Cheyenne saw Cassie, she narrowed her eyes and raised her chin and blew out a long stream of smoke.

Cassie sat down next to her and ordered a cup of coffee from the bartender. Cheyenne ordered another bourbon on the rocks. Cassie could tell by the deliberate way Cheyenne spoke that she'd been drinking for hours.

Cheyenne lifted her glass. "To my lovely father," she said. "May he rest in peace."

"So you know."

Cheyenne nodded.

"Who told you?"

"Mother called."

Cassie was surprised. "When I left I told her I thought she should call someone."

"*Moi*," Cheyenne said.

"You seem okay with the news."

"I'm more than okay. I'm ecstatic, can't you tell?"

Cassie looked Cheyenne over. She looked put-together and dangerous at the same time.

"I'm leaving now," Cassie said.

"It's about time."

"But before I do, tell me about Franny," Cassie said. "And this time try to stay cool."

A whisper of a smile floated across Cheyenne's mouth. "Give me your phone."

"Why?"

"I don't want a record of what I'm about to tell you."

Cassie had not activated the recording app on her phone so she passed it over. Cheyenne powered it off and placed it facedown on the counter. She asked, "What do you want to know?"

"Why is she in Bozeman under another name?"

"We thought it best. She might have wilted under the pressure around here. It was best for everyone that she try to live a normal life."

"Until she had to testify," Cassie said.

Cheyenne turned to Cassie and bent close to her. "She was never going to testify. She was always going to recant when the time was right."

Cassie froze for a moment. "You knew it was a false accusation."

"Of course I did. Anything John Wayne came up with was bound to be idiotic. He's really not very smart, you know."

"Why go along with it, then? I thought you got along with Blake."

"I do," Cheyenne said. "Or I should say I did. But getting him out of the trust wasn't personal. It was a business decision I made for me and my daughter. Blake has all the money in the world as it is."

That took Cassie a moment to process. Then she said, "You knew Horst didn't have long to live, so you set them all up: Blake, John Wayne, and Rand. You let it happen so all of them would be kicked out of the trust by a judge. But how can you expect to be the last one standing?"

She shrugged. "I have John Wayne on tape laying out the whole scheme to me. I have him making Franny repeat the story over and over until she had it right. I even have that idiot Wagy telling me not to worry—that he was fully on board and he could make it happen the way John Wayne dreamed it up. I recorded everything on my cell phone and I never said a word the whole time. There's nothing in those recordings that would implicate me, and it certainly *sounds* like those dumb-asses are threatening us to do what they want."

Cassie felt blindsided. She tried to get her bearings. "So, it was for control of the ranch? For the money?"

"Partly," Cheyenne said. "Not all."

"Then why?"

Cheyenne drained her drink and lifted a painted finger to signal for another. The bartender scrambled to accommodate her.

"You have no idea what it's like to be a female in that family," Cheyenne said. "It's been going on for over a hundred years and it wasn't going to change. My grandmother was abused. My mother was abused. *I* was abused. It was a matter of time before one of her uncles cornered Franny. It was a family tradition."

Cassie recoiled.

"We figured it was time to blast the men out."

"We?"

"Mom, me, and Franny."

"Your mother was in on it?"

"Not that it could ever be proven. But when Franny agreed, I knew we were set."

Cassie leaned back. She didn't want to be any closer to Cheyenne than she had to be.

"You're more depraved than I thought possible," she said.

Cheyenne smiled. "I came from toxic stock. It's in my blood."

Before Cassie could reply, Cheyenne said, "I didn't know they'd hurt Blake so badly in prison. They were just supposed to rough him up a little and help convince him to go back to New York when he could. I thought I could cut a deal with

Blake when he was acquitted. He could go back east and I'd stay just long enough to sell the ranch to the mineral people or whoever wanted it. That would be enough for Mom, Franny, and me. The men would be blasted out for good."

"My God," Cassie said.

"Not everything worked to perfection," Cheyenne said. "John Wayne is stupid but he's conniving. He didn't fully trust Franny so he had a friend of his in Bozeman serve as her guardian. They went to high school together. When I found out I warned Franny to just keep playing her role so the guardian wouldn't get wise to it. From what Franny told me today it worked perfectly. Deb Rangold didn't know that Franny was going to recant until it happened."

Cassie said, "Is Franny in danger? Are you worried that Deb Rangold might harm her?"

"No, not at all. Deb is a snitch but she isn't a criminal. She's probably snitched to John Wayne already, and I can only imagine what kind of state he must be in right now. But he wouldn't harm Franny directly. John Wayne is at his core a coward. He manipulates others to do his dirty work. He'd never do it himself."

"You've got it all figured out," Cassie said with sarcasm.

"Yes, I do. But I didn't know everything. I didn't know what role you would play in all of this," she said, clinking her bourbon glass against Cassie's coffee cup. "You really moved things along. I could just sit here and watch it all unravel all around me. It happened much faster than I thought it would."

Cheyenne took a long pull from her fresh drink. "I wish I could see John Wayne right now. His entire twisted world is falling apart, and he can't even get advice from his daddy."

"Do you know about the mineral rights?" Cassie asked.

Cheyenne nodded. "I met a man from REMR who sat where you're sitting now. It might not surprise you to find out that he told me all kinds of things that night."

"I'm not surprised."

Cheyenne made a "what are you going to do" gesture with her hands.

She said, "REMR isn't loyal to John Wayne. They're loyal to rare earth mineral deposits. They don't care who owns them."

"You and Franny may not walk," Cassie said. "I may not have a recording of your confession, but I'm duty bound to report it."

"We'll walk," Cheyenne said. "There's not enough there. No one is going to prosecute a fifteen-year-old girl who was pressured and threatened by her uncle."

Cassie knew she was probably right. "I need my phone back."

Cheyenne handed it to her.

"It was a pleasure to meet you, Cassie Dewell."

"I can't say the same."

Cheyenne tilted her head back and laughed at that. "I'll bet you can't wait to get out of Lochsa County."

"You're right about that."

TWO DCI AGENTS from Helena were waiting in their sedan next to Cassie's Honda. They got out, badged her, and asked if she had time to tell her story.

Cassie sighed and asked if they had all night.

★

IT WAS DAWN by the time she signed her statement and drove out of Lolo. She had a tremendous headache from talking all night. The sense of relief she felt when she crossed the Lochsa County line again was palpable.

The DCI agents had asked if she wanted to be there when they picked up Sheriff Wagy and John Wayne for questioning. She'd replied that she never wanted to see either one of them again although she knew she'd have to when she testified against them in court.

She couldn't wait to see Ben. And she couldn't wait to see her mother. Cassie craved some kind of normalcy.

The things she'd learned and conveyed within the last twenty-four hours were a jumble in her head, although she was proud of herself for being able to communicate a coherent time line of what she'd learned and what she'd been through to the DCI agents.

Still, though, something was missing. She wished she could define what was bothering her.

Then she remembered what John Wayne had said when she asked about Rand. He'd said, "He's making a run."

Making a run?

Then it hit her.

CASSIE WAS GRATEFUL and very surprised when Jody Haak answered his cell phone. She knew he must be somewhere other than at his place since she knew he didn't have service up the county road.

"It's happening," he said as a greeting. His tone was giddy. "My sources in town say the state cops are on their way to talk to John Wayne as we speak. They've already informed our sheriff that they've opened an investigation on him and his office."

"I know about that," Cassie said. "I have another question for you."

"Shoot."

"What does Rand do for a living?"

"You mean besides harassing tourists and laying around the Iron Cross?"

"Yes."

"He works freelance as a truck driver," Haak said. "He makes a couple of runs a week between Horston and Billings."

Cassie sat up straight and nearly drove off the road.

"He drives an eighteen-wheeler?"

"Yes, he does."

"Have you seen it?"

"If he still has the same rig I've seen it dozens of times," Haak said.

"Is it a black Peterbilt cab? Smoked windows? No chrome?"

"That sounds like it," Haak said.

"Anyone driving from Horston to Billings would go through Bozeman four times a week," Cassie said.

"I guess," Haak said.

She disconnected before saying goodbye. Then she woke up Rachel.

TWENTY-EIGHT

THE DRIVER, Rand Kleinsasser, sat high in his cab while the diesel engine idled. He'd parked once again on a residential street where he could have a good view of the grounds of Bozeman High School through his windshield. He watched as students entered the school that morning for their first period classes.

He narrowed his eyes when he saw Franny. She was within a knot of students but she was not of them. There seemed to be an invisible bubble around her that she floated in despite the other students streaming the same direction. There was no interaction with any of the other kids and she clutched her books to her chest as if wielding a shield. For a very brief moment, he felt for her. He understood what it was like to be an other. But that quickly passed.

He noted that she'd changed her look, all right. Her hair was shorter and darker, she wore more conservative clothing than he recalled, and she'd affected an awkward gait to her walk.

But it was her.

And it had been Franny on the street that day and now he was sure of it. Unfortunately, that damned boy she was with had pulled her out of the way at the last moment. But it was her.

Rand knew that she'd be going to her AP English class to start the day. Deb Rangold had outlined her schedule to John Wayne months before. The classroom was located less than seventy-five yards from the library and his cache of weapons.

WATCHING THE STUDENTS enter the building brought back unhappy memories for Rand. It all came rushing back once again, and he squirmed.

After he'd been expelled from Horston High for fighting, and despite his father's anger and threats to the Lochsa County school board, Rand had ended up in Bozeman all those years ago, where he attended Bozeman High his senior year. God, how he'd hated it.

They didn't know him there, and they didn't know that his name meant something. He'd been bullied and beaten when he tried to stand up for himself, and the girls looked down their noses at him when he tried to explain that back home he was somebody special.

He could remember the day outside the auto shop when he'd told a couple of his friends that someday he'd come back.

That someday they'd all know his name.

That day had come.

RAND HAD NEVER trusted Franny. She was too precious and too clever, too much like her mother. Even though John

Wayne assured him that he had everything under control—that Blake would go down with Cheyenne's and Franny's participation—Rand had his doubts.

Wouldn't it be better, he'd said to John Wayne, if something just happened to her before the trial? Something completely unrelated to the assault?

That way, he'd explained to his brother, her affidavit would stand there forever and be used to convict Blake. Franny couldn't screw up her story on the stand or change it.

Cheyenne might be a problem, but Cheyenne was always a problem. She was born a problem. But Franny's last statement—before she was gone—would stand like a monument.

Rand had reminded John Wayne about his suspicions—and his solution—when his brother had called him hours before in a panic. Rand was leaving Billings in his rig, bound for Horston with a load of drywall for the lumber store. He'd just delivered pallets of rough-cut logs from the Lochsa Valley, like they did twice a week.

Deb Rangold, John Wayne said, told him Franny planned to recant later that day at a lawyer's office.

"I fucking told you this would happen," Rand had said.

"What good does that do now?" John Wayne asked.

"Don't worry about it," Rand had said. "I've got it handled."

And he did. He was just waiting for the bell to go off to begin the school day.

Rand watched as a few stragglers ran across the lawn toward the front doors. Most of them made it inside before the bell went off. A couple didn't.

He wondered how many of the individual students he'd seen would come out of the building feet first.

★

THERE WAS A MOMENT of panic before Rand traded his cowboy hat for a black balaclava and got out of his cab. Out of the corner of his eye he saw a Bozeman police department cruiser flash through an opening in some tree trunks headed toward the west side of the high school. It was moving fast, he thought.

But then he lost sight of the cruiser, and he didn't see additional cops. The morning was quiet, and there were no sirens.

He figured the cop had chased down a speeding student trying to get to school on time. It was out of view on the opposite side of the big brick building.

Rand left the truck running. He climbed down and stuffed the balaclava in his front jeans pocket. There was no reason to put it on his head and risk drawing attention to himself. People were jumpy around schools these days.

He planned to leave his .22 pistol in the console of his truck, but at the last minute he snatched it out and slid it muzzle-down into his back waistband.

He crossed the lawn and didn't rush it. Like that night, he moved from tree to tree toward the back of the school. Rand could be a maintenance worker or a cafeteria employee out on his break.

At one point he glanced back at his rig. He wished it didn't look so beaten up. The black steel cowcatcher on the front of the grille was mangled, and the grille itself was smashed in. Both headlights needed to be replaced. He thought that if someone saw his truck sitting there they'd reason that it was out of commission and waiting for repair.

342

That's what happened, he thought, when you drove your truck through a motel.

AS HE WORKED his way down the side of the building toward the auto shop, Rand envisioned once again how it would go when he got inside. He'd gone over it in his mind a dozen times, but now that it was here he needed to concentrate. Which was hard. He'd always had a problem with that.

It was highly unlikely that a class would be in session in the auto shop. He recalled that vocational classes didn't start until later in the day. He assumed they maintained the same schedule. But if there were students in the auto shop for first-period class he was going to walk right past them with the mask over his face. He wouldn't threaten them or say a word. He'd just walk right by them as if he owned the place and leave them guessing. High school students weren't all that sharp first thing in the morning, especially auto shop losers like he'd been.

Then Rand would stride down the hallway toward the library without looking right or left. He'd pull down his cache of weapons and go straight to the AP English classroom and close the door behind him.

Franny wouldn't be the first to go. That would be too obvious. He'd start with the teacher and whatever targets made themselves available. Franny would be in the middle or toward the end. That way, no one would ever suspect that he was there specifically for her.

Because he wasn't. He was back for revenge. Franny was simply the vehicle to get him there.

Rand was crazy, but he wasn't stupid. He knew the

in-school cops might come after him. In a perfect world, they would. They'd take him out before he ran out an emergency door and drove away in his truck.

But it wasn't a perfect world. He'd read about other school shootings. He knew that there was just as much chance that the school security officers would cower outside waiting for backup, or hide in a closet once the shooting started.

RAND PAUSED at the corner of the building and poked his head around it. As he'd surmised, the security camera he'd disabled was still hanging limp from its mount. They hadn't even removed it yet.

Did he know how things worked in a state-run system, or what?

He fished the mask out of his pocket and pulled it over his head. He looked over his shoulder and out on the street. A car passed by but the woman driving it didn't even turn her head toward him.

The garage door shivered when he yanked on it and he could feel the latches give way. He took a deep breath and pulled up on the door and it sounded like thunder as it rolled up.

There were no students in the class, as he'd thought. Unfortunately, there were four black-clad SWAT cops wearing helmets and tactical gear and leveling automatic weapons at him. They took cover between two older-model cars inside and aimed at him over the hoods and trunks.

One of them screamed at him to get down on his belly.

To hell with that, Rand thought. Instead, he reached behind his back for his pistol. Who were they to tell *him* what to do?

It was the last thought Rand Kleinsasser ever had.

TWENTY-NINE

SIX WEEKS LATER, Cassie Dewell and Rachel Mitchell sat next to each other at the funeral of Blake Kleinsasser at Jenkins Funeral and Cremation Service in Bozeman. The ceremony took place in the smallest room in the facility because there were fewer than ten people in attendance. Blake's urn had been placed on a faux-granite column at the front of the room.

He'd died of his injuries five days before without ever regaining consciousness.

The funeral director had given a generic eulogy and no one had volunteered to say anything afterward.

The front row of seats was empty, but in the second row sat Jody Haak and Lindy Glode on opposite ends of the aisle. They'd arrived separately. Cassie and Rachel sat in the third row behind them.

Three of Blake's New York business associates were across the aisle. They'd introduced themselves but they spoke so quickly in their East Coast cadence that Cassie couldn't recall their names.

Margaret, Cheyenne, and Franny sat in the last row. They'd arrived late and Cassie noticed that Margaret looked vibrant and ten years younger than when she'd last seen her. She nodded at Cassie as if sharing a secret and then looked away.

Cassie was startled by Franny's appearance. She was dressed in funky clothing and she had a sexy, sophisticated haircut. She didn't look Cassie's way.

Cheyenne saw Cassie's obvious puzzlement and winked at her. "My God," Cassie shuddered.

CASSIE COULDN'T HELP noticing that the girl looked like a wholly different person than she had that day at the school, when Cassie arrived to find Rand's dead body sprawled out near the open auto shop garage door. At that time, Franny appeared frail and shaken. She knew what had almost happened to her, and she knew why.

Cassie had explained to her at the time that through Rachel the Bozeman PD had been on the lookout for Rand and his damaged tractor-trailer. When it was spotted on a side street near Bozeman High School, the SWAT team was dispatched inside. Their plan, until Rand decided to get out and walk into the building itself, was to lock down the school and then isolate and arrest him outside. Rand had literally walked into them as they were assembling.

"It was death by cop," Cassie had said to Franny. "Rand made the choice himself."

"That sounds like him," Franny had said.

Cassie had taken Franny in her arms and comforted her. She'd sat with her when Franny gave her statement to the police identifying her uncle and confirming that she'd lied under pressure. The authorities had treated her with kid gloves, and so had Cassie.

JOHN WAYNE KLEINSASSER was in the Missoula County Jail awaiting his criminal trial. The judge had agreed with state prosecutors that he shouldn't be housed in Lochsa County because of the very real chance that an associate might *accidentally* release him.

Sheriff Ben Wagy was suspended without pay from the Lochsa County Commissioners awaiting the conclusion of the DCI investigation into his department.

Both had been implicated by recordings that appeared on social media of them discussing how to frame Blake for rape and kidnapping. No one had claimed credit for posting the dialogue, but experts had determined that the recordings were authentic.

Prosecutors had dropped the charges against Blake Kleinsasser but he never knew it. Rachel was delicately attempting to receive legal fees for her work defending him from his estate once it was settled in probate court in New York State.

The Iron Cross Ranch was in the process of being sold to a Canadian land development company who'd already made an agreement with REMR and the conglomerate that owned the mineral rights to build a rare earth mine on the property.

Cheyenne was the sole beneficiary of the ranch sale, and rumors were circulating about the massive nine-bedroom home she was building at the confluence of the Lochsa and Bitterroot rivers.

THE FUNERAL CEREMONY didn't so much end as fade away, and Cassie looked up to find it was over. She turned her head to see Cheyenne ushering Franny and Margaret toward the back door.

"They're leaving," Cassie said to Rachel. "I'll catch up with you in a minute."

"Cassie," Rachel said, reaching out for her hand, "let it go."

"I can't."

The Kleinsasser women were almost to their new black SUV when Cassie caught up with them.

"Excuse me," she said.

Cheyenne turned and looked at her and her eyes narrowed. She proceeded to help Margaret into the passenger seat and then closed her door and turned around.

Franny stood off to the side. She seemed cold and detached although slightly taller than Cassie recalled. That was because she was no longer slouching. She looked at Cassie as if Cassie was someone she'd long ago left behind in another world.

"Yes?" Cheyenne said impatiently.

"They'll eventually catch you both," Cassie said. "I just want you to know that."

"We'll see," Cheyenne said with a smile. "But I wouldn't bet on it."

"I told the DCI agents everything. They know about you."

"I know you did," Cheyenne said. "I sat down with them for an interview. They didn't have much except your version of events and they never will. I'm quite good in those kinds of situations," she said, slyly batting her eyes and faux-fanning herself with her fingers.

Cassie said to Franny, "You broke Ben's heart. You do know that, right?"

Franny shrugged. "He's a nice boy, I guess. You should be proud of the way you raised him."

"I am. He saved your life."

Franny nodded her agreement. "He did, and so did you. I'll keep you both in my thoughts."

Cassie felt her anger rise. "You say that as if being in your thoughts is reward enough."

"What do you want?" Cheyenne interrupted. "Money?"

"No. I'm not like you. I'm just trying to figure out what Ben saw in her."

Franny chuckled. She said, "That wasn't me. That was Erin Reese. Erin was," Franny hesitated, "fun to play. She was a lot more fun than 'traumatized Franny Porché'."

Franny lifted her chin. "This is the real me."

Cassie stared at Cheyenne and Franny and shook her head in disgust. An acid taste filled her mouth.

"Don't mind her," Cheyenne said, placing her hand on Cassie's shoulder. "We move on and adapt."

"It's the Kleinsasser way," Cassie said bitterly.

"That it is," Cheyenne said. She nodded for Franny to get in, then left Cassie and walked around the front of the car to get behind the wheel.

"Take care," she said. "If I were you I'd stay out of Lochsa County."

ACKNOWLEDGMENTS

THE AUTHOR would like to sincerely thank those who helped in the research and narrative of this book, including Butch and Dana Preston of Montana, two wonderful long-haul truck drivers, for technical assistance and the staff of Chapter One Bookstore in Hamilton for area support in Montana.

My invaluable first readers were Laurie Box, Becky Reif, Molly Box, and Roxanne Woods. Thanks again.

Kudos to Molly and Prairie Sage Creative for cjbox.net for social media expertise and Becky Reif for legal advice and terminology.

It's a sincere pleasure to work with the professionals at St. Martin's Minotaur, including the fantastic Jennifer Enderlin, Andy Martin, and Hector DeJean.

Ann Rittenberg—thanks for always being in our corner.

ABOUT THE AUTHOR

C.J. BOX is the winner of the Anthony Award,
Prix Calibre .38 (France), the Macavity Award, the
Gumshoe Award, the Barry Award, and the Edgar
Award. He is also a *New York Times* bestseller.
He lives in Wyoming.